Psychic
for
Hire

The Adventures of Mr. French

By Michael Lane

Psychic for Hire
The Adventures of Mr. French

Copyright © 2021 by Michael Lane

ISBN 978-1-7364887-1-3

Psychic for Hire

The Adventures of Mr. French

CONTENTS

If you believe in the theory that there are innumerable universes parallel to our own, then somewhere there is an Earth much like our own. There, a psychic has an office visited by some very unusual clientele but, then again, this is not your average run-of-the-mill psychic.

Hiring a Secretary

"You couldna pick somewhere with a better climate?"

"No, Ainsworth. Besides, the choice was not mine to make."

Ainsworth was holding a hammer, nails, and a hand-painted wooden sign. "You sure you don't want me to do this, Myrddin?"

"Don't be such a bother, I am quite capable," the Englishman answered, taking the hammer. He climbed to the top of the ladder leaning against the porch roof.

"If you fall arse over tit, it ain't my fault, just sayin."

"I shall not fall and Ainsworth, whilst we are here, I shall not be using my true name. Names can have power to those who know the art. Now, hand me the sign."

Ainsworth passed it up. "It isn't like you aren't known by your enemies."

"True, but I don't need to be handing such a vulnerability to every Tom, Dick, and Harry that comes along either."

The Englishman adjusted the sign and began hammering it onto the roof fascia. The sign read simply *Psychic Within, Results Guaranteed.*

"Word of your arrival is spreading like a flood, you know."

The Englishman nodded. "There's always a demand for my particular services from the otherworldly community."

"But why here? San Antonio's no place for a couple London blokes—left sides a bit low."

The Englishman adjusted the sign. "Better?"

Ainsworth nodded.

"This is where the energy is focused. Can't change that now, can I?" He hammered the final nail in and climbed down. "Now all we need is a secretary."

"What time's the bird from the advert due to come by?" Ainsworth asked.

"Mrs. Brandt is not a bird and her interview happens to be at ten."

Ainsworth pulled down the ladder. "Well, I'll be puttering with the plumbing in the loo. It's still bodged up."

As Ainsworth hauled the ladder round back, the Englishman took a moment to appreciate their work. Done was the hard labor and sweat required to convert the run-down Victorian era house into a working business. Centrally located in the business district and he had picked it up for a pittance. Funny how the yanks don't value anything that's not all shiny and new. Of course the neighborhood was a bit shabby, suffering from the same flight to the suburbs that had occurred in England after the war. Still, it was exactly the kind of neighborhood that his clientele would call home. All that was needed now was someone to manage the front office.

By 10:15 there was still no sign of Mrs. Brandt. The fact that she was late was no real surprise and likely no fault of hers. San Antonio was hosting the 1968 World's Fair and the traffic was terrible. *Hemisfair,* as it was called, had filled the city with tourists. Good for most businesses, but not necessarily his. The *Otherworldly* does not go on holiday.

Mrs. Brandt finally arrived just after eleven. She walked in the door, frowned at the décor, and then turned to him.

"I am here for an interview," she said flatly. "Would you tell the psychiatrist that I am here?"

"I am not a psychiatrist, I am a psychic."

She frowned. "I don't care what you are, can you just tell the doctor that I am here to be interviewed."

"No, you don't understand," he told her politely. "There is no doctor. I am a psychic and I am the person looking to hire a secretary."

She stood there gob smacked, mouth open, and obviously confused.

He would have to start from the beginning. "Are you familiar with what a psychic is?"

She shook her head in the negative.

"A psychic is a person with faculties inexplicable to the laws of science and nature. I use those abilities to investigate the otherworldly and metaphysical."

"The otherworldly, like on *Dark Shadows*?" she asked. "Funny, you don't look like a vampire. You look more like Sabastian Cabot--sound like him too."

"Who?"

"You know, Mr. French on *Family Affair*."

"I'm afraid that I don't keep up much with popular culture," he answered. "You see, I spend most of my time investigating claims of inexplicable phenomena. Do you have any experience with ghosts?"

"No, I don't believe in those things."

"Well I am afraid that those *things* are what my business is all about."

She glanced quickly at the door, then turned back frowning. "Mr. French, I don't think this job's for me."

"My requirements *are* rather exacting. Perhaps your next interview will go better."

"I certainly hope so. The traffic getting to this dump was terrible." She stormed out the door, slamming it behind her.

The echoes of her exit brought Ainsworth from the back. "No luck with the interview?"

The psychic slumped back into his chair. "Definitely not."

"Should I fetch a spot of warm tea, sir?"

"Why yes, Ainsworth. That would be wonderful."

As Ainsworth hustled away to the kitchen, the Englishman pulled the *Yellow Pages* from a drawer in the desk and flipped to the T's. Perhaps someone from a temp agency would be agreeable.

After nearly an hour of frustrating and unproductive phone conversations, he was ready to chuck the whole idea into the waste bin when the door opened. In walked the personification of feminine beauty. She had curves in all the right places, gorgeous auburn hair, full red lips, and clear blue eyes that were entrancing--literally entrancing. This was a succubus and she was trying to ensnare him. It wasn't going to work.

"Your succubus wiles will not work on me," he said.

"No, but they never hurt in a job interview either."

The psychic peered somewhat flabbergasted over the top of his glasses. "You're here to interview for the secretarial job?"

"You find that unusual?" She was all legs in her avocado mini-skirt and white gogo boots.

"I just never considered the fact that a succubi might need to work."

She smiled and those long legs brought her across the room to the desk with amazing grace. "May I sit?"

"Of course." Her demonic aura was quite strong. She could easily be doing more to turn his libido against him but was holding back. That alone was a reason to discover what this was all about.

She settled into the chair, placed her glossy white purse on her lap, and looked up, catching him square in the eyes. "You are being polite, but yes, most succubi are gold diggers, leeching off their prey. I just prefer to earn money in a more honest way."

"And you can type and take dictation?"

She nodded. "Yes. I also have a number of infernal and otherworld connections that could prove useful to someone in your profession."

Ainsworth must have felt her presence. He arrived in the front office carrying a tray with a cup, a creamer, and a silver teapot. "Tea, sir?"

Ainsworth wasn't likely interested in whether there was a need for tea. His warrior soul had sensed the woman--the succubus French corrected himself, as a possible threat. Ainsworth could be right, she might be, but so far she hadn't done anything that would require Ainsworth's talents. Besides, what interest would a succubus have in an English psychic, well other than the fact that he was male?

"Yes, I would love a cup of tea. How about you? Would you care for tea before we begin the interview, Miss…"

"Mhyrrelle," she replied. "My true name is Mhyrrelle but Meryl is the name I use with the humans."

Offering her true name was a show of trust, if it was indeed her true name. The psychic whispered it and felt the energy in the room resonate.

Her eyebrow rose, discovering that he was indeed, no mere mortal. She scooted forward in her chair, leaning toward the desk. "And what shall I call you?"

"He is called Mr. French," Ainsworth answered quickly. He obviously didn't trust her and had no wish for his employer to do so either.

Meryl had turned at Ainsworth's voice. She turned back to the psychic, her red hair flowing about her face. "Mr. French," she said listening to the sound of it. "Yes, that suits you."

The Englishman's curiosity was piqued. She was obviously hiding something but the only way it would be discovered was by hiring her.

So he did.

With regards to an unanswered question, he was what the Americans would call *a sucker*.

***

For several months, things ran well. Meryl was an excellent secretary, office manager, and occasional bouncer, using her natural skills to defuse tense situations between clients and the things that plagued them. Mr. French had nearly convinced himself that there was no unknown element to Meryl when reality showed up and gave him a swift kick in the arse.

It was early October and still miserably hot when a gentleman in a business suit stepped into the office. He was short, maybe five-six, dark hair, olive complexion, and built like a television wrestler. Mr. French was in the front office that morning, Meryl having called in sick. That should have been his first clue.

The man in the business suit strode in like he owned the place. "I'm Brother Leo," he said, flashing an ID badge. "I have questions for one of your employees."

French recognized the ID. Brother Leo was an investigator for the Vatican's *Office of Minor Transgressions*. It didn't sound like much, which was intentional. The O.M.T. investigated and mitigated demonic and infernal disturbances. It was the Vatican equivalent to a black project--one the public should never know about. They were the long arm of Clerical law. The O.M.T. generally only concerned themselves with big disruptions in the metaphysical universe, so the question was why was Brother Leo here on his doorstep?

"So, what does the *Ghostapo* want from me?"

Brother Leo scowled, his right eyebrow rising in a manner that had more to do with Lucifer than the emotionless Vulcan from that show on the telly. "We don't particularly *like* to be called that." He pulled a chair up to the desk and sat down. "We understand you hired someone with a demonic background recently."

"If I did, it's my business."

The Ghostapo took their job seriously--far too seriously, in French's book. If it was not human, their job was to eradicate it. Demon, spirit, or fey, didn't matter, holy water would fly and the exorcism was on. French had a more enlightened attitude. Most non-humans were just like normal people. So as long as they weren't causing harm, his business ethic was to leave them be.

Brother Leo continued to scowl at French. He looked more the Mafia thug than a representative of the Vatican. Finally, the O.M.T. officer broke the visual stalemate, putting both of his meaty wrestler hands on the edge of the desk and leaning forward.

"Look Myrddin, just because you're human doesn't mean that we can't bring you up on charges."

"The name is Mr. French, and I've had dealings with your Office before. You can't bring charges against a human, so stop with the tough act. Tell me what you want and then please leave."

Instead of answering, Brother Leo angrily shoved back his chair, grinding the legs against the hardwood floor that Ainsworth and French had spent hours sanding. "Expect to see me again, French."

With that threat hanging in the air between them, Brother Leo walked out.

"Bad news, Mr. French?" Ainsworth asked.

The name *French* had stuck. Meryl liked it, Ainsworth had insisted it be used, and it was easily remembered by the public. Still, he wasn't fond of being named after a fictional portly butler. He wasn't that overweight.

French turned to Ainsworth. "Possibly, I need to get a hold of Meryl."

Ainsworth frowned. "I did recommend against hiring her."

French flipped the sign on the door to *Closed*. He was going to be busy for at least several hours. "Meryl has been an excellent secretary. If the O.M.T. is looking for her, that means she's probably in even deeper trouble."

Ainsworth just nodded, not pleased with that answer. "I shall be feeding the menagerie if you need me," he said calmly.

"When you're done, please ring round to our usual informants and see if anyone has heard anything, will you?"

"Yes sir."

French walked the hall to his study. The smell of incense, old books, and familiar odd things was pleasant and calming. He crossed the room and opened the thick red velvet curtains. Outside was the spot where Brother Leo had parked. What was Meryl into? Lost in that question, he paced the office before settling down and ringing up Meryl's flat.

No answer. If she had indeed been ill, unlikely as *Infernals* do not suffer the maladies that plague humans, she would have been at home. He tapped his pencil on the desk. What could Meryl have done that would arouse the interest of the O.M.T?

There was only one way to find out. French retrieved his car keys from the upper desk drawer, took a few other bits and bobs, and headed out into the sun bleached inferno that was October in San Antonio.

***

The employment file had provided the address of Meryl's flat. Her apartment was off San Pedro. It was a nice place, Meryl was doing well. French climbed the stairs to the second level and found number two-twenty seven. The door was open. Someone had indelicately forced the lock. Through the gap between the door and frame, French could see that there had been a struggle.

"Meryl, are you home?" the psychic asked loudly. Just barging in was not a good idea. There are things succubi can do that are not pleasurable. If she had been attacked and was still here, he had no wish to be confused with one of her attackers.

"It's your employer, Mr. French." He also didn't want any nosy Gladys Kravitz type thinking that he was the criminal. Hmm, apparently he did know a fair amount about popular culture. He owed an apology to Mrs. Brandt.

French gently shouldered open the door and stepped inside. Several chairs were on their sides and the coffee table had been overturned. Magazines and broken china littered the floor. An overwhelming emotional residue filled the space. It was remarkably strong, like it had been deliberately left. Ahh, it had. Meryl had left a clue, clever girl.

Mr. French closed his eyes and attuned himself to the emotional energy. As he focused on the memory that Meryl had psychically impressed into the room, he could see her two attackers breaking through the door. One was a large burly man of about thirty. His red hair and fair complexion had not fared well in San Antonio's hot sunny climate. The other man was tall, with a dark complexion, possibly of Spanish descent. He pulled a *docineur* from his pocket. Not a human then, but a Vanir- a human with magical talent. It was the docineur that had rendered Meryl's succubi abilities useless. The ginger-haired ruffian struggled with Meryl for a moment before brutally beating her with an iron bar. The blow would have killed a human. For an Infernal, it was sufficient to render Meryl unconscious. At that point of course, the psychic images ceased.

French walked over to where the scuffle had taken place. Meryl's necklace of aqua plastic beads had broken and they were everywhere. Amidst the beads and shattered china, something caught the sunlight streaming through the open door. It was a silver medallion. It wasn't anything Meryl would wear. Infernals don't care for silver. French stooped to pick it up. It bore the image of Pope Innocent the Eighth.

French knew immediately who had done this- the *Order of Purity*, but why would a religious order, banned for centuries, suddenly show up and kidnap his secretary?

***

On arriving back at the office, Ainsworth had good news.

"Virgil knows what's going on," he told French. "He wants to meet you this evening at the usual place."

Virgil was an incubus who catered to men. It put him at odds with both the O.M.T. and the local police. The Americans still had laws making homosexuality illegal. It was rather strange since the highest paid entertainer in the country was Liberace. The public didn't seem to find the idea of a homosexual male that offensive--the pianist certainly behaved as if he were gay, although he often denied it.

"Will you be going alone, sir?" Behind Ainsworth's question was the implication that he would prefer not to accompany him. Ainsworth had been alive since the 1300's and his attitudes were out of touch with the modern world. He couldn't accept the idea of two men together in that fashion.

"Yes," French said. "I think that Virgil is a bit uncomfortable around you. Your presence might make him less willing to talk."

Ainsworth nodded once. "The feeling of discomfort is mutual, sir."

***

Virgil's usual place was the *El Tropical* club. It was a nightclub near downtown that served as a gathering place for humans of Virgil's persuasion. The *El Tropical* on the outside was a rather nondescript local bar. The building was stained by time and wore the multiple layers of flaking paint like a vaudeville stripper's feather fan, hoping to hide the aging and naked masonry beneath. The building's windows had long ago been bricked over. Now, only the neon sign above the door gave any hint of life within the once proud building.

Inside, all subtlety was lost in an over-the-top mix of Spanish Baroque and tacky modern. Typically, Virgil could be found at the bar along the left of the room. The Infernals, like Virgil and Meryl, drink alcohol for the taste--it has very little effect on them. They do, however, enjoy watching the drunken debauchery of the Earth-bred humans as they drink.

"It's better than watching *I Love Lucy* on TV," Virgil had once told him.

As he remembered it, Virgil preferred Vodka, usually with a twist of lemon. Tonight, however, the incubus was nowhere to be seen.

As French walked over to the bar, Julio, the barman, slid his way.

"The usual?" Julio asked.

"Yes, please. Gin and tonic."

Julio turned and made the drink. As he passed it across the bar, French passed him a fiver. "Do you happen to know where I might find Virgil?"

"You just missed him," Julio said sweetly as he pocketed the bill. "He left with a well-dressed Italian gentleman about ten minutes ago. A strong, handsome type, but too short for my tastes."

"Thank you."

The Italian gentlemen had to be Brother Leo. Funny, French wouldn't have described the O.M.T operative as handsome, swarthy maybe.

He turned to face the dance floor and took a slow sip of his drink. The conifer sting of the cheap gin going down did little to improve his mood. He needed to puzzle out where a man like Leo might take Virgil. Julio had implied they were off for a tryst. That seemed to indicate that Virgil had left willingly.

French had finished the gin and tonic and was no closer to a solution when Julio came running over.

"That Italian's beating up Virgil in the alley. I saw him just now when I went to take the trash out."

"Thanks."

French rounded the end of the bar and made for the employee exit.

It could likely be a trap. Correction, it probably was a trap. In addition to Brother Leo, there were also the two thugs that had abducted Meryl. Luckily, French had brought a little surprise for whoever it might be.

French shouldered his way through the door. In the weak, yellow bug-light glare of the alley, he could make out the short, pudgy silhouette of Brother Leo. He was standing over the prone figure of Virgil. A trickle of blood was spilling out of the incubus's mouth. His left eye was bruised and swollen shut. Brotherly good will only applied to humans, it seemed.

French pulled the vial from his pocket and threw it just as Brother Leo turned. It hit him square in the chest and burst open. He went down to his knees instantly as the narcotic hit his lungs.

"French!" he managed to say before crumpling to the pavement.

The narcotic haze cleared quickly. French went over and helped Virgil to his feet. As they headed down the alley toward the car, they passed Julio standing in the doorway with a look of amazement on his face.

French reached into his pocket. "Here's a twenty. I was never here, all right?"

Julio shook his head, refusing the cash. "Just take care of Virgil."

The barman watched until the psychic had Virgil safely in the car. Then shut and locked the bar's scarred steel door.

***

By the time they made it to the office, Virgil was feeling better. Infernals can take a great deal of punishment. They also heal quickly.

French handed Virgil an icepack. "A little risky, dating an operative of the O.M.T."

"That's who he was?" Virgil placed the icepack on his face and winced.

"So why was our local Ghostapo giving you the treatment?"

"Don't know."

Virgil was still a little woozy. His pupils were dilated, indicating a possible concussion. French didn't know if that was a serious issue for an incubus or not.

"Ghostapo--You know French, that makes this even stranger," Virgil mumbled. "He wasn't threatening to take me in, just demanding information on the kidnappings."

Strange was an understatement. If Leo wasn't interested in Infernals, then something really big was in the works. "You tell him anything?

Virgil shook his head and scowled. "Hell no, and when I refused, that's when he started in on me."

Ainsworth silently entered the room and handed French the medical bag. "Anything else, sir?"

"Yes, get our traveling things together."

Ainsworth hurried out.

French turned back to Virgil. The incubus was up and out of his seat, his hands angrily in fists.

"So, you're running out on us, French?"

French placed the medical bag on his desk and took out a stoppered glass bottle. "Hardly. My traveling things are what I take with me when I go into a confrontation."

French poured some brandy into a glass from the desk decanter and added several drops from the stoppered bottle. "Now drink this and sit back down."

Virgil took the glass and settled into his chair. He tipped the snifter back, drinking the amber liquid like it was water. He smiled, which was incongruous with the blooded and beaten aspect to his face.

"Your taste in brandy does you credit, Mr. French."

"Thank you." French picked up the decanter. "My apologies for any medicinal overtones. Care for another?"

Virgil nodded, handing French the glass. His Beatle-cut blonde hair was usually so well-kept. Tonight, it was matted by blood. "Pity this doesn't affect me the way it does you human born."

French poured a very healthy portion of the 1956 vintage *Baronne Jacques de Saint-Pastou Armagnac* into Virgil's

Snifter. "So why is the Office of Minor Transgressions investigating the kidnapping of a succubus?"

"More than one," Virgil said with a growl. "Six of my brothers and sisters are missing." Virgil stared into the swirling amber liquid like it was a crystal ball promising answers. "Leo was very insistent that if I was worried for my kind, I'd tell him who was doing the kidnapping." Virgil breathed in the vaporized alcohol and then emptied the glass. "Since when does the Vatican give a damn about Infernals?"

French nodded. "An excellent question." It was the *sixty-four thousand dollar* question and one that French desperately needed the answer to if he was going to help Meryl. Another more important question he had a hunch Virgil might know the answer to.

"But you do know who is behind the kidnappings."

Incubi and succubi feed off of the energy of lust. In return, humans get the experience of a lifetime. Because of this, they are, for the most part, quite friendly and enjoy being around Earth-born humankind. Virgil was typical of his sort--jovial and almost always in good spirits. However, when he looked French in the eyes and told him who was masterminding this plot, there was nothing but loathing in his voice

"Leopold Black and the bastard's in league with those unevolved gorillas from the Order."

This was turning into a class-A, arse over tits cockup. "That's an unlikely pairing."

Virgil reached towards him with his empty glass. "Black's giving them the information and the means to hunt Infernals down."

French refilled the glass. "They had a docineur when they took Meryl."

Virgil nodded, seeing the connection. "Black's work. The word is that the Order's holding the prisoners at their east side warehouse."

There was much to consider. It was bad enough that the Order of Purity was involved. They were the type that burned people for being witches.

But then there was Leopold Archibald Black. He represented everything that the Order found as anathema. Like French, Black was a magic using Vanir. Unlike French, Black and his followers believed that humans were mere cattle to be used and discarded.

Rescuing Meryl would be a bloody balls-up mess if not planned right. Pulling it off wouldn't be easy, but in his business, things never were.

***

The following night, the operation began. Black's warehouse was dark and appeared deserted. French had parked his Mustang a block away. He hadn't used the normal spells for obscuring one's appearance on the offhand chance that Black might possibly sense that. On the warehouse's corrugated steel walls someone had repeatedly stenciled the stylized upturned fist of the *Black Power* movement. Other than those angry fists demanding equal rights, there was no activity at all on the street.

Like pulling the battery from a pocket radio, the chirping of the crickets ceased.

"There were two men guarding the front door," Ainsworth whispered, squatting outside the passenger window.

His voice had startled French. He would have sworn that he alone was on the street. Thankfully, Ainsworth was polite enough not to mention the ease with which he had snuck up. For such a big man, Ainsworth moved extremely silently.

"Nothing else?" French asked, grateful that it was Ainsworth and not the thugs of the Order.

"At the loading dock, there are also fresh tire tracks in the mud," Ainsworth whispered, "So someone is using the warehouse." He tossed a pair of necklaces with silver Pope Innocent medallions into the car. One was smeared with blood. "The two thugs were Order."

The blood bothered French. Not for squeamish reasons. In his long life, he had seen a great deal of death. No, he was worried for Ainsworth.

Six hundred years ago, Ainsworth had been cursed. He lives forever, but each night, he must suffer the pain and injury that he has ever inflicted on the innocent. What would kill a normal man simply doesn't kill Ainsworth. His body slowly, painfully heals any wound.

Ainsworth climbed into the car. "You need not worry, those two were not innocents."

French started the engine and pulled up to the warehouse. Ainsworth was out and listening at the door before French even had the car off. He hurriedly joined him.

"Don't open it yet," French whispered. "Here." he placed an amulet around Ainsworth's neck. "It's something that I recently picked up. It will confound their aim."

Ainsworth nodded, putting on the necklace with one hand while pulling a nasty looking triangular dagger with the other.

The door's deadbolt was the next obstacle. The psychic pulled out a short sliver of metal and with the ease of long practice, manipulated the lock's tumblers.

"One, two, three!" Ainsworth mouthed silently.

French flung open the door and Ainsworth bounded inside. The sound of melons being crushed was followed by gurgling sounds which mercifully ended quickly. French stepped inside.

They were in the warehouse's front office. Ainsworth was at the far door listening. As French walked forward, Ainsworth extended an open hand.

The psychic handed Ainsworth a sword. It and the dagger were Ainsworth's choice of weapons for the night's upcoming conflict. With them, he could easily deal with any of the Order's thugs. French, on the other hand, was tasked with dealing with any magical attacks Black might have waiting for them. The psychic patted the canvas bag slung over his shoulder. In it were some surprises for both Mr. Black and his friends from the Order.

"I can hear conversation so they likely have Meryl and the others tied up in there," Ainsworth whispered. "It will be a large open space so watch your back. It's likely they have men on the floor above us."

Ainsworth gestured at the ceiling with his thumb. Once again, French had been saved by Ainsworth. The office, with its low ceiling undoubtable had a floor above for additional storage. French would have neglected that little detail.

French handed Ainsworth a pair of spectacles. He put a pair on himself. "Now for our little surprise." He passed a small brass sphere over the light switch next to the door and the whole building went dark as midnight. For Ainsworth and French wearing their glasses, it was late afternoon.

Cries came from inside the warehouse and then there was a heavy, metallic whang followed by a muffled voice.

"Shut them up. Hector, go to the office and see if Parker knows what's going on," a voice yelled.

Ainsworth motioned him back. The door opened and a man stepped through, walking right into Ainsworth's dagger. Using the body as a shield, Ainsworth rushed through the door. French followed, throwing the *blitzen* up and onto the floor above. The brass sphere hit something and there was a blistering flash of lightning as it discharged its stored electricity. Revealed in the flash was a warehouse completely empty except for an iron cage surrounded by eleven or twelve men with guns.

Shots began ringing out as Ainsworth waded in, carving his way through the men like wheat before a sickle. A yellow sphere of light burst into existence near the underside of the roof. In its sulfurous glare, French found his target. Black was standing against the cage. He held a *rivener* with its silver blade against Meryl's throat.

"Call your man off, French, or I'll kill your secretary," Black screamed.

By this time, Ainsworth stood over the bodies of five men. The rest had retreated to form a circle around Black. They continued shooting at Ainsworth but the bullets shed off his skin like water.

"Fools, he's protected by magic," Black yelled. "You'll have to take him by force."

The displacement was still working. Black was talking to the building, not at French. The psychic was huddled against some cardboard boxes stacked against the back wall of the office. He released his little surprise.

"I warn you French, Call him off or she dies."

French let the displacement dissipate and stepped forward. "Drop your weapon, Ainsworth."

The timing was perfect. In that moment as their defenses relaxed, the Nigerian assassin bug French had released reached Black's right arm and latched on. The dark magician screamed as the toxins flowed into his bloodstream. The rivener slid from his paralyzed hand as the bite took effect. Seeing this, the thugs from the Order swung their guns toward French. A burst of gunfire chewed into them from the far end of the warehouse and they fell.

Virgil stepped from the shadows, gun still smoking. He had been their ace in the hole, waiting until the firefight begun to burn his way into the warehouse.

"Damn you, French," Black screamed.

With the resumption of violence, Ainsworth charged toward the dark magician. Black flung a small egg-sized stone at Ainsworth with his left hand. Ainsworth dropped and leapt sideways to avoid the stone's lethal arc, focusing again on Black. That was his mistake. The stone swerved, flying unerringly to strike Ainsworth directly in the chest. The massive fireball that resulted blew the roof off of the warehouse.

***

Fire has little effect on Infernals. Despite their proximity to the blast, the incubi and succubi in the cage had not been severely injured. Ainsworth, however, was a blackened and charred husk. Of Leopold Black, there was no sign. That he had survived the explosion, there was little doubt.

French dragged Ainsworth's body through the smoldering ruin of the warehouse and out into the street, wondering how he would fit everyone into his small Mustang. Virgil followed, leading the imprisoned Infernals out of the building. A screeching of tires at the far end of the street drew their attention.

Virgil crouched, gun aimed at the vehicle. "Who is it? More assholes from the Order?"

"I think not," French replied. "It is a bus from the St. Francis Catholic School. I do not sense their dark energy."

"Whoever it is, they're not here to pick up students." Virgil motioned for the other Infernals to spread out. "Take what cover you can!"

The bus hurtled to a jarring stop. Several men in suits jumped from the bus and rushed across the warehouse parking lot. It was Brother Leo and the Ghostapo.

"What now?" Virgil whispered.

French eased Ainsworth to the ground and pulled several items from his bag. "I am in no fit state for battle, but I will do what I can to aid your escape."

Virgil snarled. "There're only five of them. My brothers and sisters can take them."

French shook his head. "We don't know what they have with them. There are things far worse than docineurs."

Brother Leo signaled his men. They stopped in a line a car length from the building. "French, I'm here to get you and the others to safety before the police arrive."

The presence of the Ghostapo suddenly made sense. The primary job of the O.M.T. was to keep the existence of the other realm from the public.

"Where are you going to take us?" French asked, still not completely certain things were working out as well as they appeared.

"Your office, if that's what you want," Brother Leo replied.

"Think we can trust him?" Virgil asked.

"Yes," French answered. "If not, we follow your plan."

***

Apparently, it was a segregated bus. Brother Leo and the O.M.T. lads were on the left and Virgil and the Infernals were on the right. A stony silence separated the two. French was sitting next to Virgil. Needless to say, the drive to the office was not a roaring good time out with your pub mates. Then again, it wasn't the balls to the wall warfare that would have normally been the case either.

As they debarked at the office, French was less than pleased to see Brother Leo getting off the bus with them.

The O.M.T. operative stepped closer. "A word, French."

French appreciated the ride, but it didn't make up for centuries of O.M.T. oppression. "How about the word *goodbye*?"

Brother Leo reached forward and patted the psychic's shoulder. "French, I'm not your enemy."

"You're not a friend either, conveniently waiting until Black and I were done trying to kill each other before showing up."

The O.M.T. officer shook his head. "It's not like that. I came as soon as we got the tip. There was magic involved in the delivery. I just assumed it was from you."

French shook his head. "No, not me."

The stocky O.M.T. operative turned and strode toward the bus. "Call me. There are bigger things than this at work. You know the number."

He climbed the stairs of the bus and the doors scissored shut behind him. French watched in silence as the vehicle pulled out of the parking lot.

French watched until the bus turned onto Mulberry. Someone needed to tell the St. Francis Catholic School to take their bus to the mechanic, it was burning oil. The foul smell matched French's mood. He turned and climbed the steps into the office.

Inside, the atmosphere was far more jovial. A great deal of laughter was coming from down the hall, inside his study.

French stepped inside. Virgil was emptying what was left in the decanter into his glass.

"I see that you have liberated my private stock."

"We needed a proper celebration!"

"I suppose that's true."

Behind French in the doorway, Meryl wrapped her arms around his waist.

"Thank you." She placed her chin on his shoulder. "Ainsworth's in his room and is resting. He's in bad shape but his burns are showing signs of healing."

French put his hands on hers. She was radiating a happy contentment with definite overtones of sexual desire. Virgil was holding the decanter upside down and looking at French questioningly.

"In the right bottom drawer," he told the incubus.

Virgil bent down and reappeared smiling and holding two more bottles of the Armagnac.

Meryl kissed him on the neck. "So, why are you such a wet blanket?"

"Some unfinished business Brother Leo brought up."

She kissed him again and nuzzled into his ear. "You can worry tomorrow," she whispered. "Tonight, we enjoy living."

Meryl pulled him into the hall. Her succubus wiles were on high volume.

"What the hell." French took the gorgeous succubus in his arms and kissed her. "A little rumpy pumpy might be just the ticket."

Although danger is always a possibility when dealing with the paranormal, a psychic's life is not all battles and bloodshed. Sometimes there can be rather pleasant experiences, especially when succubi are involved.

My Girlfriend is a Succubus

A young man in a *Dr. Who* t-shirt bulldozed through the door in the undignified way of most modern Americans. The door banged against the brass door stop, rattling the glass. The young man failed to notice. "Please, you gotta help me."

Mr. French nodded to the desperate young man and motioned for him to follow him through the curtains and into the parlor. The house was built in 1885. It had dignified things like parlors and sitting rooms. It also had far stranger things as well, but this young man would not need that kind of help. He was twenty-something, athletically built, relatively handsome, but obviously exhausted.

"So, what does a young college student need from a psychic?"

"You deal with things like demons, right?" he asked.

French nodded. "Yes, on occasion. Why don't we start with a bit about you?"

"You can't do that? I thought you were a psychic?"

Always the first question from clients. "Jason, I am quite capable of entering your mind but that is considered a violation of personal space by those in my occupation. Without having to snoop, I can tell that the incident for which you have come started at the college where you are a student. Am I correct?"

"Yeah, uh I mean yes sir and I'm here about a girl."

In addition to the mental anguish afflicting the young man, it was quite obvious that he was also suffering from an acute drain of Odic energy. "But not just any girl."

"I think she might be a demon," Jason whispered. "Do you deal with demons like succubusses?"

"The correct plural is succubi, but yes."

The young man was on the verge of collapse. French motioned for Jason to sit. Luckily, the young man had sought help just in time.

Jason slumped into the couch like liquid flowing into a bottle. The antique Victorian settee creaked under the sudden weight.

"I have a problem. It's my girlfriend; she's a succubus."

"Yes, there is the spoor of demon about you." Mr. French settled into his trusted old wingback armchair. It didn't belong in the Victorian setting, but was very comfortable. Besides, most of his clients would never notice the interior design *faux paus*. "You are encountering issues?"

"Issues!" Jason exclaimed. "Yeah, like I can barely get up in the morning anymore." The exertion of the statement had the boy sagging even lower in the couch.

Mr. French lit one of the healing candles on the side table. It would help. "Do you wish to rid yourself of the succubus?"

French already knew the answer. The young architecture student would keep the succubus. It was how the Infernals worked. Mortal men were willing to die rather than lose the affection of a succubus. The lust they generated was the most potent of spells.

"No, I love Jynieth." Jason paused. "Sounds so strange when I hear myself say it-- I love a succubus."

"They are far more common that you might imagine."

"*Suck*- ubus. Sounds like a good thing, right?"

Mr. French smiled. The adrenalin of Jason's frantic search for help was waning. Even with the boost the candle was providing, the boy would soon fall unconscious without some revitalization of his core energy levels.

"Your relationship has left you drained," French said. "Before we go on, I believe that you could use some tea." The psychic rang the small hand bell sitting on the side table.

Jason nodded. "Yeah, a caffeine buzz would help."

The curtains parted and a pale man in a well-tailored suit entered.

"Ainsworth, tea please, the *Sumatran Enchantment* blend, if you would."

"Yes sir," the manservant said before disappearing through the curtains.

The boy was nearly asleep. "While we wait, tell me Jason, how did you meet this succubus?"

Jason clawed his way out of his stupor. "I met Jynieth at the coffee shop by the college. She caught my eye when she came in. I mean, what's not to notice--she's beautiful with great big eyes and the reddest lips, and her bod--wow! Hot, hot, hot, wearing the sexiest yoga pants ever."

"Succubi typically choose a physical form that is highly desirable."

"Then she did a great job," Jason replied. "Anyway, she got in line behind me and I'm thinking how I can start a conversation with her, when she taps me on the shoulder. Really! I mean like how lucky is that?"

Most succubi study their prey in detail before beginning the hunt but there was no need to deflate Jason's ego. This Jynieth had obviously tailored her appearance to her victim, Jason's, preferences. That moment in the coffee shop had been the start of her active stalk of the boy.

"So we started talking," Jason continued. "Things were going good so when we got to the counter, I offered to buy her coffee. Usually, that's the moment I get dumped but amazingly, Jynieth accepted. The only place left to sit was in the couch by the corner window. It was pretty cold out that morning and she cuddled up to me for warmth. It was great. I so failed to show in my math class but it was worth it."

Ainsworth opened the door, rolled the tea trolley to the side of the wingback chair and left silently. French poured a cup for Jason and handed it over. He'd added no cream or sugar to dilute the effects.

"When did you find out her true nature?" French asked. He poured a second cup for himself to which he did add cream and took a sip. Excellent, Ainsworth had brewed it to a double potency.

Jason sipped tentatively at the tea. His eyes brightened and he took another longer sip. "Jynieth told me the first night."

French nodded. Some of the slump was leaving the boy's shoulders as the tea bolstered his Odic energy levels.

"Of course I had no idea what she was talking about. Later, we were, you know, doing it, and she changed into this demon thing-- leathery wings, spike tipped tits, and teeth around her, well down there. I tell you I would have completely lost my chubby, if she hadn't dug her claws into me and screamed that she wanted more. Her hips were gyrating and pumping. Wow, what a ride!"

The energy of the encounter threatened to spill over into French's mind. "This was several weeks ago?" the psychic said to get Jason's mind back on topic. French was no voyeur.

"No," Jason answered. "Closer to a month ago, just before Thanksgiving."

That was a surprise. "Really? You must have quite the constitution."

French put his teacup and saucer on the side table and pulled a pair of wire-frame spectacles from the inside of his coat. The lenses were an apricot shade of pink.

Jason looked on quizzically.

"They allow me to see auras," he explained.

Jason nodded and continued sipping at his tea.

French looked the young man over. The aura was the bordered by a chrome yellow indicating an individual in the pursuit of knowledge. No surprise there but there were also flares of orange and a very definite streak of brilliant crimson. The later was indicative of vibrancy. Odd as the young man was feeling anything but vibrant at the moment. Interesting as well were the tangerine orange flares--they didn't belong in a human aura spectrum at all. French pondered the puzzle for a moment; then it became quite obvious.

The psychic leaned back and retrieved his tea. "Jynieth must love you very much, Jason. She has placed a part of her Chi into you. It is preventing you from expiring during your love-making sessions."

"Yeah, I think she said something about that," Jason mumbled. "Didn't really understand what she meant but she said that it would keep me safe."

"How often is she feeding off of you?" French asked.

"Do you mean how often do we fuck?"

Mr. French coughed, the tea caught in his throat. He had forgotten that what was once completely vulgar and uncouth, was now just a normal part of the lexicon. He recovered himself.

"Yes, the sexual act is when a succubus feeds off of her victim's energy."

Jason was clueless to the disturbance he had caused in his host's composure. The young man emptied his teacup. "It started as just once a night. Now we are up to three or four times a day. I've had to drop my classes and I'm falling asleep at my job."

French nodded. There was something else, a black spot of trepidation lurking in the aura. Was there something the young man wanted to say, but was afraid to?

"There is something else?" French asked.

"Jynieth is worried that you'll banish her."

The black spot flickered.

"I am not one of those kinds of psychics," French answered. The darkness in the boy's aura faded. "You may reassure Jynieth, that I am not about to try and dispel her back to the infernal reaches of hell."

Jason relaxed. "Yeah, she was kinda worried about that."

Mr. French smiled, bolstered by the tea. "You came to the right person for help. I have a fair amount of experience with regards to living with a succubus. My secretary is also a succubus. You might mention that to Jynieth. It should convince her of my good will."

Meryl had been his office manager for nearly as long as the office had been in this house. The relationship was much deeper than that but Jason need not know those details. "Your Jynieth will know her by the name of Mhyrrelle."

"I'll tell her."

The tea was working; Jason was no longer slumped like an understuffed pillow.

The very potent Sumatran Enchantment blend was having its effect on French as well. The psychic felt strong enough to lift the house. He stood and walked over to the darkly stained oak bookcases behind the desk. Amongst the antique books, brass instruments, and a taxidermied bat under a glass dome, there was a small enameled box. French retrieved the box.

"There are ways of satisfying the hunger of a succubus that won't leave you so lethargic." French opened the box and pulled out an unshaped lump of Baltic amber on a gold chain. "This pendant you must wear at all times. It will draw excess Odic energy from the world around you. When you are making love to Jynieth, your body will draw from the pendant, replacing what you lose to her appetite."

Relief spread over the young man's face. "Thank you."

The tea had Mr. French in particularly fine spirits and that always made him talkative. "It's odd, the first question from someone involved with a succubus is usually *Will I go to Hell*. You haven't even asked about that?"

Jason shook his head scornfully. "Naw, my mom believes in that seven-levels-of-hell stuff but it's not even in the Bible. Dante made all that crap up."

Mr. French thought about that for a moment. Would it do any harm if the boy believed as he did? Probably not. He didn't need to know that Dante Alighieri, as a result of heavenly clerical mistake, had in fact been to Hell. His descriptions, although overly dramatic and seen through the lenses of his time and culture, were fairly accurate.

"You might find it interesting to know," Mr. French said finally, wishing there were biscuits to go with the tea, "That there was even a Pope, Sylvester the Second I believe, who was involved with a succubus. She was named Meridiana, although I doubt that was her true name. She helped him to become Pope."

"A Pope?" Jason said in amazement.

Mr. French nodded enthusiastically, nearly sloshing his tea. "Of course Sylvester confessed and repented all of this before his death."

"They didn't teach me anything like that in Catholic school."

"Certainly not," French said a bit too loudly. "The official doctrine of the Church is that creatures from the infernal region are forbidden from the Earth."

"But they know the truth?"

"Of course they do," the psychic answered. "One entire wing of the Vatican is devoted to Otherworld Management. They have teams all over the globe hunting down and hushing up demonic incursions."

Jason's smile faded. "Crap, will they come after Jynieth?"

Mr. French shook his head. "No, no. The succubi are small potatoes in their game. Besides, Jynieth isn't a predator, draining lives right and left. That's only the offspring of Agrat Bat Mahla."

"Who?" Jason asked.

"One of the succubi queens. Infernals like Jynieth and my secretary are the offspring of the original four succubi queens and the angel Samael," Mr. French explained. "They were expelled from heaven for this sin. Agrat's anger was terrible, and her offspring seek to avenge this dishonor by destroying Mankind."

"Really, they were cast out of heaven for having kids?"

Mr. French finished his tea. The morals of sexuality had changed so much. "Yes, I'm afraid so. The other *Daughters*, as the succubi prefer to be called, are unlikely to drain a person to the point of death."

Perhaps it was the tea but Mr. French did something that was most unusual. "If Jynieth is a daughter of Naahmah, the two of you should come by for dinner."

"Naahmah?"

"Another of the succubi queens," Mr. French explained. "The offspring of the four do not get along well each other; only mingling with others of similar maternal lineage."

Jason shook his head. "I should be taking notes. I had no idea that dating could be this complicated."

***

It was late in the evening as they closed the Book for the day. A fairly busy one at that. Recalling the invitation he had given to Jason, French turned to his office manager. "Meryl, we may be having guests for dinner."

The succubus, with her curves and auburn hair deliberately designed to satisfy the psychic's personal tastes, nearly dropped the Book as she placed it on the shelf. "Dinner guests, really? Someone I know?"

"Possibly," French answered. "A Daughter who goes by the name of Jynieth."

"Don't think I know her," Meryl said. "Is she of Naahmah?"

"That I do not as yet know."

The discussion was interrupted by the office phone ringing. It wasn't unusual for the business to get calls at night. Indeed, many of the more interesting and sometimes dangerous clients preferred the night. Meryl picked up the phone. After a few moments she began scowling at French.

She placed her hand over the mouthpiece of the 1940's era black telephone "It's your succubi and her boyfriend. They want to know what they should do if she got pregnant?"

More typical of a psychic's work is dealing with the Life-Challenged, what the average person would call a ghost. Mr. French has dealt with quite a few in his time. Usually they are merely misguided individuals caught in an afterlife loop. Once provided with the equivalent of a map and they are on their way. On Occasion, however, things don't go quite that easily.

The Family

"EVP session, July eighth, old Weselyn asylum, second floor lobby. We are here to contact the spirit of John Riggers."

Jenn held her camera and digital recorder with the absolute confidence that she would get an answer. Caitlin wasn't so sure. They had been on several investigations before where Jenn had guaranteed results, only to spend hours listening to nothing but their own voices. That had been lame. Of course, lying in bed, struggling to hear ghost voices on a recorder would be better than this place. It stank of mildew, decay, and hobo piss. Such things never seemed to bother Jenn.

"John, are you here?" Jenn asked the darkness.

She and Jenn stood silent for several seconds. The pause was to record any possible response. All Caitlin heard was the buzz of mosquitoes and the distant hum of traffic.

"Think he answered?" Caitlin whispered.

"Won't know 'til later. I need to upgrade to one of the recorders that lets you listen live."

Jenn clicked off the recorder. "Looks like this was a nice building once upon a time."

Caitlin swung the beam of her own flashlight around the lobby and shrugged. "Maybe but I doubt the patients noticed."

Along the floor and baseboards, snowdrifts of paint peels had collected. In this lead-based winter wonderland, a path had been trampled.

Jenn prodded the curls of paint with her toe. "Something's wandering these halls."

The path led through the lobby and down each side corridor.

"Rats, maybe," Caitlin speculated. "Or other curious teenagers."

"Or the ghost of John Riggers," Jenn countered excitedly.

"Do ghosts leave tracks?"

Jenn turned to Caitlin, disgust on her face. "There are hundreds of recordings of ghostly footsteps. If they're walking, they leave tracks."

"That makes sense."

Caitlin wasn't sure she agreed with that logic but as long as it made Jenn happy, she was willing to pretend to believe it. She and Jenn had been friends since elementary school and Caitlin couldn't imagine her life without Jenn in it.

She scrapped her foot along the floor. Below the paint dust was the original hygienic floor tile. It was broken and missing in places. "You know, these old floors were usually made of asbestos. Should we be wearing a mask?"

"Only dangerous if we start busting them up," Jenn replied.

Caitlin had expected some such answer. Jenn would never admit that the building was too hazardous to enter. She'd completely ignored the danger sign hanging on the fence they'd crawled under.

Jenn swung her K-II meter around. "No sign of any EMF. Get the IR camera out and see what you can find."

"Okay."

Caitlin pulled the device from her backpack. The compact IR camera was Jenn's big Christmas present last year and was her pride and joy. Caitlin flipped the device on and the screen lit up in rainbow colors. Except for Jenn's glowing red and yellow aura, there was only the cold background blue of the partially painted walls, asbestos tile floor, and plaster ceiling.

"Nothing but you."

Caitlin was glad to have the camera in the nearly absolute darkness of the old asylum. It was comforting to have something that saw everything.

"Thanks for letting me turn this on," she told Jenn.

Jenn focused her light down the left hallway. "No prob. You've always been scared of the dark."

"Yeah, too many horror movies and supernatural video games."

Jenn turned back and began poking at an object buried in a paint snowdrift. "Doesn't usually bother me but this place has me on edge. Maybe because it was an asylum."

There was a clunk down the right hallway.

Jenn swiveled to follow the sound. Clicking on the digital recorder, she walked over to the hallway opening. "John. Is that you?"

She paused for the few required seconds. "If it is, can you make another sound?

Caitlin focused the IR camera down the hallway. On the tiny screen, something around the size of a baseball was walking across the floor thirty feet away.

"It's a rat," she announced.

"Sound possibly caused by rodent," Jenn said for the recorder.

"Possibly? I can see the rat on the IR camera. The clunk was a board falling over."

"Fine," Jenn said, somewhat irritated. "Now back to the investigation."

Jenn took her ghost investigating very seriously. Something as mundane as a rat was not allowed to interrupt.

"John Riggers is it true that you were a patient here in the asylum?" she said to the darkness.

As Jenn waited for an answer, Caitlin watched another rat scampered out to join the first. Bright beady eyes turned her way.

"Creepy, the rats are watching us."

"They're just worried we're a cat."

Caitlin wasn't so sure. They were rather bold for rats; walking around in the wide open of a corridor. "Must be pretty boring here, if two nerdy high-school girls are prime-time entertainment."

Jenn giggled. It was a welcome sound in such a spooky place. "Let's take a break for a bit," she said. "The humidity's killing me."

Caitlin nodded and the two sat down on the grand staircase leading to the second floor. It had once been the centerpiece of the building. Now, buried under layer upon layer of paint, the decorative carving had been reduced to a series of undecipherable lumps and bumps.

"Forecaster said we wouldn't get below eighty until just before morning."

Jenn wiped the sweat from her brow. "At eleven at night, it should be cool."

"Texas in the summer," Caitlin shrugged.

"We love it here," the two said in chorus, mimicking their favorite comedian.

Both Caitlin and Jenn had lived their whole lives in San Antonio. Even so, the heat and cloying humidity of a Texas August wasn't something even natives ever got used to. Like most people in the south, they spent their days hiding inside air-conditioned isolation, coming out only for the special occasions of barbecue, beach trips, and the big adventure of an amusement park.

Caitlin glanced down at the IR's screen. "The two rats don't seem to mind the heat."

"They're just glad we're not cats here to eat them."

"They're watching us."

Jenn pulled the recorder from her pocket. "They'll leave if we get close, now it's time to get back to work."

The quirky blonde stood. "John, is it true that you were left here when the asylum closed for good?"

Somewhere on one of the upper floors, a door slammed shut.

Jenn sprinted up the stairs. "Going to the second floor!" she said for the recorder.

"Could've been the wind," Caitlin cautioned, just steps behind her friend. "Building's got a lot of broken windows."

As a rule, you don't assume everything is paranormal. Good investigation uses the scientific method to eliminate any possible solutions. It was often disappointing but it made for good research.

Joining Jenn at the second floor, Caitlin did a quick scan of the lobby and hallways. "Nothing showing on the IR camera, not even rats."

Jenn was starring expectantly into the darkness. The electric blue-tinged highlights in her hair caught the reflections of her flashlight. "John, we think we heard you. Can you talk to us?"

Caitlin waited. There were no further door slams and not even the clunks of rats walking on unstable boards.

"Are you here John?" Jenn clipped short the response time and ran over to the nurse station in the center of the lobby. It had once controlled this floor, a bastion of proper medical care with commanding views down both side hallways. With no more patients, it sat empty and powerless.

Jenn began shuffling through a mound of file folders which littered the surface of the old nurse station. The decades of disturbed dust hung in the air like fog.

"No sign of John Rigger's patient file," Jenn said.

"Wasn't he on the third floor?"

"Yeah but all this stuff was dumped here. Could be anything in these files."

The petite blonde sneezed. Her frail high-pitched kachew echoed along the empty corridors and abandoned patient rooms like a marble tumbling in a dryer.

Caitlin suppressed a giggle. "John Riggers certainly knows we're here now."

Jenn wiped at her nose. "It's not my fault. It's all this dust. I have allergies."

"Yeah, allergies to asbestos and lead paint."

"Smart ass," Jenn said smiling.

Like reptiles shedding their skin, the walls were in the middle of a decades-long exfoliation treatment to scour their surface of paint. Partially revealed was the archaeological history of the asylum's interior. Oldest and rarest and found only at the very bottom of the stratified layers, was the asylum's original paint—an institutional pale green.

Caitlin glanced down at her K-II meter. "Nothing on the meter either."

"Well, something slammed a door."

Caitlin panned the IR camera up and down both halls. "None of these doors are closed and no sign of any temperature variations."

Jenn flashed her light down the abandoned hallway. A modern layer of spray paint had been added by recent visitors. Garish names and lewd suggestions filled the walls where reproductions of Waterhouse and Beardsley had once hung. "Probably on third floor then. Let's head up."

The two climbed the stairs and found the same layout as on floor two. To their left, a pair of doors stood open flanking a dark hallway opening. It was mirrored on the left with one of the doors hanging askew. Stenciled on the wall above the door opening was *Ward 3E*.

"Wasn't that where John was kept?"

Jenn nodded, and walked toward the corridor opening. She wiped at her nose then drug her hand across the seat of her shorts. "John, we think we heard you. Can you make another sound?"

The responding gravely moan nearly made Caitlin pee her pants. "We've never had that kind of response."

Jenn's eyes glittered. "John Riggers, is that you?"

On Caitlin's IR display, something large and man-shaped darted across the lobby. She screamed.

Jenn hurried over. "What?"

The two girls huddled over the thermal camera's display. Caitlin replayed the image for Jenn. She insisted on watching the video three more times, her excitement growing with each viewing. Never had Caitlin seen her so happy.

"This is so effin amazing!" Blonde hair bounced as she glanced up to look down the corridor. "Let's see if we can find him."

Only one of the pair of doors that had led into the patient ward remained. It hung broken and twisted from just the top hinge.

"The apparition appeared to go into a patient ward on the east side of the building. Entering there now."

Huddled together over the camera, the two girls made their way past the broken door and into the corridor. Stripes of light pierced the darkness, painting the ceiling with the sodium vapor peach of parking lot lighting.

"There's a little bit of light in here at least."

Jenn gave the barest nod. "Patient room windows are not covered by plywood on this level," she said for the video. "We're now moving down the hallway following the apparition. Checking the first patient room on the right."

She stepped forward and through the patient room door. Her shadow hung menacingly above on the ceiling.

"What's in there?" Caitlin asked from the doorway.

Jenn swung her flashlight quickly around. "Nothing. Only paint chips, shards of glass, and bird poop but no ghosts."

She turned back to the door and Caitlin. "John Riggers, are you here?"

Caitlin counted down the five seconds for a ghost to answer. "The parking lot lighting is coming from the Mallmart."

Visible through the broken and missing wire glass was the retail giant's sign four blocks away.

"There's nothing on the thermal," Caitlin stated.

Jenn stepped closer and clicked off her flashlight. On the glowing screen of the thermal camera, nothing showed but the cold silent blue of residual heat.

"Let's try the next one."

She followed Jenn back into the corridor.

"Checking room two."

Jenn bravely stepped through the open door. Caitlin followed and swept the room for anomalies. This side of the building was dark.

"Again, nothing on thermal."

Jenn's flashlight swept the room. "There's gotta be something, we heard it."

Caitlin held up her hand. Even though the windows were empty of glass, there was almost no breeze. "No air movement so that debunks my wind theory."

Jenn stepped back into the corridor and glanced around. "And there's no loose boards for the rats to knock down."

Caitlin pointed at the disturbed flakes of paint. "But there is a path. Think it's a ghost or a homeless person."

"Ghost," Jenn answered. "Why would a homeless person come in here? There's no furniture and no protection from the weather."

"Could be a druggie shooting up."

Jenn shook her head. "Addicts wouldn't climb to the third floor. Besides, there's no needles. Remember what we found on the Donaldson investigation?"

At that house, they'd found no evidence of ghosts but loads of syringes. "Yeah, well we've still got a couple more rooms and then those double doors at the end of the hall," Caitlin offered, trying to be positive.

"Exactly, moving to room three."

Caitlin followed Jenn inside. The blonde's flashlight was focused on a tiny body on the floor.

"Oh, poor bird. I wonder what happened," Caitlin whispered.

"Wasn't a cat," Jenn answered.

Caitlin tried not to giggle.

The other three rooms were the same, with only flaking paint, bits of glass, and menacing shadows to be found.

"Maybe the sound came from the patient ward on the other side of the lobby."

Jenn shook her head. "No, Riggers was in 3 East and this is 3 East. That leaves the doorway at the end of the hall."

"But both doors are wedged open."

"Maybe he slammed some other door," Jenn answered. "But whatever we saw on thermal came this way and through those doors is the only place left for them to hide."

Slowly and cautiously, the two girls stepped inside. The room was a large rectangular space with big windows along the far wall.

"This must have been a security room," Jenn said. "There are steel security bars outside the windows."

The retail giant's parking lot lights cast an imperfect pattern on the darkness. The shadows were as tortured and damaged as the patients once housed within the room.

"No sign of life in here either," Caitlin announced.

"Nothing? Not even the orange or red blobs of rats?"

"Nope, and no red edged yellow smear of a man running," Caitlin answered. Honestly, she was grateful. Unlike Jenn, she'd prefer not to meet John Riggers' ghost.

Perhaps Jenn was having second thoughts as well. She was huddled right against Caitlin. The petite blonde took a deep breath. "Was this your room, John?"

There was no answer.

Jenn flipped on her flashlight. Metal framed beds lined the far wall of the room below the windows. A stack of mattresses lurked in one corner. They sagged with age and neglect, their pinstripes now lost to a black pattern of mold.

"We just want to talk."

"Yeah, we aren't here to harm you, honest," Caitlin added.

She focused the IR camera on two large ceramic sinks bolted to the corridor wall. One had been vandalized and was broken, its pieces strewn across the floor.

"John, are you here?" Jenn asked again.

There was a thud!

***

Caitlin opened her eyes. Her head hurt. "Eww, what is that smell?"

Then she remembered being hit in the back of the head.

She tried to sit up. "Shit, why can't I move?"

Caitlin yanked against the rusty wire tying her wrists and ankles to the steel bed frame. Crap, nothing. In addition to the wire, there was a chicken wire cage wrapped around her torso. The raw edges pricked at her skin.

"What the hell's this for?"

It couldn't be good. Her mind ran wild and she panicked. Her screams echoed dully off the security ward's sound absorptive walls.

Out of breath and her still heart racing, Caitlin could feel a line of blood running down her neck. Her thrashing had gained her nothing, only a gash to the throat. Rational thought began to reassert itself.

A moan came from her left. Just visible in the amber glow of the Mallmart parking lot lights was Jenn. Like Caitlin, she was also strapped down to a bed.

"Jenn, wake up," Caitlin yelled.

Jenn's eyes slowly fluttered open.

"I think some homeless freak attacked us. Can you get loose?"

Jenn struggled against the restraints. The squeaking of the bedframe's steel springs and her cursing in pain were a replay of Caitlin's efforts earlier.

"No, I can't."

"Shit, we've gotta figure some way out of here."

"Is he still here?" Jenn asked.

Caitlin cast a panicky glance around the room. "I don't know. I haven't heard anyone since I came to. Maybe he ran off."

"Why tie us up if he was just going to run?" Jenn countered. Her logic was correct but hardly comforting. "And what's up with the wire cage?"

They both screamed as Jenn's phone went off.

"Can you get to it?" Caitlin asked.

"No, it's in my back pocket. Might as well be on the moon." The frustration and anger that filled her voice mirrored Caitlin's own feelings.

"Maybe it was your dad. When you don't answer, he'll drive over to check on us," Caitlin speculated, looking for a lifeline.

"No, he thinks we're at the movies," Jenn replied and then began to sob. "Oh, I never should have dragged us off doing these stupid investigations."

Caitlin sighed. "It's not like you had to force me." She sounded far calmer than she felt.

"You're just being nice," Jenn said between sobs. "We're going to get raped and killed because I wanted to see a ghost. What a stupid way to die. It's not like anyone will even care if we contact the ghost of John Riggers..."

"John..." a gravelly voice muttered from the darkness.

In any other neighborhood, two girls screaming would have attracted attention. The asylum, however, was in a bad neighborhood and their screams didn't even scare away the rats. A growing number of the rodents were calmly watching from a spot against the far wall. Their eyes glittered in the darkness.

A silhouette separated itself from the shadows. It was stooped and bent with age. As it approached, the black outline became clearer. Arms dangling limp and lifeless, hands with their long, thin fingers ending in claw-like points, and the thin ragged wisps of hair, clumped in places, surrounding a bald head like an obscene halo. And the eyes, those eyes shining in the dark like an animal's, those eyes shone with desperate hunger.

The sight of John Riggers had Jenn on the scalpel edge of sanity. "But you're dead. They left you here alone, left you here to die!"

The specter moved closer. The effluvia of rotting flesh and unwashed human traveled with it. "John not alone," the gravelly voice said. "He has friends."

Caitlin was desperate. "We can be your friends too." Could she talk their way out of this?

"You're no friends to John," he spat. It dripped down his pitted and cancer-ridden face to hang in a line between his lip and chest "Your like come here often. I do as I always done. I's gonna feed you to my real friends."

As he said that, Caitlin noticed that the floor surrounding John Riggers was now filled with rats. He lifted his arm, pointing at the two girls. The rats rushed forward, scampering under the beds, swarming across the bed frame, and crawling over Caitlin's imprisoned legs. Their smell, a mix of filth and urine, filled the room. She shuddered involuntarily.

"You're going to feed us… to the rats?" Jenn asked in a voice from the far side of sanity.

John Riggers wiggled his bony fingers. "Only parts of you," he hissed.

One rat, much bigger than the others, climbed onto the end of Caitlin's bed. It sniffed at her Doc Martins then scampered up her leg and over the chicken wire cage to stare her in the eye.

Riggers giggled. "I only lets my friends eat the tough, stringy bits. Dat's why I puts you in dem cages." He stared down at Caitlin. "Dat ways, I get the juicy parts for myself."

The rat on Caitlin's chest turned and stared at John Riggers. He and the rat locked eyes for a moment. Rigger's beady eyes glowed in the dark just like the rats surrounding him. "No, you'll has to wait. All da family not be here yet."

As he said this, more and more rats were filling the room, gathering in a circle around the two girls. Several had scampered up Rigger's body for a better view. It wasn't the first time they had made such a climb. The shoulders of his threadbare asylum jumper were stained from the traffic of tiny, dirty little feet.

Jenn began screaming. Caitlin supposed that it was the rational thing to do. For some reason, she was transfixed by the rat on her chest and the way he used his front paws. They were just like hands, with fingers and everything. He seemed to be twiddling his thumbs. Probably impatient to start eating her. She wasn't sure why she was so calmly noticing all this. Shock maybe.

Then John Riggers placed his hands together. The rats all turned to face him.

"Thank you Lord for the feast that we are about to receive," he said.

The rats continued to stare, watching him, waiting.

"Amen," John said finally. With that, the rats fell upon the two bound girls in a swarm.

Caitlin screamed finally, squirming as teeth bit and claws tore into the flesh of her face, arms, and legs. She shook her head violently against their attack. The big rat from her chest was holding onto her hair with his little hands in a tight grip. She knew that he wanted to bite her ear. Her hands, in fists kept the rats from her fingers but the backs were already shredded and bleeding.

She'd closed her eyes instinctively to protect them. Through the skin of her eyelids, there was a bright flash, orange red followed by a thunderous bang. The rats jumped from her body as the sound echoed through the decrepit building. Caitlin caught the whiff of gun powder.

She opened her eyes. Riggers and the rats were gone. In the doorway to the room, a police officer was standing holding his gun. His flashlight swung around and found the two girls.

"Thank God you're here," Caitlin said. Her voice was trembling.

The officer rushed over. "I'll have you free in a moment."

"Jenn first," Caitlin told him.

He holstered his gun and pulled some sort of folding tool from his belt. As he snipped the wire holding Jenn's arms, she threw them around his shoulders and began bawling.

***

Caitlin had done her share of crying too. It turned out that Mr. Johnson, the man Caitlin thought was a cop, was actually a security guard for Mallmart.

"Thanks for coming to visit us in the hospital, Mr. Johnson," Caitlin told him. "You're a brave man. I don't think I would have gone into the asylum in the middle of the night if I'd heard screaming."

"All part of the job, I s'pose."

"Somehow, I doubt that saving dumb white girls was in the job description," Jenn snarked.

Despite what had happened, it did mean that she and Jenn had more time together. Even connected to tubes and with no makeup, Jenn was beautiful. Caitlin agonized over telling her so. Did Jenn feel the same way about her?

Mr. Johnson smiled. "I was thinking more about the oath I took at the academy to protect the public."

"We're sure glad you showed up when you did," Caitlin said. "Did they find Riggers?"

"Not yet, but he's wounded so he can't go far. The Police dogs followed a trail of blood and found where he'd been living. He had a spot tucked into the asylum's crawlspace up above the ceiling." He paused. "Probably shouldn't tell you the next part."

"What?" Jenn asked.

"They found lots and lots of bones in his nest—cats, dogs, possums, raccoons, and human. You two weren't his first victims."

"Saw that on the news," Jenn replied. "Forensic pathologist said the marks on the bones were from both rats and human teeth."

Mr. Johnson shook his head slowly side to side. "Terrible thing. So, you two gonna be okay?"

"Doctor Davison said we were lucky; nothing serious enough to require plastic surgery."

"The shots are serious," Jenn interrupted.

"Antibiotics and rabies," Caitlin explained. "And the rabies shots really hurt."

"Be glad when those are over."

Mr. Johnson nodded sympathetically. "Done that; got bit by a dog when I was a kid. It's no fun."

He eyes searched the room for another topic but found nothing. "So, they lettin' you out soon?"

"Friday," Caitlin answered.

"And next week, we get to push the button to blow up the building," Jenn added. "Mayor called and told us himself."

"I saw that a crew was workin' on the building. Must be what they're doing."

There was a knock at the door. It was the nurse. "I need to take your vitals," she announced.

Mr. Johnson stood. "I needed to be going, anyhow. You girls keep getting' better, okay?"

"Will do and thanks again."

***

Blowing up the asylum had been cool. The news crews had recorded Caitlin saying *Sorry Rat Man, I blew up your house*. The interview had gone viral. Even the national news had picked it up. She was famous.

Even though John Riggers was supposed to be dead, somehow Caitlin knew that he was really angry with her. She went to her mom and tried talking about it.

"He's sent his rats after me."

"They aren't his rats, honey, and they may not even be real," her mother replied.

"These aren't illusions, mom, they're real."

Her mom had just rolled her eyes. Despite what she thought, Caitlin saw Rigger's rats everywhere. One like to hide in the neighbor's bushes, there was a big black one that sat inside the storm drain, and there were always several peeking out from under the convenience store dumpster.

They watched her with their beady little eyes every time she left the house.

Her mom put her arm around her shoulder. "Even if you are seeing rats, they aren't his. He's dead. The police said so."

"They never found his body," Caitlin argued.

"Honey, have you discussed this with your counselor?"

Caitlin shrugged. "Yes. He's just like you and the police, assuming Riggers crawled into some hidey hole in the asylum and died."

"See, dear, you might just be imagining all of this as a result of the incident."

"Mom, they're not a trauma induced illusion, the rats are real."

She gave up. Why wouldn't anyone believe her? Phantom rats don't leave turds on your window sill. No one listened.

After several days, she began to wonder if it was all an illusion. Then came the night John Rigger's ghost appeared in her room although it didn't look like him to begin with. Instead, there was a ghostly rat, huge and hungry looking. It slowly morphed into John Riggers.

"My family still be hungry," he said before fading away.

If she hadn't been fully awake when it happened, Caitlin would have discounted it as a nightmare paired with sleep paralysis.

Caitlin pulled her phone from her pocket. "Time to call Mr. French."

She'd been debating that already but with the specter's appearance, the decision was made for her. French was a psychic that guaranteed his work. Odd thing for a psychic to do but she'd seen him work. Mr. French had located a jar of old coins her grandfather had buried. Hopefully, the psychic was just as good at dealing with rat-loving ghosts.

The psychic's office was just off Broadway in an old Victorian home. Caitlin pulled into the parking lot and turned off the Volkswagen bug's engine. The vintage VW was still coughing to an asthmatic stop as Caitlin shut the door and headed for the building.

A tall, beautiful redhead was watching her from the porch of the old house. A cigarette dangled from her right hand and in her left, she held a highball glass filled with *Jonnie Walker* on the rocks. The half-empty bottle was sitting on the railing. It was just after noon.

She smiled at Caitlin. "Mr. French is expecting you," she said cheerfully.

Caitlin walked up to the porch and found herself wondering that if the psychic's secretary was drinking on the job, this might not be as good an idea as she'd thought.

The woman must have read Caitlin's mind. "We've been up all night dealing with a Voodoo Loa," she explained. "Go on in, his office is down the hall and to the right."

The auburn haired secretary took a long draw from the glass of whiskey. Caitlin climbed the porch stairs and entered the building. Inside, the front office was crisp and clean. The smell of incense filled the air. Chrome and glass tables joined an overstuffed leather sofa and chair to fill the space. It felt more like someone's living room than an office. On the far wall was a door to a hallway. It was open and the sound of conversation was spilling out. Caitlin gathered her courage and headed down the hallway. The voices became clearer.

"You are going to have to confront Marinette," a male voice said.

Caitlin recognized it as the voice of Mr. French. He had a very refined English accent that was hard to miss.

"I'm more of a passenger when she takes over," a second voice said.

The second voice was female, and probably not much older than she was, Caitlin decided.

"You are going to have to exert your will, Charlotte. Marinette can't be taking your body out to do her dirty work," Mr. French told the girl.

"They were pimps preying on underage runaways. They deserved it."

Mr. French sighed. "I happen to agree, but you do not need to be Marinette's tool to extract vengeance," he said calmly. "What we desperately don't need at this point, and I believe that your friend Officer Durand would agree with me, is a recently dead, embalmed, and buried young woman to be discovered somehow alive and murdering pimps and child molesters."

"Marinette is really strong," the female voice said. She didn't sound hopeful.

"You are too, Charlotte. You just haven't realized it yet." French's voice said confidently. "Now go to the loo and clean up. You are dripping blood in my office, off with you!"

Caitlin had stopped in the hallway, politely waiting until Mr. French was alone. Suddenly she wondered if it might look as if she was eavesdropping. As she decided to head back to the waiting room, a college-age girl came out of the office. She was blonde, splattered with blood, and was carrying something that was a cross between a meat cleaver and a huge knife. She must be Charlotte.

The girl turned as she noticed Caitlin. "You waiting for French?"

Caitlin just nodded, frozen to the spot.

Charlotte leaned back into Mr. French's office. "Is this your day to solve girl problems?"

"Ah, that must mean that Miss Stevens is here. Come on in Caitlin."

Caitlin stared as the bloody girl turned and walked down the hall. The back of her shirt was torn open in three massive splats of blood, each revealing fist-sized bullet wounds.

"Well, if Mr. French can help a blonde zombie pimp killer, my problem with John Riggers might not be so tough," she mumbled. Caitlin took a deep breath and stepped into Mr. French's office.

"Hello, Mr. French, I don't know if you remember me, you helped my grandmother once."

The psychic stepped forward and shook her hand. "Of course, the lost jar of coins," he replied.

Like the time he had visited the house, Mr. French was wearing a gray wool suit jacket with a blue tie and vest. Today, however, the suit was somewhat rumpled.

He gestured for her to sit and Caitlin settled into a Victorian carved oak sofa with velvet cushions facing his desk.

"Gramma really appreciated finding those for her. Sorry that my parents acted so strange."

The psychic collapsed into an old wingback armchair by the window. He seemed exhausted. "It is a common response when people discover that not all in my profession are charlatans."

French's office was like a set from one the BBC historical dramas Caitlin enjoyed so much. His desk was simple but huge and looked to be at least a hundred years old. In the dark stained oak bookcases beyond were a library of antique books and what must be the paraphernalia of a psychic—odd bits of glass, silver bowls, intricate brass devices, and a taxidermied bat carefully preserved under a glass dome.

"From what Meryl told me, you need a fair bit more than a treasure located."

"Yeah, I have a ghost problem."

Behind French's wingback chair, velvet curtains in rich burgundy held open by gold tassels straddled a tall window. On the satin wallpapered walls were a patchwork of fading brown photographs of people and buildings. The gilded frames and convex glass reflected the light from the room's crystal chandelier.

"So, tell me about your incident with this ghost," he asked.

Caitlin was a little surprised. No one had believed her about the rats. She'd known better than to mention the ghost to her mom or the counselor. It was nice to finally be believed.

"Well, I've been seeing rats everywhere. Then three days ago, a rat showed up on my window sill. The way that it looked at me, I knew that *he* had sent it."

Mr. French reached over and retrieved what looked like a brass hand-held compass from his desk. "John Riggers, you mean."

Caitlin nodded. "Yes, and then last night, I was up late working on homework—you would think that being fed to rats by a psycho would be enough to get you out of schoolwork. Anyway, I had just finished my history when the bulb in my desk light burned out."

Mr. French stood and walked about the room with the compass. He cocked his head. "And then what happened?"

Caitlin noticed that the small needle on the compass stubbornly continued to point towards her no matter where he went in the room. "Well, in the dark, I got kind of panicky. I turned to go flip the room light on and there it was."

"It? Not him?" he asked before walking over and returning the compass to his desk.

Caitlin could feel her heart racing. This was the really crazy part. "No, definitely an *it*, at least at first. What I saw was a rat the size of a German Shepherd in my room. Slowly, its face changed into John Riggers. *My family still be hungry*, he said to me."

The psychic settled into his wingback chair and interlaced his fingers. "Could be a lycanthrope."

Caitlin shook her head. "No, I threw my textbook at him and it went right through. It was a ghost."

The psychic frowned. "Pity, a lycanthrope would have been rather simple." He shifted in his chair, leaning his chin on his hand. "Something must be keeping Mr. Riggers here. Typically, a post-life individual is drawn from this universe. Very odd, and he told you that his family was hungry?"

"He meant his rats," Caitlin explained. "He called the rats his family."

"Ah, of course. I suspect he is drawing from their Odic force to remain here."

A crudely made table sat next to Mr. French's chair. On it was a small brass bell. He picked it up and gave it a little shake.

Caitlin was fairly literate in paranormal lore but she was completely lost. "What kind of energy? And what does the bell have to do with it?"

Mr. French returned the bell to the table. "Odic energy. It is created by living things and is the basis of magic. By drawing on the rats' Odic energy, a magic using creature can direct that energy to perform tasks. The bell, however, is merely to summon my butler."

"Magic?" Caitlin asked.

Mr. French nodded once more. "Yes, there used to be a great deal of magic in the world, but that was long ago. The beings that could harness the Odic energy were called Vaettir. They left our world when humans began to persecute them. Those that remain, harbour ill will to human kind." He turned and gently ran a finger along the antique table's detailed carving. "Much of their anger is justified. This table for instance…" His voice trailed away and he was silent.

Caitlin looked closely at the rustic table. It seemed out of place but was undoubtedly old. Four stout legs supported the top and other than the wood pegs tying it together, there was nothing in the way of ornament.

"I was given this table by a client. It had been in their family for years. He was a proper English gentleman, tut tut and that sort of thing but his family had been cursed. They were in the ship building business and had been since the time English sailing ships and commerce still spanned the globe. Unfortunately, one of his ancestors in the process of procuring lumber to build those ships cut down a particularly large tree."

"What's so special about the tree?"

"Ah, you see this tree contained the spirit of a dryad. It took quite some doing, but I was able to convince her that the family had suffered enough. She resides here in the table still. She and I have pleasant conversations during the months of spring."

Caitlin sat fascinated. She had always considered the Harry Potter stuff as pure fantasy. Had J.K. Rowling had based her books on the Vaettir? She was about to ask when a man entered the room.

"You require something sir?"

The man was tall and had an old fashioned handlebar moustache. His black suit and tie didn't quite hide the muscles and grace of movement indicating he might be more than simply a domestic servant.

Mr. French nodded. "Yes, some tea and biscuits- the *Sumatran Enchantment* blend please. I am still rather drained from last night's affair. Oh, and if you would, please bring the summoning circle. Thank you, Ainsworth."

"Of course, sir."

Caitlin watched Ainsworth leave. She'd never seen a butler in real life, only on television. She turned back to Mr. French. "Summoning?"

"Yes. We are going to bring Mr. Riggers here to discover what is binding him to our plane of existence."

Caitlin shuddered. "Here?"

Mr. French smiled. "Not to worry my dear. He will not be able to harm you. That is the purpose of the circlet."

Even with Mr. French's reassurances, Caitlin didn't like the idea of seeing Riggers again.

"Without the energy of his rats, it would be a rather simple task to open a portal and return him to the other side. Of course for that, you could have called up any Tom, Dick, or Harry."

Caitlin shrugged. "You're the only psychic I know."

Mr. French smiled quite pleasantly. "I suppose that I do stand out in the crowd."

There was a rap on the door and Mr. French's face brightened. "Ah, at last, Ainsworth's here with the tea trolley."

Caitlin turned to see the butler rolling a cart into the room. On it was a silver tea pot, two cups and saucers, and two matching containers, one of sugar and a creamer.

Ainsworth picked up the tea pot and poured some tea into one of the cups. "One lump or two?"

Caitlin wasn't quite sure what to say. She didn't often drink tea and then it was iced tea from the Old Miller's barbecue drive-thru.

Mr. French saw her confusion "Just one for now, I should think, Ainsworth. She can always add another if it doesn't suit her taste."

The black suited butler used a set of tongs to plop one sugar cube into the steaming cup of tea before handing the cup and saucer to Caitlin.

Ainsworth prepared a second cup. To this one, he poured some cream into the cup before adding the tea.

"The circlet is on the cart. Will there be anything else sir?"

On the lower shelf of the cart was a gold ring about eight inches in diameter. It was simple in design but there looked to be symbols or writing incised into the surface.

"Perhaps Ainsworth, but I will ring if that is the case."

The butler nodded with a slight bow and exited the room.

Caitlin sipped at her tea. It was quite hot but smelled amazing. Iced tea didn't smell much, she realized. Her curiosity got the better of her. "What happened to that girl earlier?"

"Ah, Charlotte. Fairly messy situation, that." His left brow rose. "Let's just say that if you ever have the chance to read from a magical book, just don't. Agreed?"

Caitlin nodded.

Mr. French inhaled the aroma of the steaming tea and settled back in his chair. "Back to your problem, when we do the summoning, we must both hold onto the circlet. It will draw Mr. Riggers here and contain him, so you have no need to be afraid. Whatever happens, do not let go of the circlet. If you do, he will disappear so try to maintain your hold until we have finished questioning him."

He took a sip of the tea. "Whatever happens, we must discover what it is that he wants from you."

Caitlin's hand was shaky as she lifted the teacup to her lips. She was glad that Mr. French was polite enough not to notice.

"There was a case several years ago that illustrates what we must do rather perfectly. A client came to me upset that he was being haunted by his mother. Upon summoning her, we discovered that she was upset with her son for quitting college. My client returned to school and once graduated, poof, the mother's ghost was gone. That is what we have to do with Mr. Riggers. Complete whatever task he feels is unfinished."

Mr. French placed his teacup and saucer down on the table and retrieved the gold circlet.

"Are you ready to begin?"

Caitlin nodded reluctantly.

The psychic stood and pulled the velvet curtains closed before joining Caitlin on the Victorian sofa. "Hold the circlet firmly with both hands."

She wrapped her fingers around the gold ring. It was warm and smooth.

"Good. Ready?" he asked.

She took a deep breath. "Yes."

"Then we shall begin. John Riggers, you have chosen to remain in this world. You have also chosen to contact this girl, Caitlin Stevens. Now, we reply in kind. Appear and tell us why you choose to remain. What part does Caitlin Stevens play in completing your cycle of existence?"

Just as in her room, the lightbulbs, this time in the chandelier, shattered one by one, plunging the room into darkness.

"John…" a voice hissed from the confines of the circlet.

Caitlin shivered. It was him. In the circlet, a cold mist was forming between her fingers and those of Mr. French. It began to swirl, rising from the circlet, bringing with it the stench of the asylum. Within that swirling vapor, John Rigger's face formed to stare at her.

"My family not fed," the ghostly image said. It swelled and grew until a fully formed man floated in the air above them. He was complete down to the stains on his asylum jumpsuit and the claw-like boniness of his hands. He glared down.

French nodded. "And when your family is fed?"

"Dey's have no more home." Rigger's pointed his bony finger at Caitlin. "She done blowed it up."

Mr. French took a deep breath. "So, if we keep your family fed *and* find them a home, you will be satisfied?"

The ghostly image of John Riggers turned his gaze to Mr. French. "Should be loved too. Dey like being family." He turned to Caitlin and stabbed his finger in her direction. "You fix dis. You broked it."

Oddly, Caitlin was not so afraid of John any more. Sure he was a psychopath who had tried to kill and eat her but she could feel that he truly cared for his rat friends. She nodded. "Okay, I will."

The image of John Riggers faded, collapsing back into the circlet. As the last of him faded away, he seemed to be smiling.

Mr. French let go of the circlet and the mist disappeared with a pop. He stood and walked to the curtains, pulling them open, bathing the room in sunlight. Caitlin turned from the brightness and saw sitting in the doorway, two rats. The larger of the two was standing on his hind legs. He ran forward and scampered up the side of the sofa. Caitlin steeled herself. Rather than jumping onto her, the rat sat on the arm of the sofa and stared. She knew what she had to do and shuddered. Slowly, she extended her hand to the rat.

It sniffed her fingers and then looked at her expectantly.

What did it want? "Oh, of course, you're hungry. Just a minute." She picked up several cookies from the tea cart and offered them to the rat.

In the doorway, the other rat scampered forward. Caitlin jumped a bit as it scurried up her pant leg to sit in her lap. She offered it a cookie. He hungrily took the cookie in his little hands and began nibbling.

The first rat carefully watched. He hadn't even picked up his cookie.

Caitlin frowned. "It isn't poison!" She retrieved the cookie and took a bite. "See!"

The rat on her lap watched all this while busily nibbling away. She offered the cookie to the big rat on the sofa arm again. He rushed forward and took the cookie and began eating.

Caitlin shook her head. "Really, you'd let your friend rat eat a poison cookie and do nothing? We really need to work on your manners."

"It is a part of their hierarchy," Ainsworth said calmly from the door. Caitlin jumped. She hadn't noticed the butler arrive. "As a group, they learn in this manner, letting the weaker members of the group take the risks to protect the whole."

"I'm not sure I like that idea. It seems mean."

Ainsworth nodded. "True but the world they live in is a mean place."

Mr. French leaned forward. There was concern on his face. "You are adapting to the rats exceptionally quickly."

Caitlin was watching the smaller rat eat. He was very skinny. "Yeah, I should be scared shouldn't I, but even at the asylum I was fascinated by their little hands."

French stood and walked to his bookcase. The rats eyed him warily. He found a small box and took a set of brass-rimmed optical lenses from inside. He turned and stared at Caitlin through first one, then another, and then a third of the odd monocles.

Caitlin waited. Finally, French noticed her staring.

"I'm sorry. These will identify if you might have been, ah shall we say, contaminated by Mister Riggers. Your sudden empathy for his family concerns me."

"And these will tell you if I am?"

"Yes, your pale will be distorted."

She nodded as if that made perfect sense and sat silently as he continued.

After a long period of flipping, rotating, and combining lenses, Mr. French seemed convinced. "Apparently, you just find rats interesting. You are a very strange and intriguing girl, Ms. Stevens."

She smiled, taking it as the compliment French intended it to be. Caitlin had always equated strange with interesting. It was nice to find an adult that did so as well.

The psychic placed the box of lenses back on the shelf. "So, I have devised a plan, but there are several things that Ainsworth and I will need to procure before we begin. Can you join us this evening around nine?"

She looked up from the rat on her lap. "Sure, I'll just say that I am going to a study group. I do that all the time."

***

That evening, when Caitlin arrived at Mr. French's office, she was surprised to see a moving truck. Mr. French and Ainsworth were standing next to it. She parked the Volkswagen and walked over to join them.

"You're moving?" she asked.

Mr. French nodded. "Yes, this area is gentrifying and my clientele are finding the bright lights and all of the attention rather distasteful."

Ainsworth smirked. "That and we can't stand the mindless muck-spouts and loiter-sacks that have moved in. Annoying gits have more cash than is good for 'em."

Mr. French sighed. "I do not care for the hipsters either, but that is no reason to resort to name calling."

Ainsworth scowled. "Call 'em what you will. I'll be gladly rid of them once we've moved."

"Where are you moving too?" Caitlin asked.

"I have purchased a house on Hickman, just north of Five Points. You shall see for yourself as we will be going there later tonight." The psychic pulled a set of keys from his vest pocket. "In addition to the house, I purchased an abandoned warehouse that is just across the corner. It shall be your rats' new home, but first we must collect them. Inside the lorry, please, if you would."

Mr. French stepped over to the cab of the truck and opened the door. He held it for her as she climbed in. She slid across the bench seat to the passenger side and belted in. There was a plastic hula dancer mounted to the dash and several Mickey-D's Kiddo Meal toys in the center console. It seemed very unlike Mr. French.

"No fuzzy dice?" she asked as he climbed in.

He turned and smiled. "No. As you've guessed, it is Ainsworth that generally drives the lorry."

It didn't seem much like the quiet and reserved butler either, but Caitlin didn't comment further.

Mr. French started up the truck. "If you are interested, I have an employment opportunity to discuss with you."

That caught Caitlin by surprise. "A job?"

"Yes. You are going to become a farmer," he said, as he struggled with the gears.

On the porch of the old house, Caitlin saw Ainsworth cringing as the clutch caught and the truck began to move.

"Your newly found family members will need to earn their keep. One way that they can do so is as an energy farm for me."

Caitlin was completely lost at this point. "A farmer?"

"Yes, a rat farmer. There are devices in your rats' new home that will absorb the excess Odic energy they produce. It will not hurt them in any way. Rodents are creative and energetic little buggers and as such are an excellent Odic resource."

He turned out of the parking lot onto Broadway in an overly wide arc. He straightened the truck out and they were on their way.

"You have been directing them to return to the asylum as I requested?"

She nodded. "Every time I saw a rat today, I focused on food and then the asylum. They scampered off as I did so. Do you think this will work?"

"I have contacted and instructed Mr. Riggers to do so as well. Your new family should be waiting for us."

Caitlin suppressed a shudder. *Her family*. It hadn't been that long ago that her family was trying to eat her. She took a deep breath.

"Do not worry," Mr. French said, misreading the attempt to calm herself as a sigh of concern. "We might miss one or two but they are intelligent. Any we miss will find their way to the warehouse. They found us this morning, didn't they?"

She nodded, visualizing the back of the truck full of rats. It was a good thing that Jenn wasn't here. She'd be screaming.

***

It turned out that Mr. French was a better psychic than he was a truck driver. On arriving at the asylum, he pulled into front drive as far as possible. What little remained of the asylum was now surrounded by an eight-foot chain link fence with razor wire strung at the top and *No Trespassing* signs every twenty feet courtesy of the San Antonio police. In the brightness of the truck's headlights, thousands of beady little eyes watched. If Mr. French noticed, he gave no indication. He set the parking break and turned off the ignition.

"Now we get out and entice your rats to join us in the back.

Her rats. Caitlin hid a shudder and climbed out.

After a moment, French joined her. "There is a large bag of deer corn in the back," he said. "Once we put down the lorry's loading ramp, you can then summon the rats to come eat. Then we shall wait for them to arrive."

Caitlin looked around. There were rats everywhere. Did French not notice? Summoning really wasn't going to be necessary.

"I think they know we're here," she said as she followed French to the back of the truck.

French undid the latch and slid up the back door. The metallic rumble was loud as thunder in the still, humid night. Caitlin looked around nervously. The only people nearby were at the bus stop down by the Mallmart four blocks away. Luckily, they were keeping to their own business. Caitlin wondered if Mr. Johnson was on duty tonight.

"I shall require some assistance with the loading ramp," French said.

He unlocked the loading ramp and motioned for her to grab her side and together they pulled it out, and placed the end on the ground. Hungry eyes were watching them with focused interest. Even French must have seen them by now.

He lifted and locked the ramp into place. "Time to lead your family inside."

"*Lead* them inside?"

Mr. French glanced down at her feet. Around her, ten to twelve rats had gathered. Another was in the street, staring at her. At the Mallmart, a white Ford *Taurus* pulled out and was heading this way.

"Get out of the street," she yelled.

That rat scampered over to join the horde massed around her tennis shoes.

Mr. French stepped away from the back of the truck. "The lorry is something quite alien to them. They will not enter without you leading them."

She shuddered, thinking of being in the confined space of the truck with all the rats. "Do I have to?"

He handed her a pocket knife. "Here, you will need this to open the feed bag."

The back of the truck was now surrounded by a sea of rats. She gestured up the aluminum loading ramp.

"That way."

A rather large rat climbed over the others and scampered up the leg of her jeans, clawup up the back of her tee shirt, and sat on her shoulder.

Caitlin turned to the rat. "I was wondering where you were."

It was the large rat from this morning. He was twiddling his thumbs. She turned back to her milling congregation and pointed into the truck. "The food's in the truck. Everyone inside."

At her direction, several of the smaller rats scurried up the ramp and began exploring. Ainsworth had been right—the smaller and weaker rats were the ones that took the risks. One of the risk-takers, an albino rat far smaller than the rest, scurried around the interior perimeter of the truck and then ran back. Whatever it said with a glance to the others resulted in a sudden flow of rats up the ramp.

Caitlin followed. She could only take shuffling baby steps to avoid stepping on tails. Once inside, she opened the pocket knife and slit open the bag of deer feed. She put the knife in the pocket of her jeans and scooped a double handful onto the scarred plywood floor of the truck.

"Here you go!"

It was like throwing beads to a Mardi Gras crowd except there were no flashing boobs. With the last of the rats inside and happily eating, Mr. French walked over and unhooked the ramp from the truck.

Caitlin panicked. "What are you doing?"

French looked up at her. "I have seen a great many things during my life. In my oddest imaginings, I could never have conceived that one day I would be assisting a sixteen-year old girl to transport a lorry-full of rats."

He was ignoring her question. The churning mass of rat bodies had her traumatized subconscious ready to run. It was only the open door that was keeping her panic at bay. "I have to ride back here with the rats?"

She knew the answer from the look on French's face.

"I'm afraid so, but perhaps this might help. Turn and look at the rat on your shoulder."

Caitlin turned and stared at the big rat. He paused his nibbling on the kernel of corn. His little whiskers twitched happily and he leaned his little head to one side.

"You want to be scratched?" she asked. He leaned forward, making it apparent that yes, indeed, that was exactly what he wanted. She reached up and began rubbing his neck with her finger. Caitlin could feel his happiness. "More to the right? How's that?"

She turned back to Mr. French. "Okay, I guess I'll ride back here. Just watch the bumps, okay?"

"I shall avoid the bypass," he said. "There shouldn't be much traffic on the local roads this late at night."

Caitlin shoved the feed bag over, emptying it onto the floor. "Remember that I don't have a belt. No sharp turns."

Mr. French hoisted himself up the back of the truck and grabbed the line to pull down the sliding cargo door. "I don't believe that this particular vehicle can make sharp turns."

Caitlin shooed the rats from a spot on the floor and settled nervously to the plywood surface. The little white albino leapt onto her lap. He plopped down at the bend of her hip and began gnawing at the corn kernel he held securely in his tiny hands.

"And please don't shut off the cargo light," she begged.

"I shall not."

"Thanks." Several other rats joined the albino. She began absent-mindedly stroking their backs as the door slid closed.

***

It had been several weeks since they had brought Caitlin's rats to their new home. The warehouse held the psychic's menagerie as well as Caitlin's new family. Additionally, it had a proper laboratory for research as well as storage for his treasures and mementoes. That was what they were doing today. The gentlemen from *Two Juans and a Truck* had stacked everything by the loading dock. Now, the problem was finding a place for it all.

Caitlin was examining one of the boxes. "This one doesn't have a label."

She handed it to Mr. French.

He took the box and lifted off the top. Inside were a ring of old-fashioned keys, an apron, and several scraps of scorched tracing tissue with the faint lines of sewing patterns still visible. All of it smelled of smoke.

He wrinkled his nose at the acrid charred wood smell. "I had forgotten about this one. It was my first case in America." He pulled out a flame seared business form and handed it to the her.

"The logo says it's from the *Triangle Shirtwaist Company*."

French picked up the ring of keys. "There was a fire and one-hundred and forty-six men, women, and children died," he told her. "The exit doors had been locked by the manager."

"Why?"

"The workers were spending too long on their breaks."

"That's terrible."

"Yes. Five years later, New York University leased the building. No matter what they did, the doors were constantly being unlocked and opened. That's when I was called in. It took a demonstration of both the newly installed fire sprinkler system and the panic hardware on the exit doors to finally convince the deceased former employees of the building's safety."

Caitlin handed the paper back to Mr. French who returned it to the box.

"So, Ainsworth tells me that you have been helping him feed my menagerie," he said.

She nodded. "Yes. Well, not the Vartilliamenthum. It doesn't like me."

Bob, the rather large alpha male rat, scampered across the floor and climbed up to her shoulder. His coat was shiny and bright and his little clawed hands remarkably clean. She was not going to have filthy clothes and had insisted on baths once a week. Oddly enough, they didn't seem to mind. Caitlin had posted a video of Bob lounging in his tiny tub and he was quite the internet star now.

French was using a china marker to scribble a note on the box of artifacts. "With regards to the Vartilliamenthum, you are not alone. It does not care for me either."

Caitlin didn't reply. Her mind was focused on a question that she knew had to be asked even though it might mean ending her time with Mr. French.

"No witty response?"

French turned and must have seen the serious look in her eye. "What?"

"Mr. French, there's something I need to tell you."

"What's that?"

"I should have told you this when I got here this morning but I was afraid what you might think," she blurted out.

"Afraid, why?"

Caitlin turned to Bob, gave him a scratch, and then at the menagerie. "Because you might decide I'm crazy after all and make me stop working here."

"You are not crazy, Caitlin."

"Even though I saw John Riggers' ghost in my room again last night."

"He has returned? Interesting. Generally a spirit dissipates once their task is done," French replied quite calmly. "His family has been here for a week now. Strange that he waited so long."

Caitlin nodded. "That's why I thought you'd think I was crazy."

French chuckled. "The average spirit dissipates but I dare say that Mr. Riggers was hardly average. What did he want?"

"To say he's happy with what we've done."

A stray lock of hair escaped Caitlin's ponytail. Bob took the loose bit and tucked it behind her ear.

"You're not crazy. The rats would not listen to you if you were," French explained. "But as to seeing Riggers again, do not worry. The fact that the rats are fat and healthy simply gave him enough energy to stay. The man had a troubled life. Trust was something that was lacking in his life. My guess would be that he stayed to make sure you took care of the family."

"So I can keep working here?"

"Ainsworth would have a conniption if I were to let you go."

Caitlin threw her arms around the psychic. "Thank you. The rest of my life is so fucked up right now. Everyone thinks I'm mental because I'm working with rats. My parents want me to quit. You're the one person that understands."

French tsked. "I have no more concerns with regards to Mr. Riggers. Even if I did, you know that Ainsworth can take very good care of the family. With that in mind, would it be easier if you were to quit?"

"No, well, maybe, but I like working here! It's the one place I belong. Even my best friend Jenn doesn't understand." Her shoulders collapsed and she sighed. "At least Jenn believed me about seeing John Riggers as a ghost. I knew better than to tell anybody else about that."

Mr. French considered the situation for a moment. "What is it exactly that your parents believe you do as a part of your employment?"

"I told them that I was helping Ainsworth with your menagerie. I kinda want to take Bob home with me occasionally so I told them it included some rats."

Mr. French lifted his eyebrows. "I hope you didn't mention any of the, um shall we say, more exotic specimens."

Caitlin shook her head. "No, I only mentioned the rats."

"Then I shall draft a letter explaining that, in addition to my other animals, I am having you work with the rats as therapy to overcome any possible phobia that might have developed. Will that help?"

"I think so. At least my counselor will understand that."

She turned to face Bob. "I guess that means you don't go home with me."

The rat's shoulders dropped in disappointment.

She reached up and scratched his neck. "Don't worry, when I move out for school in a couple of years, I can bring you home as often as I like."

What most people believe demons to be is amazingly inaccurate. Demons do not have horns, or tails, or bodies at all. They are formless hungry things from other dimensions and not hell as the Vatican would have you believe. As French finds out, trying to get them to return to those dimensions is always something of a challenge.

The Box

Winston Jones stumbled through the office doors carrying a Mallmart plastic bag and the stink of a demon. And it wasn't the run-of-the-mill resident of the infernal regions, this was old, powerful, and hateful.

"I called earlier. I'm told you can help me," Mr. Jones stammered.

Meryl, the secretary, stood and motioned for the elderly gentleman to follow her. "Right this way. Mr. French is expecting you."

In addition to being a secretary, Meryl was also a succubus. She had little patience for fools like Mr. Jones. Anyone who takes home a box they found in the cemetery deserves the disasters that follow.

The psychic was waiting inside his office door. "A pleasure to meet you, Mr. Jones. Won't you have a seat?"

The elderly man nodded, settling into the Victorian settee. "Thank you for seein' me. I'm at my wit's end. This demon is ruinin' my life."

"First, I should clarify that what you're calling a demon, is not, technically, a creature from hell." French took a spot in the wingback chair by the window. "The idea that demons come from hell to torment the wicked is an archaic superstition created by the Church. What you have is a malevolent force from somewhere quite separate from hell."

Mr. Jones was confused, as most people are by the true nature of the underworld.

French tried another tack. "Let me explain. You see, what humans know of as Heaven and Hell is a region of reality populated by a race of non-corporeal beings. These beings are known as the Devine and the Infernals. Though they are the same species, they long ago split into two factions over an age-old argument of how humans should be treated."

"So, one of these is hauntin'me?" Mr. Jones asked.

"No, the Devine and the Infernal are both quite benign," French explained. "I merely started here to clarify what hell is and isn't. This demon you have is not from hell. It is from somewhere far worse."

"Great."

"So, to begin, tell me about your problem in some detail. You mentioned a few things over the phone, but a more complete version of the story would help my investigation."

Mr. Jones took a long, deep breath, letting it out slowly. "This all started when I was walkin' my dog in the cemetery."

"That would be city cemetery number one."

Mr. Jones nodded. "Yep. The dog started diggin' at this thing in the dirt. When I went over, it was this wooden box."

He pulled a dirt crusted wooden box from the Mallmart bag and handed it to the psychic. It was the size of a package of business envelopes with corroded brass fittings and a broken padlock. The psychic undid the hasp and lifted the lid. Inside was unquestionably the mummified remains of a human tongue.

"And you took the box home?"

"Yes, it was still locked at that point. I didn't break the box open 'til I got home. That's what released the demon."

French nodded. "Yes and no. The box and lock are merely symbolic parts of the magic that held closed a portal. When you opened the box that set in motion the magic which created a passageway to whatever other-dimensional realm this thing existed within."

"Well, the damn thing's here now, and it's livin' under my house."

French sighed. "Yes, and getting it to return to its place of origin will not be easy. In the past, these creatures were called upon to perform a task. Once done, they would leave. They are rarely called upon any more as they could not be trusted. The demons took great delight in perverting the intentions of the summoner, causing mayhem and havoc in the process. It's unusual that this one chose to remain and torment you after it had been freed. Usually, their tortures are reserved for the person who summoned and trapped it."

The old man scowled. "Don't need to know all that, just need to know how to get rid of the damn thing? I tried burning sage and using holy water."

"A good start," French replied. They actually weren't. Sage worked on certain types of hauntings—human spirits, not demonic. Holy water had some small effect, usually limited to making things wet.

He handed the box back to Mr. Jones. "Where exactly in the cemetery did you find this? If you would picture it in your mind, I will share that thought with you, if that is acceptable."

"Sure. Whatever you need."

The image was of a path running alongside several limestone tombstones. A cluster of large juniper trees were nearby. They would serve as a landmark.

"Thank you. I shall pay a visit to the cemetery. Perhaps one of the individuals interred nearby had a history with this entity. For now, if you would please continue with what has happened since the box was opened."

"Well, as soon as I broke open the lock, every light in the house went out. Blew out, I should say. It weren't the power, although the fuses had all popped too, but I mean every single bulb either burst or burnt out."

"Oedic energy pulse. Not uncommon in portal breaches. Continue."

"Bulb in the flashlight was out too, so I found some matches and lit a candle. I managed to replace the fuses with some spares. That's when I found all the light bulbs dead. I only had three replacements. While I was gettin' the lights in the kitchen working, it felt like something was watching me, something in the edge of the shadows that I could almost see. At the time, I just ignored it as the jitters."

"The human mind is conditioned to filter out the paranormal," French explained. "You may find yourself seeing a great deal more supernatural things from now on. I'm afraid that once the mind has been made aware of such events, it rarely goes back to way it was. So, then what happened?"

"I drove to the store to buy more bulbs. By the time I got home, I was thinkin' that this wasn't normal—a freak electrical pulse just happened to occur as I opened the box? Too much of a coincidence. An' I was right. As I pulled into the driveway, I done seen through the windows this blood red light floating in my bedroom. Right then, I knew I'd done something mighty foolish by bringing that box home."

"Interesting manifestation. How large was this light?" French asked.

"About the size of a basketball. Evertime it moved, lightning bolts would shoot like legs. I done sat there for some time wondering what to do. Finally, I took the prayer beads from the truck's rearview mirror, got a hammer from the toolshed, and marched to the back door. Then, my courage done failed me. I stood there on the stoop like an idiot for quite some time afore I opened up the back door."

"And was the manifestation still present?"

"Found it in the front room. As soon as I entered, it done zapped me with its lightning bolts."

Mr. Jones pulled open his shirt. "Done this," he said, pointing to two spots on his chest covered by Band-Aids. "You need to see the wounds?"

French shook his head. "Perhaps later, if that proves necessary. Continue with the story for now."

"I done tried hittin' it with the hammer. Didn't do much, although it did make the motherfucker spark like crazy."

"It was still non-corporeal at that point."

"I guess. After it shocked me, I had the thought that if this thing is electrical, maybe I could cause it to ground out. I had some electrical cable in the shed, so I done run out and got it. I secured one end to the outside faucet, then went back inside. By then, the thing was in the kitchen—lookin' for me, probly. I stuck that wire into the bastard and damned if he didn't start a flashing. Asshole blew out the new bulbs in the kitchen, then ran off, back to the front of the house. I'd a chased after him, but the cable weren't long enough."

French was puzzled. "Odd that this worked. Oedic energy and electricity are quite different. Let me check once again, just to be certain this wasn't some natural phenomenon such as ball lightning."

The psychic pulled a set of old-fashioned spectacles from his pocket. He placed them on his head and rotated several additional lenses over each eye. "Well, that settles that. It wasn't natural. You have the unmistakable traces of demonic power about you."

French placed the glasses back in his pocket. "Sorry, continue."

"So, by that time, I was near scared to death, so much so, I slept in the truck. In the morning, I drove to the Hardware Depot and bought two-hunnert feet of wire. I figure'd to run ground wires through the whole damn house. When I got back, ready to do battle with this sumbitch, it was nowhere to be found. Ran the wires anyways."

French leaned back in the wingback chair. "But this was not the end of the matter?"

"No sir. Nothin' else happened for a day or two, so's I just attributed it to some freak phenomenon, like that there ball lightning you mentioned. Then I began hearing things underneath the house. Now, that ain't uncommon. You get the possum or the skunk under there occasionally but they're usually pretty quiet. No, this here was struggling and squealing. Somethin' was afightin' under there. After that, the house started smelling of somethin' dead, so's I figured I'd better go under there and drag whatever corpse was in there out. I was a thinkin' this was just some feral dog or something, maybe killing rats—that there's what the squealing sounded like. Anyways, I done got me a flashlight, a shovel, and my shotgun, just in case, and I got on my belly and crawled under there."

"You were thinking this was just an animal," French said.

"Yessir. Shoulda put two and two together, but I didn't."

"Understandable," French said.

"So, I'm under theres, and as I come near the front of the house, these two glowing eyes are astarin' at me. And I don't mean reflecting my flashlight, I mean honest to God glowing, like coals in a barbeque pit. It roared at me, scariest sound I ever done heard, and charged. I flipped the safety on that shotgun and let the thing have it. All it done was slow it down some. Seein' that, I started scootin' backward as fast as could. I fired several more times, keepin' the thing back. When I got out of there, I tell you, I damn near shit my pants."

"And how big do you think this thing was?" French asked.

"Hard to tell. It was just this darkness, blockin' the light from the vents in the house skirt. I couldn't make out anything, not a face, or hair, or nothin'. And the odd thing is, at times, it seemed to spread out, taking most of the space under the house, and at other times, usually when I was about to shoot, the damned thing made itself all narrow-like."

"But the gunshots slowed it down. Interesting. Did it seem like it was taking damage, or was it just scared of the light and noise?"

"Bit of both, I think," Mr. Jones replied. "Seemed to blast bits of the darkness off, but not enough to hurt it much."

"Are you still in the house?"

Mr. Jones shrugged. "Don't got much choice. Cain't afford no motel. Been sleepin' in the truck. Just cooking and doing my business in the house. Scary, sitting on the pot, knowing what's roamin' around under the floorboards. When I was unnerneath fighting the thing, my shootin' done blowed three holes in the floor of the front room. Found that out when I went back inside. I could see that motherfucker through the holes, red eyes aglaring at me. I got up the courage to shove some plywood over the holes, but I ain't been brave enough to go back in the front room since."

French steepled his fingers. This was going to be a difficult case. Demons usually were. "So, you think it is eating rats?"

"More 'n that, now. It goes out huntin' at night. My neighbors been complaining about missing pets. I think the thing done ate 'em."

French scowled. That was not good news. "Your demon is using the material it consumes to create a physical form for itself."

"It's getting' big. Gonna be huntin' humans soon, as I figure it. That's why I come to you. Don't wanna be next on the menu."

"Certainly not," French said. "Have you observed the entity leaving to go hunt?"

"As a matter of fact, I have. Slinks along near the ground, all lumpy like, then kind of rears up to go over the fence."

"When does this occur? Is it at the same time each night?"

The old man nodded. "Yessir. After my neighbors told me the pets done gone missing, I stayed up, watching for the damn thing. Left just after midnight and came back around three, draggin' sumpin' with it. Gotta unnerstand, I was watching from the truck so's I didn't see too good. Still, that was close enough. Damn thing sure does stink."

"So you've only seen it the once?"

"Mostly, but it wakes me up ever night now. It's getting' big and makes a fair bit o' noise."

French ran his hand over his beard, thinking. "I would recommend you stay here tonight. I believe that you are correct with regards to this thing's next source of sustenance, and I doubt that your vehicle will provide adequate protection."

"That's a might kind of you, Mr. French."

Meryl would be upset, but he couldn't, in good conscience, leave the man in such close proximity to the creature. "My secretary will show you to a room. Meanwhile, I must make preparations to send this creature back from whence it came."

"What'cha gonna do?"

French took a deep breath. "There is only one thing that will guarantee a return of such a creature. I must go to the reality it came from, and find the object the creature is using for an anchor. A demon cannot fully leave its realm. It uses a spiritual thread tied to something in its reality. If I can disrupt that connection, the creature will be drawn back to defend it. Once it has returned, I need only close the portal behind it."

"You're makin' it sound simple an' easy, but I'm bettin' it ain't either."

"You are correct, Mr. Jones, It will not be."

***

Mr. Jones' house was typical of the pier and beam construction from the 1920's. Much of the white lead-based paint had long ago peeled away, leaving the house the gray of weathered wood. At twenty-seven minutes past midnight, the thing crawled out from underneath the house. In the darkness, even with the light-enhancement provided by his spectacles, the thing was more shadow than object. The old man's description was spot on. Parts of the thing were more solid than others—probably incorporating bits and pieces of the creatures it had fed on. The 1958 movie *The Blob* came to mind. Unfortunately, Steve McQueen wouldn't be able to freeze this creature like he had that monster from outer space.

The thing lurched over the fence. Once it was well down the road, French went to the back door of the house and let himself in. In the front room, just as Jones had said, a sheet of plywood was on the floor. French shoved it aside. The three holes were not large enough to allow French's body to pass. He'd assumed as much. Reaching into his bag, he pulled out a battery-powered saw. The old home's pine flooring offered little resistance.

He flipped to the fifth lens on the glasses and ducked under the floor. The lens illuminated objects of demonic or magical origin. A string of red light, like a laser only curved and fluid, led to a hole in the skirting around the house. Somewhere, in the other direction, it would lead French to the portal.

He crawled over the desiccated earth. Bits of bone and partially consumed flesh littered the ground. What was unquestionably the femur of a human lay in a slight depression. It was here that the glowing thread disappeared into the aether.

French checked his watch. It was fifteen minutes before one giving him only two hours to find and destroy the creature's anchor. French took hold of the thread and threw himself into the portal.

A reality shift is never pleasant; less so when the reality you find yourself in has very few similarities to your own. Here, there was no up or down, just multiple sideways. Each step altered the surroundings like the turning of a kaleidoscope. Finding his way back to the portal would be problematic once the creature's life-thread was cut.

He needed his own anchor. French pulled a ball of twine and some duct tape from his bag. The only objects nearby were some star shaped crystals. He picked one up. The crystalline lattice folded eye-bendingly into a fourth-dimensional origami star. It would have to do. French duct-taped the string to the star, then tossed it back through the portal. So far, so good. As insurance, he made several loops in the string and wrapped it around one of the star's larger cousins. With that done, he began walking, following the psychic thread. Where it ended, he would find the creature's anchor.

It was no easy walk. With each step, the direction of gravity shifted subtly, sending French falling onto the broken glass sand on numerous occasions. Thankfully, the glass shards only appeared sharp. Rather than cut the skin, the glass attached themselves to his bare hands and arms. Whatever these creatures were, they sought to feed on his essence. He scraped the hungry things off with a knife from the bag. Metal, apparently, they had little taste for, releasing their grip as the steel of the knife came close.

"My old armor would have been a good choice of attire today," French muttered to himself. His voice echoed off facets and walls unseen, to return twisted and bent, distorted into a parody of his voice.

"A tire toooo day. A tire toooo day. A tire toooo day." For some reason, that part of the echo refused to die.

Ahead, a black monolith bisected the plane that was this footstep's reality. French took another step more. The monolith remained, though now at a different angle. Several more steps, and the monolith was ninety-degrees rotated, pointing like an accusing finger at French. He paused, checking the psychic thread. It was heading toward the monolith despite each shift of the kaleidoscopic reality.

"Whatever that large object is, it's likely the anchor."

Two more steps and something at the base of the monolith moved. Several somethings. They were black—not the shiny black of a sports car or the dull radar-reflective black of a stealth fighter, but an inkiness, like a hole-in-reality black. They stuttered forwards, angling to catch French between them. How far away they were was a difficult thing to tell. Distance meant very little here. Mr. Jones had mentioned that the beast in his house had been affected by electricity, or more correctly, as if it was electricity. Perhaps these things might be as well. The glass sand creatures had avoided the knife's steel, and steel was a good conductor.

The two black somethings, guardians probably, were nearly in position for their ambush. It was time to do something. French brought up a protection bubble, then threw lightning at the nearest of the two. Perhaps a circuit could be overloaded.

With the crackle of ozone, lightning the color of rust, smashed into the guardian. The thing swelled, fractal surfaces growing larger and larger.

French ceased his attack. "That was a bloody bad mistake."

Now twice the size of the monolith, the thing loomed over French and the other guardian. The smaller creature shied away, sensing menace from its larger brethren. It backed cautiously, then turned and ran, skittering away on multitudes of cilia legs. The larger creature's response was immediate. A sliver, black as the void between stars, stabbed out, impaling the smaller guardian. It wiggled helplessly, like spaghetti on a fork, as the larger guardian devoured it.

Obviously, energy-based attacks were out. Fire, maybe?

French found the lump of Baltic amber in his coat pocket. It was a *staubecken*, an object in which magical energy could be stored. This particular staubecken had been with French for over three-hundred years, given to him as payment for dispatching a banshee. French drew from the magical battery, throwing a conflagration of flames at the beast. Unlike the lightning attack, this seemed to be working. Engulfed in fire, the guardian screamed in pain, flailing about as the flames chewed at its obsidian nothingness. The creature careened into the monolith, smashing it to the ground with a sound of universal proportions. If Vesuvius were to battle the San Andreas fault, and a tidal wave was mixed in for harmony, it would approach the horror and spectacle of this sound.

French felt the spirit thread jump. Things were definitely not going as planned. Might this be his last adventure? Time for the better part of valor. He turned and ran, following his limp white line of string.

French was near where the glass sand creatures had first attacked him when the portal was torn open. Hands, paws, claws, and hooves forced the opening wider. The thing from under Mr. Jones' house had returned home. Its body, an ebony stew of misshapen body parts, organs, bits of bone, eyes, and mouths filled with teeth, thrust its way through the portal. It saw the guardian and charged.

French threw himself to the side, sliding through the hungry glass sand, scrambling for cover behind a bush-size origami star.

Like a flea watching a dog fight, French was helpless, cringing in terror, as the beast and the guardian, like two great titans, crashed into each other. The fabric of reality heaved, casting French, the sand, and the multi-dimensional stars into the air. Glass shards scrambled for purchase, adhering to French for safety, not sustenance.

Locked in combat, the beast and the much-larger guardian fought, tentacles of darkness interlocked with the claws and teeth of Labrador and rat.

With the two creatures occupied, French scrambled to follow the thin hope offered by the string.

Mr. Jones' beast spied him with one its salvaged eyes. It screamed through the vocal chords of a hundred dead creatures as the psychic reached the portal. Whatever foul intelligence the thing possessed, it knew French intended to imprison it here once again. It turned to keep that from happening.

The guardian seized that distraction, slashing at the nightmare beast with multiple stiletto blacknesses. Ichor and organs spilled onto the panicking glass sand below.

The thing shuddered; death was now imminent. As this was the beast's domain, as it died, so would this reality. Faceted fractals began dividing, shedding existence. Origami stars unwound, spilling lattice blood into the air, while glass creatures sang dirges, clear and beautiful.

French dove through the portal, landing on the dry dirt underneath Mr. Jones' house. Behind him, an injury in space-time struggled to survive French pulled the box and lock from his bag, panic making his hands fumble. At last, the latch of the padlock snapped into place. Like the closing of a fist, the twisting rent between realities disappeared.

The psychic collapsed onto the dirt.

"This calls for something much stronger than tea."

***

Back at the office, after a much-needed drink of Scotch, French had Meryl bring Mr. Jones down to his office.

He handed the elderly gentleman his house keys. "Your beast is gone. The box, I shall keep for safe-keeping."

"Better you than me, an' good riddance," the old man replied.

"I'm afraid I did additional damage to your floor. I shall send a contractor to make repairs."

"Hell, there's no need for that. I can fix it meself."

French smiled. "This is no ordinary contractor. He will also be installing a permanent barrier so that we never see that beast again."

Mr. Jones pocketed the keys. "Thanks again."

French escorted Mr. Jones to the door and watched him drive away. He returned to his office and admired the newest addition to his collection of oddities. Sitting on his desk was an eye-bending Mandelbrot star. Origami lattice had unfolded, spreading out to capture the early morning sun.

When confronting the Life Challenged, there are always perils and it should never be attempted by the inexperienced. Dealing with just one ghost can be tricky at best. When two or three ghosts are involved, the potential for danger rises exponentially. But what should the average ghost hunter to do if they run into an entire town full of ghosts? Call Mr. French, of course.

Ghost Town

Jerry was falling asleep. Not a good thing when driving through the Texas Hill Country. He shouldn't have agreed to do the ghost investigation. Jerry rubbed his eyes. Better stop for a caffeine boost in Comfort—had to exit there anyway to pick up state highway 473.

Strange name for a town, *Comfort*, but strange town names were common in Texas. Comfort's original settlers were a bunch of German free thinkers and academics who came to Texas in 1854. They found the back breaking work of agriculture a damn sight harder than they'd expected and named the town Comfort because there wasn't any.

Jerry's mind was wandering. Thankfully, exit 523 was just ahead. He put on his blinker and exited the highway. The brightly lit Alamo truck stop at the intersection promised caffeinated salvation.

He parked the car and stepped out. The hot humid Texas evening attacked him with a ferocity that rivaled that of the swarming mosquitoes. Luckily, the road side junk food wonderland offered air-conditioned respite. Once inside, Jerry grabbed two Red Bulls and a Milky Way, then headed to the register.

A bored woman in her forties with bottled red hair and creases on her upper lip from her three–pack-a-day habit glanced up from the paper she was reading behind the register.

"Evening," she said as Jerry placed the two cans and the candy bar on the counter. "You in town for the auction?"

Jerry shook his head. "Just passing through on business. A client ran into some trouble. They're renovating an old building into a bed-and-breakfast."

The redhead nodded as she swiped the Red Bull across the register scanner. She eyed Jerry's dress shirt and tie. "You a contractor?"

"Structural engineer," Jerry answered, although it had not been for his engineering skills that he'd been called. Engineering was just easier than trying to explain paranormal investigation. "It's a place called the Old Whorehouse Inn. Ever hear of it?"

"Nope," the woman said, ringing up the total. "Where's it at?"

Jerry pulled out his phone and pulled up Google maps with the address. "About ten miles down Old Number Nine road. I'm supposed to turn right onto a street called Wildfire."

At the mention of Wildfire, the woman recoiled slightly. Her frown didn't help her looks. "Ain't never been up there," she said tersely. She tossed the Milky Way on top of the bagged cans, and shoved it across the counter at Jerry. "Best tell your client to give up. Wildfire road and Higgins creek are cursed ground. Somethin' bad happened 'round there once, long time ago."

That woke Jerry up better than a caffeine boost. "Really, like what?"

"Never cared to know," she said, done with the subject. "You drive careful." She turned and made herself busy wiping down the back counter.

**

The rest of the drive, Jerry mulled over what the cashier had said about the land being cursed. Information like that was absolute gold for a paranormal researcher. Too bad he hadn't recorded their discussion. Did the owners of the bed-and-breakfast know they were on land considered cursed?

Jerry turned off 473 onto Old Number Nine road. It was a narrow and dark farm road that twisted through the scrub oak and juniper landscape with no apparent logic. Had probably been a cow path originally. Jerry crested a ridge and the land below was lit with an orange glow. The summer had been hotter and drier than normal. Dry lightning may have started a brush fire. He lost sight of the glow as the road dropped down the far side of the rise. Jerry rolled the car window down. There was no scent of smoke. He continued to scan for any signs of fire, wondering if that was what the orange glow had been.

The Google app shattered the silence. "In one mile, turn right onto Wildfire road."

Jerry slowed the car and followed the app's directions. A mile later, there was no street sign, just a dirt track leading south. If it hadn't been for the Google app, Jerry would have missed the turn. He flipped on the brights and turned down the road. The BMW 3 was not happy with his navigation choice and transmitted every bump and pothole directly to his butt.

Three miles and ten minutes later, Jerry could see the Old Whorehouse Inn looming up in the headlights. He rattled over the cattle guard at the gate and pulled into the drive. A Cadillac Escalade was parked near the building. The bed-and-breakfast was a long, two-story building of rough shaped Texas limestone. A balcony on both levels surrounded the building. Tall, narrow doors rather than windows opened onto the balcony.

Jerry turned off the engine. He glanced at his watch. It was nearly eleven. At the building, one of the tall doors opened. The silhouette of a woman stood in the escaping warm, yellow light.

"Is that you, Mr. Stoner?" a female voice asked.

Jerry got out of the car. He locked the door, paused and then laughed at himself. Not too many car thieves way the hell out here.

"Yes, Mrs. Dean," he waved.

"Thanks for helping us. We're at our wit's end."

An outside light flipped on. Mrs. Dean was in her early fifties. Her blonde hair was covered under a faded red scarf. She wore an old concert t-shirt with the Car's *Candy-O* album on it. The shirt was tucked into her jeans. Judging from the fresh plaster and paint stuck to her pants, it was a purely utilitarian look, but the jeans and tight shirt accentuated an hourglass figure that Mae West would have been proud of. Jerry knew that Mrs. Dean was a realtor when not out here at the B&B. Her husband Robert was an investment broker.

Jerry grabbed his suitcase and the two equipment cases from the backseat. "Be right there."

"Sorry that Robert isn't around to help with your luggage. He's upstairs putting drywall in one of the rooms."

Jerry lumbered up to the porch. "It's just these bags. I'm fine, really."

She held the door and Jerry stepped into what had probably been the lobby and bar of the old building when it had been a saloon and whorehouse. Now, the smell of plaster and fresh paint had replaced the odor of stale beer and cigars. Along the right hand wall, an ornate wood and iron staircase ran up to the second floor. The cast iron railings gave the room a hint of New Orleans.

Jerry placed his cases down. "You've done an amazing job considering you started with just the rock walls."

She nodded. Her smile creased the wrinkles around her eyes. "Eventually, we hope to get some of the other buildings repaired too." She paused, appearing nervous. "There used to be a little town here."

"Really?"

"Yes, but you'll get a chance to see that tomorrow," she answered. "For now, let's get you into a room. Robert has the guest rooms on the south wing complete."

She picked up his suitcase. Jerry grabbed the two equipment cases and followed Mrs. Dean to the stairs.

"We salvaged the stair railing. It survived the fire."

"Fire?"

"Yes, the whole town was destroyed by a wildfire in 1871. Very tragic and likely why we're having such trouble."

Jerry nodded. "You didn't go into detail over the phone."

She stopped and turned to face him. "No, we decided to let you experience things for yourself."

That was ominous. "Did this start with the renovation?" It was very common for paranormal activity to be spurred by construction.

"No. We've been working on the property since we bought it last November. It cost us almost nothing. Everything was fine until several weeks ago. That's when the lights in the woods began showing up. Robert was concerned, thinking it was a grassfire but there we never found any sign of anything burnt." She turned and resumed walking up the stairs.

Jerry worried he'd bang the antique railing with the hard edges of the equipment cases, and followed slowly. "I saw what looked like the glow of a fire on my drive in."

She nodded. "Yes, it isn't just single lights anymore, but whole areas of the woods are lit up like they're on fire."

Mrs. Dean turned to the right and led him down a hallway. The walls were true to the period. Dark wood wainscoting protected the base of the wall. Above, a bawdy red flocked wall paper of repeating trefoils stretched to the beadboard ceiling. As they walked along, the salvaged longleaf pine floorboards creaked and complained.

"Not long after we first saw the lights, the town showed up," she added.

"The town?"

She stopped and turned to face Jerry. "We have a ghost *town*, Mr. Stoner. Every day for over a month now, it shows up at 11:47 in the afternoon. At first, it was more of a mirage that only lasted less than thirty minutes."

She paused. Jerry could see that she was scared but trying not to show it.

"It lasts longer now?" he asked.

"Yes, and it's not a phantasm like it was at first. You can touch the buildings and there are people. The first time we saw one, Robert and I were working on the barn. He led a horse into the barn. Both went right through the car. I don't think they could go through the car anymore—not if they're like the buildings. Then, last Monday, we could hear their voices and the sound of the horses walking. It lasts until nearly dusk now."

"I've never heard of anything on this scale," Jerry answered. "But it sounds like a residual loop haunting. Sometimes a traumatic event, the fire maybe, creates an impression on a place. That stored emotional energy can play back like a movie. It's usually nothing to be afraid of."

One of his jobs as a paranormal investigator was to make his clients comfortable again in their homes. Of course, in this case, it was an entire town. He might need help for this one.

She shook her head. "It's not a loop. Things change day to day and I think they see us now. I was in the middle of the street this afternoon and a man deliberately walked around me."

Crap, that didn't sound like a residual haunting. "Well, they don't sound aggressive anyway," he said, to bolster her spirits.

Mrs. Dean reached the end of the hall and used an old fashioned brass key to open the door. Small ceramic numbers were affixed above each opening. His was room number 12.

"No, nothing bad has happened," she said, turning back to Jerry. "But I can't run a B&B with ghosts everywhere."

She was wrong in that assumption. The paranormal crowd would beat a path to her door if what she described was true. "Do you mind if I set up some equipment tonight?"

She nodded, handing him the key. "Of course, anything you want. This skeleton key opens everything. We won't be here. We've been staying at a hotel in town since this started. We'll be by in the morning with coffee and donuts."

Jerry nodded. "Thank you."

"Let's get your things into your room and I'll introduce you to Robert."

Once inside, Mrs. Dean placed his suitcase on an antique Turkish fainting couch. The burgundy upholstery matched the Victorian wallpaper. Opposite the couch was a large, brass bed. Jerry put the two equipment cases down next to it. Four overstuffed pillows sat atop the wedding ring patterned quilt. The Deans had done a great job. Except for the light fixtures and outlets, the room looked like it might have 150 years ago.

Behind them, a man who must be her husband Robert stepped into the room. He pulled his cloth dust mask down, and extended his hand. "Thanks for coming out Mr. Stoner."

"My pleasure."

Mr. Dean was six-foot tall, in a plaid shirt and jeans, and had a strong build that he didn't get from sitting behind his desk. His nicked and battered hands indicated a love of do-it-yourself projects. That suited Jerry fine. He was a bit of a construction hobbyist himself.

"As our first official guest, we hope your stay at the Old Whorehouse Inn meets your expectations."

Jerry smiled. If only half of what he had been told was true, this would prove to be an amazing investigation. Usually it was just the rare electronic voice phenomenon and the occasional moved object. "I'm sure everything will be great."

After a bit more chit chat, Jerry followed the Deans downstairs. Once outside, the couple made their goodbyes and got into the Escalade and drove off. Jerry locked the door and turned off the porch light. On the way up to his room, he removed his tie and jacket. Ghost hunting did not require business attire.

After unloading the infrared cameras, he trekked through the building, placing them in strategic locations. With the last camera in place, he went back to the room and collapsed onto the bed. In the open equipment case, the digital recorders were still sitting.

"Screw it, they can wait for tomorrow."

He'd had a hell of a week and was exhausted. The drawings for the parking garage at the College had gone out this afternoon. This would be the first night since Tuesday that he'd get a full night's sleep.

Jerry rolled off the bed, grabbed his overnight bag from the suitcase, and made his way to the bathroom. The bleary eyed person in the mirror agreed with his decision for sleep. He washed up, peed, flipped off the lights in the room, and walked to the bed.

He stopped. Silhouetted by the moonlight was a woman standing at the French doors to the balcony. It had to be a ghost. No one had been standing there when the lights were on. His mind struggled to rationalize the situation. Could she be outside on the balcony and this was a trick of the light that made it appear like she was in the room?

"My name is Jerry," he said. "Who are you?"

There was no response and the woman didn't move. Perhaps his mind was just matrixing shadows. Jerry took a few steps closer. She was still there so it wasn't his eyes creating a silhouette from the background shadows. Whoever she was, she was real and inside the room.

"Hello," he said again.

Still, she did nothing.

Jerry took another step closer. He was now close enough to reach out and touch her if he wanted. She looked to be in her twenties. Her hair was gathered up on her head with a bow, with two braids hung looped at the back. She was staring out the window, focused on an orange glow in the forest. Her frilly knee-length underdress looked more like a night gown than an actual dress. Jerry found her quite attractive.

This wasn't like any full-body apparition he'd ever heard of. She seemed solid and he could hear her breathing. It would be a shame if she turned into some skull-faced horror like in the movies. He calmed his mind and reached out and gently placed his hand on her shoulder.

"Excuse me," Jerry said quietly.

She turned, startled. "Oh!"

Oh, thank god she didn't turn into a zombie dripping ooze. "I'm sorry to disturb you. I am Jerry Stoner."

The woman recovered her composure and gave a slight curtsy. "I'm dreadfully sorry, sir. I was watching the fire." She extended her hand palm down. "I'm Sophie Meyer. I'm so pleased to make your acquaintance, Mr. Stoner. I haven't had visitors in years, it seems." She glanced out the window again and then turned back. The orange glow reflected in her eyes. "I am most grateful for your companionship on a night like this."

Jerry took her hand. It was warm. Was he supposed to kiss it? What was etiquette in the 1800's? He shook gently and let go. He was debating whether to mention the consequences of the fire. He decided against it.

"It seems like quite a large fire," he said instead.

Sophie turned back to him. "The Major has organized everyone to help build a firebreak."

"Everyone but you."

She nodded. "The Major and the city council have requested that those of us who are employed here not sully the streets with our presence."

"Why?"

"You are in a whorehouse Mr. Stoner. The upstanding citizens of our little town would rather that Ophelia Mae's little doves not remind them that such incivilities as prostitution still exist in their chaste and proper utopia."

"Ahh, that," Jerry said, not knowing what else to say.

Sophie reached over and took Jerry's hands in hers. "Besides, my presence would be useless. The fire will jump the firebreak as it always does." She put his hands on her waist, wrapped her arms around him, and placed her head on his shoulder. "Hold me. I do not wish to witness it again."

Jerry pulled her tight. She smelled of lavender. "You know that the fire destroys the town?"

"Yes, but as always, the Major insists on trying to stop it."

That was it. It made sense. "He's what's keeping you here?"

She turned her face to his. "Yes, Major Higgins runs the town like he runs his ranch and the people are content to allow him to do so." Her arms traveled up Jerry's back and pulled him close. "Now, kiss me and make me forget about the fire."

Jerry leaned down and kissed her. It was a gentle and polite kiss. She smiled at him and he kissed her again, this time with more passion. Her hands traveled to his chest and began undoing the buttons to his shirt.

"I have missed the feel of a man's arms holding me tight," she whispered. "It's been a very long time."

Jerry smiled down at her. Sophie was a good six to eight inches shorter than he was. "You are very beautiful."

She smiled and kissed him again. "Take me to your bed, Mr. Stoner."

Jerry reached down and swept her up and into his arms. She giggled. He kissed her again and carried her to the large brass bed.

Several times as they made love, Jerry's mind reminded him that this was a ghost. He ignored that logic and loved Sophie all the more fiercely. After sating their desire, they spooned together. Jerry had his arm over Sophie's waist and was gently kissing her neck.

Sophie interlaced her fingers with his. "The fire is almost here."

That brought Jerry back to reality. When the fire arrived, what then?

"Will you go?"

"Yes," she said sadly.

Jerry could think of nothing else to say but just pulled her tight. After several minutes, there was an orange flash outside the windows and Sophie disappeared.

Jerry rolled over and turned on the light at the bedside table. In the bed where Sophie had been, there was a powdering of fine ash. Jerry coughed. The room was filled with the smell of wood smoke.

"Shit!"

***

Jerry was up at daybreak. He went down to the B&B's kitchen and found two bananas to eat. He sat down at the table he checked the video from the IR cameras on his laptop. Hmm, nothing. That was a bit of a surprise, you'd think the bar would have been a focus of activity. Then again, Sophie had told him everyone was out fighting the fire.

Jerry went outside and began poking about the property. He was investigating the fallen walls of a building as the Deans drove up.

Holding a box of donuts and a thermos, Mrs. Dean stepped from the Escalade. "Beware geeks bearing gifts," she said happily.

"You are in very good spirits, pardon the pun, for someone dealing with a ghost issue," he replied "How are you this morning, Mrs. Dean?"

"It's Dorothy, please. Anything happen overnight?"

Jerry wondered how she would take the story that he had to tell. "Nothing on the cameras, but I had a very intense personal experience."

How would he explain the ashes on his sheets? He'd been wrestling with that problem all morning. Was there a way to explain having Sophie in his bed for some reason other than sex? He was still drawing a blank. After Sophie had disappeared, he had shaken the sheets out on the balcony but there was still a noticeable gray area on the burgundy fabric. They also smelled heavily of smoke.

"You'll have to tell us over breakfast," Mr. Dean said. At the front door, he patted his wife's bottom as she walked past.

She turned and frowned at her husband. "Robert, stop that. We have guests."

"It's the building," he answered. "It's all the pent up sexual energy. It made me do it."

She scowled. "Sure. So what was your excuse yesterday when we were shopping?"

He turned to Jerry. "Can ghosts affect you away from the haunted site?"

Dorothy tsked and put the donuts and coffee on the table. "Don't help him Jerry. He's a perverted old sex addict and won't admit it."

Robert moved in behind his wife and wrapped his arms around her waist. "And you wouldn't have it any other way."

"You are incorrigible!" She pulled several plates and cups from a cabinet. "Now sit. I want to hear Mr. Stoner's story."

Jerry followed Mr. Dean's example and sat at the table as Dorothy poured coffee for everyone.

"There was a visitor in my room last night," he told the couple. "Apparently, the town's people are still trying to stop the fire that burned everything to the ground in the 1800's."

"A visitor?" Dorothy asked as she joined them at the table. "What was this visitor like?"

Jerry took a small bit of donut, chewed several times and swallowed. Here it was. "Um, her name is Sophie. She worked here at the brothel."

"So did you two, you know?" Robert asked, pushing his index finger in and out of his other hand's open fist.

Dorothy whacked her husband in the arm. "Stop that!" Then she cocked her head, noticing something about Jerry's reaction to the question. "Wait, you did?"

"She's lonely. She's trapped here in the building by herself."

Rather than expressing disgust, as Jerry had expected, Dorothy seemed intrigued.

"Oh, how romantic. What's she like?"

"Very attractive, in her twenties, with her hair up like in the old photos." Jerry turned and stared out the window. "A man called Major Higgins is holding the town here."

Robert's brow rose "We bought the land from a family named Higgins."

Dorothy turned to her husband. "Do you think they might know something about this?"

Jerry recalled what the cashier at the truck stop had said about the land being cursed. Undoubtedly that was why the Deans had paid so little for the property.

"Are they local?" he asked.

Robert nodded. "They have a small ranch several miles back toward the highway." He pulled out his phone and brought up a map. The entrance to the Higgins ranch was just before the turn onto Old Number Nine road.

Jerry took a sip of the coffee. "I think I might drop by and ask some questions later."

Robert licked the donut icing off his fingers. "Better do it today. They should be there doing last minute clean up. Tomorrow at noon is the auction for their ranch."

"Thanks," Jerry replied.

"Back to the story," Dorothy interrupted. "What happened to Sophie?"

"As the fire reached the house, there was an orange flash outside and she was gone. All that was left was some ash in the bed and the strong odor of smoke. The room still smells of it."

"I wonder what happened to the other prostitutes." Robert asked.

"I'm not sure. I captured nothing on my cameras but Sophie did say she was alone here."

Dorothy was thrilled. "Well, that confirms the building really was a whorehouse. Did Sophie say what it was called?"

"No, but she did mention that they were Ophelia Mae's little doves."

Mrs. Dean nodded. "A soiled dove was the less offensive term at the time for a prostitute. I'll go online later and see if I can find any kind of reference."

Robert nodded toward the window. "Mr. Stoner, you might want to head outside soon. It's 11:30 now."

Jerry remembered that the town was supposed to appear at 11:47. "Thanks, I'll run upstairs and get a camera and some recorders."

***

First thing to do was photograph the ruined walls and foundations he'd discovered earlier. He had the limestone and charred timbers in focus when suddenly it was intact. At the same instant, there was the banging of a smith hammering on an anvil, the clip clop of horses, and the sound of a group of men laughing. There was even the smell the coal stoked forge and the ripeness of recent horse droppings.

He took pictures of everything. Most of the buildings were constructed of board-and-batten siding or rough stone that had been mortared together. Red primed metal roofs were the norm but a few were simple cedar shingles. The wide main street had a general store with a dentist on the floor above, a hardware store, Otto Koehler's dry goods, a milliner, several saloons, and a white wood church with its steeple stabbing at the sky.

Jerry reached out to touch the wall of the dry goods store. Mrs. Dean was right, it was solid and real. Inside, a father was buying his son a hard candy. The boy pointed out the window right at Jerry. The father looked Jerry in the eyes for a moment, then patted his son's head and turned back to the cashier at the counter.

Nothing like this had ever been encountered on any of the paranormal shows he'd seen. Jerry was in over his head. He pulled out his phone. He knew of a psychic in San Antonio that handled strange occurrences like this. Jerry'd used him once and the man was amazing. Jerry texted the basics of what was happening.

He sent the text message and checked the time. It was nearly one. Time to go visit the Higgin's ranch and see if they had any answers.

***

The Higgin's ranch was a well-kept two story Victorian home of cut ashlar stone. A single octagonal tower stood at the east end of the house. There were several people in the yard; one pruning bushes and the other hand watering the lawn. They didn't seem surprised or alarmed at visitors. Jerry parked behind a Toyota Tundra. Next to it was a blue Prius. Both were from San Antonio car dealers.

Jerry stepped from the car and walked up to the door. It stood wide open, spilling air-conditioning into the hot Texas summer. A table just inside the door was stacked with flyers about the ranch as well as an *Information-to-Bidders* sheet. Jerry took one of the flyers.

From a side room, a man in his late sixties came over and extended his hand. "I'm Robert Higgins. Are you going to be bidding tomorrow?" His grandfatherly face had seen too much Texas sun. The lines of experience crisscrossing his face were accentuated by thick glasses.

Jerry shook the old man's hand. "Jerry Stoner, sir. Actually, I was hoping to get some information on the ranch and its history."

"The brochure has some of that. Was there something that you were particularly interested in?"

"I was curious about the fire," Jerry answered, getting straight to the point.

The façade of polite friendliness crumbled from Mr. Higgins face like a brick wall before a wrecking ball.

"That piece of the family history has already been sold," he said coldly.

"Yes, I'm gathering information for the current owner," Jerry answered. He didn't want to frighten the old man off. "I'm not a lawyer. I'm just a paranormal investigator looking into the lights at night." Jerry felt that it was best not to mention the town itself just yet.

"It's their problem now," Mr. Higgins said rather shortly. "Was there anything else you needed before you leave?"

That wasn't very subtle. "No, I suppose not," Jerry answered and then added "Are you a descendant of the Major?"

Mr. Higgin's shocked look was a blatant admission that he was. "My great-great-grandfather had nothing to do with the fire. In fact, he did everything he could to stop the blaze from destroying Freiburg."

"And he's still trying," Jerry replied. "I just want to discover why."

Mr. Higgins scowled. "Isn't it enough that he gave his life trying to save the town?"

Jerry had hit a nerve. "I am not denying his bravery but something is keeping him here."

"I don't believe in such nonsense," Mr. Higgins said, gesturing toward the door. "Thank you for coming by." He turned and walked away.

Jerry took the not-so-subtle cue and stepped out the open door.

"You want to know about the fire," said a frail voice to his right.

Jerry looked over. An elderly woman in a black dress was sitting in a rocking chair on the porch. She gestured for Jerry to come closer.

"Yes, I am trying to determine what happened that night."

The old woman was very frail and appeared to be in her nineties. Her hands were twisted by arthritis and shook with palsy.

"The family doesn't talk about it," she said motioning for Jerry to sit with her.

He pulled up the other rocker and sat. "But didn't the Major tried to stop the fire?"

"Yes, but that's because he ordered it set," the old woman replied. "He was trying to burn some squatters off our land but the blaze got out of control and jumped the creek."

The pieces suddenly fit. "So his guilt is making him stay?"

She nodded, her thin white hair bouncing in the breeze. "But you are the key to ending this," she said cryptically.

"Me?"

She didn't have time to explain. A voice from behind Jerry interrupted. He turned. It was Mr. Higgins.

"I thought that I made it plain that you were not welcome," Mr. Higgins said angrily.

"I was just speaking with…" Jerry turned to the woman. The rocking chair was empty.

The anger drained from Mr. Higgins face and he grew ashen. "A woman in a black mourning dress?"

Jerry nodded. "Yes, although I hadn't realized it was for that reason."

"That was my great-grandmother," Mr. Higgins whispered. "We see her from time to time. She was the Major's daughter. I never knew her. She died several years after I was born."

Jerry turned back to look at the rocker. "Damn," he muttered.

"Mr. Stoner, my sisters and I are trying to put this behind us," the old man said flatly. "It is why we're selling the ranch. My sisters, Margaret and Caroline, believe that if someone other than a Higgins owns the land, the hallucinations will cease."

"Hallucinations? There's a whole town…"

Mr. Higgins held up his hand to stop Jerry. "Yes, but my sisters chose to believe otherwise. Good Day, Mr. Stoner. I do truly hope things go well for your clients."

Jerry glanced again at the rocker, then stood and walked to the BMW. He got in and checked the phone. No response from the psychic. Not too surprising. Mr. French was a good psychic but something of a neophyte with technology. If past experience served as an example, it would be his secretary who would ultimately reply to the text message.

***

The drive back to the Old Whorehouse Inn was uneventful. Once past the cattle guard, however, he had to avoid several people and a horse-drawn wagon as he drove through town. The B&B didn't face the main road but was one street back. Sophie was right, the citizens really didn't want to know a brothel was in their midst.

As he parked, Jerry looked up. Sophie was standing on the balcony. She was in a fancy dark blue Victorian dress with black lace and a bustle. She smiled and raced back into the house.

As he entered the building, Sophie was hurrying down the stairs. A very startled Mrs. Dean was standing at the kitchen sink. She starred open-mouthed, the plate in her hand forgotten. Sophie ran to Jerry and threw her arms around his neck. He kissed her happily.

"This is Sophie?" Mrs. Dean asked cautiously.

Jerry nodded. "Mrs. Dorothy Dean, may I present Miss Sophie Meyer."

Sophie nodded. "I am most honored to make your acquaintance, ma'am."

Mrs. Dean wiped her hands on a towel and walked over. Somewhat tentatively, she took Sophie's outstretched hand. "The pleasure is mine."

Sophie looked around at the lobby. "I am most delighted to see that you are bringing the building back to life."

"That's mostly my husband," Mrs. Dean answered proudly. "Oh, he'll want to meet you. Let me give him a call." She reached over to the counter and picked up her phone. With a few swipes on the screen, she put the phone to her ear. "Robert, come down to the kitchen and hurry."

Sophie was regarding this odd behavior rather curiously.

"It's a type of telephone," Jerry told her.

She nodded. "I am afraid that I happen to be a bit out of fashion. Things seem to have changed a great deal." She glanced at the lobby's chandelier. "I find the mode of illumination quite amazing."

They could hear Robert running down the hall before he ever reached the stairs. "What's wrong?" He bounded down the stairs three at a time. He came up short as he noticed Sophie. A relieved look filled his face. "Oh, I thought you had hurt yourself," he said to his wife.

Mrs. Dean smiled at her husband. "Sophie, this is my husband, Robert."

Sophie extended her hand. "Mr. Dean, it is a pleasure."

Robert looked at his hands. They were covered in drywall mud. He wiped them on his shirt and took her hand with just his fingertips. "Sorry, I'm refinishing one of the rooms."

Sophie nodded. "Yes, I was just saying what a nice job you and your wife are doing."

"Thanks," he answered, still somewhat out of breath.

"Why don't we all sit down? I'll get some tea," Mrs. Dean said pleasantly.

Jerry was surprised how quickly Mrs. Dean had adjusted to Sophie. Of course, she appeared to be quite real so maybe it wasn't that amazing. He pulled a chair out for Sophie at the table. She sat and he took the seat next to her. She smiled and placed her hand on his.

"Robert, get some glasses from the cabinet." Mrs. Dean opened the refrigerator and retrieved a pitcher of tea. "Oh, I found some things about Ophelia Mae online. They were listed on a website about the history of San Antonio."

Sophie cocked her head. "I suppose they must have stayed in San Antonio after the fire. Miss Ophelia and the others had gone there for the return of the cattle drovers. One can always count on cowboys to not be frugal with their earnings."

Jerry took the glass of tea offered by Mrs. Dean. He turned to Sophie. "But why didn't you go?"

Sophie sighed. "I have a bit of the consumption, I'm afraid, and I do not travel well as a result. Miss Ophelia thought it best for me to remain here."

"Ah," Jerry said, wondering if ghost tuberculosis was contagious.

Robert, still standing by the counter, quickly emptied his glass. "Well, I need to get back to work."

Mrs. Dean frowned at her husband. "Robert, don't be rude. Sophie is our guest."

Robert turned to Sophie. "You aren't going anywhere are you?"

Sophie shook her head. "No sir."

He turned back to his wife. "I'll be polite at dinner when I'm done working. Until then." Mr. Dean made an overly dramatic bow and headed back up the stairs.

Mrs. Dean shook her head. "I apologize for my husband. He has the social grace of a bull in a china shop."

"It is quite alright. I am rather used to the brusque manner of men," Sophie said smiling. "We have visitors here of all types, from farm boys to fine gentlemen, and as broad a range of etiquette. In the end, they regard us as fine ladies and we treat them as upstanding gentlemen."

Mrs. Dean stared at Sophie for a moment. "You really are a ghost. I keep forgetting that. I'm sorry."

Sophie smiled. "I am just glad to have the pleasure of fine company again." She turned to Jerry. "So, Mr. Stoner, what manner of occupation do you engage in?" she asked with a slight squeeze of his hand.

"I'm an engineer."

"Odd, you do not dress in the manner of an engineer, nor smell of the coal and oil of a train. Do modern locomotives not require such things?"

Jerry chuckled. "Not that kind of engineer. I'm a structural engineer. I design tall buildings."

Sophie's eyes brightened. "That is a most honorable profession," she said relieved. "I would not abide having the engineer of a locomotive as a husband as he would rarely be at home."

Jerry laughed, thrilled with the idea that Sophie found him suitable as a husband. He tried to phrase his response appropriately. "I would return home to you every night without fail if I were so honored to be your husband."

She squeezed his hand. "And I would be twice honored to be your wife," Sophie replied happily.

Mrs. Dean raised her glass. "To the new couple."

Jerry and Sophie looked at each other with a measure of embarrassment. Then Jerry raised his own glass. "To us!"

Sophie shook her head and with a giggle, picked up her glass. The three clinked the glasses together then Jerry leaned over and kissed Sophie.

She kissed him back for a second and then pushed him away with a smile. She turned to Mrs. Dean. "See, men forget their manners in public constantly. It seems that it is the lot of us women, to constantly be reminding our men of their proper place."

***

That evening, Jerry decided to confront the Major and end his hold over the town. He loved Sophie but she couldn't stay as a prisoner here forever. He waited until just before dusk and then went outside. At the edge of town, the townspeople were already digging a trench for a firebreak.

Jerry went up to one of the men digging. "Where can I find the Major?"

The man turned to look at Jerry. With a scowl, he nodded in a direction further up the trench.

The diggings made a slow turn and headed back to parallel the main street. Just past a pile of cut juniper trees, he saw the Major. There was no mistaking the man in his blue Union army greatcoat. He was coordinating the men digging and drawing a line in the dirt with a cane to designate where the firebreak should be widened.

Jerry walked up to the Major. "Sir, I would like to discuss a matter with you," he said bravely. Honestly, his stomach was in knots at the moment.

The Major ignored him. "Can't you see, sir, that we are busy?"

"Yes I can, but to what purpose?"

The Major turned on Jerry with a vengeance. "Are you daft? We must protect our town from the coming wildfire."

"Major, you have tried this before. No amount of preparation will keep that fire away."

A blaze erupted in the Major's eyes and his skin grew black and burnt. "Belief in God and our own hard work will protect this town!"

Jerry took a step back from the horrifying vision. Bits of flesh were shedding from the Major's skull with each movement. The once dapper Union officer was now a decaying and burnt corpse. The terrifying vision lifted his cane and swung. Charred muscle and bone driven on by rage slammed the cane into Jerry's temple. He fell, seeing stars. Jerry looked up. Now fully aflame, the Major, was pulling the cane back to strike again.

Jerry scrambled out of the way and the cane struck the bare earth with a dull thud. Jerry stood and ran for the safety of a nearby house. Once around the corner, he huddled panting. Had that really just happened?

"Well, that sure didn't work," he muttered to himself.

He got his breath back and retreated to the whorehouse. As he reached the building's porch, his phone beeped to signal that he had a message. He pulled it from his pocket.

The message was short. *French says it sounds interesting. He'll be there tonight before ten.* As expected, it was from the psychic's secretary. For a psychic that guaranteed his work, you'd think he could manage to operate a phone.

***

"You did what?" Sophie asked.

"I confronted the Major but he refuses to face reality."

"He could have killed you."

Jerry hadn't expected Sophie to be so angry. "Well, then we would have been together."

She glared at him. "It doesn't work that way."

"Anyway, I have a psychic coming and he'll sort this all out."

"Spiritualists are all charlatans. This will only anger the Major further. Oh Jerry, what have you done? I…"

Whatever else Sophie had to say was lost as she collapsed. Jerry caught her and eased her to the floor.

"We need to get her out of that corset," Mrs. Dean instructed. "All this excitement was too much for her."

Jerry picked Sophie up and headed for the stairs. "I'll put her in my bed but I don't have a clue how to take off a corset."

Mrs. Dean tsked. "You're too young to have gone to *Rocky Horror* or you'd know. I'll help."

***

It was nearly ten. Jerry was out on the porch of the old whorehouse pacing. French was due to arrive any time now. Jerry'd been outside waiting since nine-thirty. Suffering in the heat was better than facing Sophie's wrath. She was still furious that he had confronted the Major. Being on the porch had been Mrs. Dean's suggestion, hoping his absence might calm Sophie down. Hopefully it had.

Two minutes before ten, Mr. French arrived in his candy apple red 1969 Plymouth Sport Fury convertible. He had the top up. The stark white canvas was a beacon in the near darkness.

"Glad you could find the place," Jerry said, as French stepped from the car.

"Not a bit of trouble. Your directions were spot on."

Mr. French was an old man in a well-tailored black suit. His dark hair was streaked with grey at the temples as was his mustache and beard. He looked more like a banker than a psychic.

He joined Jerry on the porch. "Interesting case. I would have been here sooner but it took me a while to find this." He handed Jerry a gold chain with a pendant.

"What's this for?"

"It will protect and hide Sophie from the other post-life individuals."

Jerry looked up from the pendant. "Post-life?"

Mr. French frowned. "Yes. Political correctness has invaded even my industry."

Jerry looked at the pendant. It was a gold disc with a polished piece of amber. Maybe this would help calm Sophie down.

He turned to Mr. French. "She's upstairs. Follow me."

The psychic followed Jerry inside. "I've had reports of this place now and then over the years. It's about time I came up here and did something about it."

"Really? What is it you plan to do?"

"My part is fairly inconsequential," French replied without actually answering the question.

With French, that was rather common. One thing that Jerry had learned the last time was that the psychic didn't like to give solid answers.

"So, who does play an important part?" Jerry asked. "Sophie isn't the critical element, is she?"

Mr. French shook his head. "No, she is quite safe. You, on the other hand, are the ghost investigator and the one in grave danger."

"Crap. Well, whatever else you do, don't tell Sophie that. She's already livid that I confronted the Major."

Jerry glanced upstairs towards his room and Sophie. "So what do I need to do?"

French merely smiled. "First, we shall calm your fiancée and then I will tell you what must be done."

"Fiancée?"

"So Sophie believes," Mr. French said. "From what I am reading from the girl, she took your discussion this afternoon as a proposal of matrimony. Do you not wish to marry her?"

Jerry thought about it. He did love Sophie and even though he hadn't known her more than a day, it was thrilling to envision them married.

"Yes, I do, but how? Sophie's a ghost."

Mr. French *tsked*. "Happens all the time. We can work that out later. For now, you and I just need to worry about calming your fiancée down."

They arrived at the room and Jerry opened the door slowly. Mrs. Dean was sitting next to Sophie on the bed. Sophie sat up as soon as they stepped in.

Jerry hurried over and offered her the necklace and pendant. "Mr. French says this will protect you from the Major."

Sophie glanced over at the psychic. Despite her objections to a spiritualist, a look of complete calm crossed her face. "Thank you for your kindness, sir."

Jerry placed the necklace about Sophie's neck. The chain seemed to close itself as he brought the two ends together. Jerry checked anyway to see that the clasp was closed. As an engineer, redundant checks were something of an occupational hazard.

He pulled his hands back and held Sophie's face as he kissed her. "I love you wife," he whispered.

Sophie flung her arms around him. "I love you husband," she whispered back.

Mrs. Dean shook her head. "Why are you whispering? I can still hear you."

That set Sophie to giggling. Jerry took off his class ring from A&M. "Here, this will have to do as a ring for now." He slipped it on her thumb.

Mrs. Dean shook her head once again, this time rolling her eyes. "That won't do." She pulled the pair of rings from her left hand. "Here. Sophie, our hands are about the same size. Wear this." Mrs. Dean handed Sophie the engagement ring.

Sophie slipped the ring on her finger. It was a nearly perfect fit. A tear was running down her cheek. "Thank you."

"Something borrowed…" Mrs. Dean said as she turned to Jerry. "And this is something old."

She handed her wedding band to Jerry. "This is for when you two get married."

"But you can't give up your own rings."

"Oh, it's time Robert and I got new rings anyway," she said. "We can renew our vows in Cancun the next time we go."

Jerry reached over and hugged Sophie. In addition to her lavender perfume, the room still smelled of smoke.

Sophie pulled back, her eyes staring into his. "You're going out there aren't you?"

Jerry nodded. "I have to."

"If you do drive off the Major, I'll disappear."

Jerry shook his head. "French doesn't think so. Besides, you've stayed over a century for the Major, someone you don't even like. If you can stay around for that asshole, you can stay around for me."

Sophie smiled nervously and then pulled him tight against her. "Be careful. I don't want us both to be ghosts."

Jerry brightened. "That's the worst that could happen, isn't it? If I die fighting the Major, you and I can still be together!"

"It doesn't work that way."

"I'll make it work that way," Jerry insisted.

Suddenly, he felt confident. The thought of going head-to-head with a flesh shedding, crispy-fried phantom wasn't so frightening anymore.

"Besides, I'll be fine," he added, nodding towards Mr. French. "This time I've got reinforcements."

***

Mr. French's plan did involve Sophie, but just slightly. She and the other townspeople had to be there when Jerry confronted the Major. According to French, it had to happen just as the wildfire struck the town.

Jerry glanced at his watch. It was nearly that time. Jerry, the Deans, and Sophie followed the psychic to where the church had once stood. In the darkness, the ghostly shadows of the town's buildings wavered at the edges of their vision. French led them to the church. The faint outlines of the steeple were barely visible against the night sky.

French placed a suitcase from his car on the ground and opened it. The psychic took a bronze censer from within and placed it on the ground. After drawing a circle in the hard-packed dirt, he lit two pieces of incense. With some muttered words, the psychic placed the incense within the censer's bowl.

"That should open the portal."

After pulling a leather-bound book from the suitcase, French walked around the circle, chanting something in Latin. After one full revolution of the circle, he turned and walked the opposite way twice more.

He stopped and looked at Jerry. "It has begun."

Jerry's stomach was in knots. With the last of French's incantation, the town had become real again. Lanterns hung from porch posts, horses were tethered at the saloon, and the smell of smoke was everywhere. In the distance, the sky burned red with the reflected light of the fire. Townspeople were running his way. At the church door, a man in a stark black suit beckoned to the people.

"Hurry, our prayers will deliver us from the fire."

Sophie appeared beside Jerry. "We need to go inside the church with everyone else."

They joined the group of people crowding inside. At the pulpit, the minister began singing a hymn. Quickly, the crowd joined in. Jerry didn't know the words so just hummed. He seriously hoped this wouldn't affect their safety.

Behind them, the doors burst open and the Major entered the church. He caught Jerry's gaze and pointed with his cane. "Blasphemer, what are you doing here?"

The minister stopped the hymn. "All are welcome within this church," he said calmly.

The Major took several steps forward. "This unbeliever has no faith in our ability to overcome this hellfire."

Jerry was now within swinging distance of the cane. As the crowd around Jerry cleared away, he took a step forward. "This fire is a creation of man, not Satan."

"You lie!" The Major drew back his cane. His eyes burned with rage.

"No, I do not." Jerry pointed at the Major. "You set the fire to drive squatters off of your ranch!"

The Major took a step back. "I would never do such a thing."

"You did and the fire grew wild and jumped the creek!"

The skin on the Major's face began to shrivel.

A man in overalls stepped forward. "Is this true, Major?"

"You are in the house of God, Major Higgins," the minister interjected. "It shall do you no good to lie."

The Major glanced around. His skin began to blacken and char. Outside the church windows, flames were dancing, lighting up the night.

"We can still stop the fire!" the Major screamed.

A woman holding a baby stepped up to him. "You started the fire? You lied to us." She looked down at her child. "We died because of you."

"NO!"

The Major's flesh was falling away in clumps now. Around him, the wooden walls of the church were ablaze. The crowd ignored the flames. They simply watched as the Major collapsed screaming into a heap.

Even though they were in the heart of the fire, there was no heat. Jerry held Sophie's hand as the minister began leading the people once more in a hymn. Above them, the roof beams were engulfed in flames. Jerry did his best to sing along.

The hymn finished and the minister smiled and gestured at Jerry and Sophie. "Today, we welcome a newly married couple into our congregation. Let us greet them."

The crowd of smiling town's people congratulated Jerry and Sophie with hugs and handshakes, then, with a sound as loud as thunder, the roof collapsed, crashing down in fiery destruction.

Jerry blinked. The church, the fire, and all of the people were gone. He turned in a panic. Thankfully, Sophie was still with him. He squeezed her hand and wrapped his arms around her.

"I love you, Sophie!" He was giddy. "Do you hear that world, I love my wife!" he yelled into the dark night. He kissed her again and let his hand slide down to grab her bustled butt.

"We are in a church," she told him with a smile.

"If you two are quite done, I think that it's time for a stiff drink," Mr. Dean said.

"I'll want a double," Mrs. Dean told her husband. "By the way, we're going to Cancun this summer, right?"

Jerry led Sophie over to Mr. French who was busy snuffing out the incense and packing his things into the suitcase.

"Thank you for everything."

Sophie reached over and took Mr. French's hand. "You are a dear and honored friend."

French lifted her hand to his lips and kissed the back of her hand. "I am very grateful to have met you Miss Meyer."

"It is Mrs. Stoner now," she corrected him.

"Of course. How forgetful of me." He picked up his suitcase. "I have several things for you both in the car."

They followed him to the '69 *Fury*. After placing the suitcase in the back, he pulled two business cards from the glove box, handing the cards to Jerry.

"What are these?" Jerry asked.

"The first is a doctor that I am familiar with," Mr. French explained. "She will get the four of you on antibiotics for tuberculosis."

"Well that answers the question of whether you can catch tuberculosis from a ghost. And the other card?" Jerry asked, trying to read it in the moonlight.

"Ah, that," French said with a smile. "That is someone you should visit rather soon. He is an excellent obstetrician."

Having a few friends over for dinner is always a grand idea but what if the guests don't like each other. Things can quickly escalate into a bitch-fight, threatening to ruin your social standing. But what happens when a party crasher is also thrown into the mix? A full-on disaster is what, but that's also when things get really interesting.

The Dinner Party

Special thanks to Emily for inspiring this story

"Smells good. What are you making?" Meryl asked. She settled into a chair at the kitchen table. Meryl was Mr. French's secretary and occasional front office bouncer. She was also a succubus. The later was something of a plus considering that Mr. French was a psychic.

French turned from the sauté pan on the stove. "Bacon at the moment, but ultimately a shrimp fettuccine Alfredo. The bits of bacon aren't exactly true to the Italian recipe but they add a nice hint of savory."

Meryl frowned but it had nothing to do with the choice of cuisine. "I'm not sure this dinner was such a good idea, French."

"Why?"

He glanced at the clock. "Our guests should be arriving any time now. I think I've remembered everything. The Antipasto salad is chilling in the fridge along with several bottles of pinot Grigio. The buttered brussel sprouts are in the oven along with the garlic bread. Just need to crisp the bacon and add it to the sauce. Nothing else can be done until the guests arrive. I can't prepare the fettuccine until then if it is to be perfectly *al dente*.

"You're changing the topic," Meryl said. "You do realize that the Daughters of the four original Queens don't get along."

"Yes, that's true in general. You in particular, however, seem to play well with others." French peeked into the oven to check on the bread. "I should think that you and Jynieth could manage to tolerate a dinner together."

"I'm a Daughter of Naahmah and Jynieth is of Lilith. That's one thing," Meryl explained. "Naahmah and Lilith's Daughters are fairly rational, but you invited an offspring of Eisheth Zenunim—and an incubus at that. Zen's Daughters are an emotional wildcard and her incubi are even less predictable."

French scowled. "You and I have worked with Virgil for years. He won't be a problem. Besides, he's great fun at parties."

Meryl smiled. "Yes, I've been to quite a few of those parties. The last one, as you recall, was broken up by the police." She straightened a stray lock of her auburn hair.

French said nothing, but just smiled.

"You're flexing your wiles a bit. Keep that up and the two of us are going to have quite a good time once the guests leave," he said finally.

"Sorry, unconscious response. I'll try to keep it down."

"Don't do it for me, I rather like it."

She scowled at the psychic.

Meryl was the ideal of feminine beauty. In particular, Mr. French's ideal of beauty. As a succubus, Meryl had tailored her appearance to his desires before she'd first approached French. That had been nearly sixty years ago. She now considered this curvy red head form as her own.

The doorbell rang. Ainsworth, who had been leaning in the doorway, straightened. "I'll get that." Ainsworth was Mr. French's manservant, hired muscle, and trusted friend.

French donned oven mitts and pulled the bread pan from the oven. The smell of garlic, butter, and yeast filled the kitchen.

"Young Jason and Miss Jynieth, sir," Ainsworth announced, showing the newlywed couple into the kitchen.

There was a distinct tension in the air as the two succubi shared the small space. It faded quickly. Perhaps Meryl was right. Had this been a bad idea?

"Sorry," Jynieth said. "Thought I was ready for this."

"Me too," Meryl replied. "Plain stupid reactions. I'm Mhyrrelle," she said, using her true name. "It *is* nice to meet you, despite what my body is saying."

"Nice to meet you too," Jynieth replied. "My hormones are all out of whack with the pregnancy. Let's blame it on that."

Meryl's face lit up with a smile and she elbowed French in the side. "This one hasn't stopped talking about your pregnancy since the night you called and told us."

Everybody's eyes turned to the psychic.

French ignored them and added fettuccine noodles to the pot of boiling water. "It happens to be exciting news and everyone knows I'm a bit of a gossip," he said without turning.

Ainsworth rolled his eyes. "Liar. Busybody maybe, but you are the most tight-lipped person I've ever met and I've met quite a few people in six-hundred years." Ainsworth had been cursed by a witch. One aspect of the curse was that he couldn't die. The things that he'd survived and slowly healed from were horrifying.

"Yes, but this isn't some tragic secret, this is good news," French countered.

The sound of the doorbell ended any further discussion. Meryl and Jynieth shared a look.

"His name is Virgil. He's an incubus of Eisheth Zenunim," Mr. French said calmly.

"This might be bad, right?" Jason asked. He and Jynieth were engaged to be married. It wasn't a common occurrence for succubi, but Jynieth was not your average succubus.

"Get the door, will you Ainsworth," French said. "Nothing to worry about—Virgil and Meryl get along fine. He's really quite a pleasant chap and a fun sort to be around."

"Zen's children usually are," Jynieth said. "Then the fun gets out of hand."

Meryl nodded. "Last time we had a party, the *Ghostapo* showed up. We had to bail Virgil out of the O.M.T lockup."

The Ghostapo was the derogatory term for the Vatican's *Office of Minor Transgressions*. The O.M.T. investigated and mitigated otherworldly disturbances—things the public was forbidden to know about, things like succubi, although they were small fry in the O.M.T.'s grand scheme of things.

"That was not his fault," French explained. "The lycanthrope that crashed the party was who they were after. Virgil just got caught up in the excitement."

"Did I hear my name being said in vain?"

An attractive blonde male in his early thirties stepped into the kitchen. His boyish smile was infectious and the riled up senses of Meryl and Jynieth faded immediately. Like the oil and vinegar in the marinade on the antipasto salad, Virgil was the polar opposite of threatening. His hipster casual brown jacket, vest, and trousers were perfectly accented by the hand-loomed scarf.

"These two were concerned about my choice of invitees for dinner," French told the incubus.

"I'm no trouble," he said, still smiling.

Meryl couldn't help but prod the incubus a bit. "And the last time you were here?"

"Hey, he insisted I climb on his back."

Meryl eyed the incubus over the top of her glasses. "You rode the werewolf down the length of Broadway!" she exclaimed.

"Yeah, that was fun. What ever happened to that guy?"

"Watch out, coming through with a hot pot," Mr. French said, carrying the pasta to the strainer in the sink. "I proved to the O.M.T. that it was a human and not Mr. Gaines that was doing the killings," he said over his shoulder. "I believe that he resides in Austin these days—works as a game designer, as I recall."

"Yeah, he was no killer," Virgil added. "Those O.M.T. goons just have it out for our kind."

"You rode a werewolf?" Jason asked?

Virgil nodded, his fashionable flop of hair bouncing with each nod. "Yup. The hard part was keeping my knees clamped tight on his hips."

Meryl suppressed a giggle.

"Yeah, I know. I was the perfect person for the job, eh?" Virgil said with a naughty, sly smile.

Jason didn't get the reference.

Jynieth leaned over and whispered into his ear. "Virgil is gay, honey."

"Oh, good. I thought I was underdressed," Jason replied. He was wearing a simple red dress-shirt and jeans. "Oh crap, was that rude?"

Virgil shook his head. His smile was even larger than it had been. "No, I over-dress for everything. You never know when you might meet some cute guy."

"You Zen types, always looking for fun," Meryl commented.

"Better than being a nun of Naahmah," he snapped back with a devious smile.

"She's no nun," French muttered as he stirred the pasta noodles into the white cream sauce.

Meryl snapped her head around to glare at French. "I'm not sure how to take that."

French's hand abruptly stopped stirring. "Well, I meant only to say that I, for one, am very glad that you are not a celibate nun."

"Just quit now," Ainsworth said, shaking his head.

"Probably a wise decision," French agreed. "Time for us to migrate to the dining room anyhow. I don't suppose our other guest will be joining us for dinner."

"Other guest?" Meryl asked confused.

"Yes, I extended an invitation to Agrat Bat Mahlat asking her to send one of her Daughters."

Looks of stunned disbelief stared back at French.

"What? There are things that need discussion."

"Don't her Daughters want to kill all humans?" Jason asked in a whisper.

French shook his head. "No, no, they only prey on the vile sort of human that deserves killing."

"How do you know that?" Meryl asked. "In the few experiences I've had, her Daughters were obnoxious bitches."

"That about sums it up," Virgil added.

"Me too," Jynieth said.

French gestured toward the door. "I have my sources, now head into the dining room please. Ainsworth, could you grab a bottle of the wine?"

"Of course."

Jason and Jynieth followed Meryl. The Victorian house that French used as an office had a large formal dining room. In it, a mahogany table was set with china and silver for seven.

Meryl stopped and turned back to stare toward the kitchen and Mr. French. "He really did invite a Daughter of Agrat. I thought he was joking."

Jason looked puzzled.

Jynieth pointed at the table. "Seven place settings. There are only six of us."

"Oh yeah, obvious. Sorry to be such a doofus, babe. I'm still sort of out of my depth dealing with all this stuff."

"You knew enough to be scared of a Daughter of Agrat."

"Yeah, well when a demon queen has sworn to kill all of humanity to get even with God, you kinda remember those things."

"The Queens prefer to be called *Lilin*, not demons," Virgil added. "*Demon* is a term the other side uses in a somewhat unfriendly way."

French stopped any further discussion of the Daughters as he arrived bearing the Antipasto. "Sit down everyone. Ainsworth, see to filling the glasses, would you. We're informal here, just serve yourselves. I'll pop back and get the bread."

Meryl stepped to the far side of the table and pulled out one of the scroll backed chairs. "French and I can sit over here. Virgil, you, Jason and Jynieth can have the near side."

As they sat, Ainsworth filled their wine glasses. French returned bearing the loaf of warm bread.

"So, how did the visit to the OB-Gyn go?" he asked Jynieth.

"Still no answer as to how I became pregnant. Dr. Maks checked, and I still have my passages blocked. It wasn't a fault of my body's. I shouldn't be pregnant."

It had come as a surprise to Jason that succubi had the ability to control their fertility. The visit to Dr. Maks, a specialist in the biology of *Infernals,* as succubi and incubi were commonly known, had been eye opening.

"Just as I suspected," French replied, settling into the chair by Meryl. "It was why I wanted a representative from all four Lilin here tonight."

Meryl turned to French. "You aren't referring to that old fairy-tale?"

"Could be a core of truth there," he responded.

Jynieth shook her head. "You think my child is the one to unite the Lilin?"

Jason took Jynieth's hand. "Is this good or bad?"

"I don't know," she said in a subdued voice.

"The prophecy refers to a child born of a human to a virgin Daughter," Meryl explained.

Jason relaxed. "Well that's not you babe. The way we've been going at it for the past year, we're both long past being virgins."

Virgil laughed, swirling the wine in his glass. "For us, *Virgin* means pregnant when the woman's passages are blocked."

Jason's worried look returned. "Oh," he said glumly. "So what else does this prophecy say?"

"It's rather vague," Meryl answered. "Supposedly the Daughters will stop fighting amongst ourselves and unify under one leader."

"Our baby is going to be the leader of the succubi? Cool."

Jynieth sadly kissed her husband on the cheek. "Except that we will be at war when this happens."

"I have done some research," French added. "The exact prophecy went *A child, conceived of man, born to a virgin Daughter, will bring the four together as one. This Daughter shall lead the four in the war against the dark.*"

Jynieth clutched at Jason's hand.

Meryl noticed. "What?"

"The ultrasound showed it's a girl," Jason explained.

"Do you really think my daughter is the one?" Jynieth asked French.

"Doesn't matter what I think," Mr. French said. "What matters is what the Lilin and their Daughters think."

"Can't we just keep it a secret?" Jason asked.

"Too late for that," Meryl said. "Lilith felt the pregnancy. She contacted French several days after you told us."

French nodded. "Yes, and I happen to know that Lilith has been speaking with the other three Queens."

Jaws dropped around the table.

"Even Agrat?" Meryl asked, somewhat stunned.

"Yes, and from what I was told, it wasn't just Lilith that sensed the pregnancy—they all did."

The stunned silence was broken by Virgil. "I really can't see Zen talking with the old bitch Agrat. Honestly, I can't even conceive of the four of them in the same room together."

Mr. French heaped a spoonful of Antipasto onto his plate. The kalamata olives, prosciutto, genoa salami, finely cubed aged provolone, marinated artichokes, and mushrooms would have normally been the center of attention but not today. "I doubt that Agrat is as terrible as her reputation," he said, passing the platter to Meryl.

She eyed him sideways then took the antipasto. "You're not telling us something."

There was a massive bang from the front of the house. It was like a car had slammed into the front door only louder. Then it happened again.

Ainsworth had jumped up at the first bang and by the second was rushing down the hall toward the entry.

"We have visitors," he yelled.

Mr. French stood, pointing for everyone to move toward the kitchen. "Who?" he yelles at Ainsworth.

There was another massive crash.

"Devine war party from the looks of it," the man servant yelled back.

"My wards should hold for a few minutes." French glanced out the window above the sink. "Damn, they're back here too."

Ainsworth reappeared carrying a sword and shield. "Yes, they have the house surrounded. I'll hold them as long as I can. Use the tunnel. Get everyone to safety." He ran to the front of the house as another crash, much louder, rattled the entire house. This time there was the sound of splintering wood.

An older woman stepped into the kitchen.

"Mrs. Mallet, what are you doing here?" Jason asked the woman.

Mr. French turned to the woman and then to Jason. "You two know each other?"

"She's my landlady," Jason answered.

Mrs. Mallet ignored Jason's question. "It's a good thing you invited me, French."

"Yes, I suppose, but now the issue is how to get everyone out of here."

The medieval sound of metal striking metal came from the front office. Jason peeked into the hall and saw Ainsworth fighting a man wearing golden armor. The armored man had wings.

"Is that an…"

Mrs. Mallet interrupted. "Yes, now everyone, gather round me please."

French shook his head. "Wait, you're not taking us there…"

He was interrupted as the floor fell away and everything went black.

***

Jason was in darkness. He tried to move but his muscles were frozen solid. He could still feel Jynieth's hand in his so that was something. The roaring sound filling his ears began to lessen and slowly the stygian blackness was replaced by a red mist. Haze and the overpowering smell of Fourth of July fireworks made it difficult to breathe.

Breathing, hey, those muscles worked. Jason tried squeezing Jynieth's hand again. Nope, still no good. Apparently just the voluntary muscles were frozen, not the lungs and heart. Around him, the mist and smoke flickered, illuminated by bonfires yet unseen. Then the dark descended again. The feeling of falling slowly eased and Jason felt his feet reach a solid surface. In that instant, light slammed into his retinas. He squinted, blinking away the purple and red dots burned into his corneas. What he saw made no sense.

"Hurry up, we need to get off the street," Mrs. Mallet told the group.

Everyone but Mrs. Mallet was disconcerted and blinking at the brightness. Jason didn't feel quite so much like a newb now.

"Where are we?" he asked.

"One of the resort islands of Tartarus. I find that the seaside air does wonders for my skin," Mrs. Mallet told him.

Around them, what looked like a quaint Italian town went about its business, quite undisturbed that five people had just appeared out of nowhere.

"So you're a succubus too?" Jason asked.

"The college educated human gets it in one," she responded.

"Sorry, still new to all of this." In the four months that he and Jynieth had rented the apartment, he hadn't ever really talked to Mrs. Mallet. She was an older woman, sort of heavy set, with a gray streak in her hair, who was not much for conversation. When Jason dropped the check off, she usually thanked him with a scowl. So far today, she had said more than all their previous conversations combined.

She shook her head, pre-empting anything else Jason might ask. "The answer to your next inanely stupid question is *Yes, this is hell. No, it isn't what you expected, and yes there are places where the souls are tormented.*"

"Why?" Jason asked while admiring the Romanesque style architecture. Jason's father was a mason so he had a soft spot for rock walls and stone arches. Helping his dad had been a hell of a lot of work. It was why he was going to college to become an architect—to avoid the family business.

"Why are the souls tormented, you mean?" Mrs. Mallet asked.

"Yeah. Seems kinda unfair to punish someone for eternity for a mere lifetime of sinning."

Mrs. Mallet snickered. "You humans insisted. It wasn't our idea."

"*We* insisted?"

"Yes, the plan was just to recycle you when you died but your religious leaders demanded that sinners be punished. The Devine created a whole bureaucracy to manage the punishment."

Jason was thoroughly confused. "Humans created hell? Recycled? A bureaucracy?"

"You apes are so clueless," she replied and turned to French. "We need to get out of the open. Even here we aren't safe from the Devine hit squads. We need to find a place to hole up."

"Agreed, but we are far from my stomping grounds. I am assuming that you have an idea where we should reside."

"The Hotel Tiramezzo would be safest…" she replied.

"I detect that there is an unspoken *However*?"

"Yes, well the Daughters of Agrat held a party there a century ago and are no longer welcome, but the Tiramezzo's security is the best. The Devine will be blocked from manifesting within the building."

"So what you are saying is that someone other than yourself will need to secure our lodging," French said. "What form of remuneration does one use in Tartarus?"

"Visa or Mastercard are fine, or cash. Remember, it was Infernals who set up the human banking system."

"Yes, that's right, after the fiasco with the Templars and Philip the Fair." French turned and surveyed the street with its stone cobbles and rows of quaint shops. "So how does one find their way to the Hotel Tiramezzo?"

"This way," Mrs. Mallet answered, taking off at a brisk pace.

She looked like the typical American tourist in Europe. Her floral print polyester blouse was a size too large and should not have been tucked into the Gloria Vanderbilt designer *mom* jeans she wore. Unlike the blouse, the pants could have been a size bigger. Mrs. Mallet's somewhat large backside was testing the tensile strength of the vintage jean's double sewn seams.

Jason turned to Jynieth. "So humans are recycled?"

She smiled. "Reincarnated is a nicer way to put it but yes."

"Why?"

"Around five or six-thousand years ago, our race discovered the plane of your existence. It was of little interest at first until a Devine scientist modified the life on Earth to produce the energy that our life forms consume. With a hint here and there, your species thrived and was soon quickly spreading across the planet."

"You speak of us like livestock."

Mrs. Mallet dropped back and added to the conversation. "That was all you were in the Devine plan. Note that we Infernals opposed humans being treated in that way."

Jynieth nodded smiling. "It was what caused the division within our race. We Infernals believe in giving you something for what we take."

Jason's face squinched up in confusion. "I know how the succubi feed but how do the Devine?"

"Church," Mr. French answered. "The gathering and directing of one's self toward Heaven."

Jason's jaw dropped. "Wow, is my mom going to be unhappy. Do the church leaders know this?"

"Yes, Meridiana, the succubus that helped Pope Sylvester II told him. Since then the Vatican has kept the knowledge to itself."

"What a scam!"

Suddenly, Jason had one of his premonitions. He called them his *spider sense*. He turned. Down the alley to their left was one of the armored angels. He was holding a staff, shifting it in the frozen slow motion of the moment to point towards Mrs. Mallet.

"Get down!" Jason screamed, rushing towards the older woman. His shoulder slammed into her side, knocking them both to the ground as the wall above them erupted in an explosion of stone and broken rock. Bits of masonry pelted them like the sting of a million angry bees.

Mrs. Mallet said something and flung her hand at the angel. A wall of fire engulfed him. Jason looked around. Jynieth was with French. The psychic pulled a small stone from his pocket. It began sparking, creating a thick black cloud of smoke.

A very serious Virgil was suddenly by Jason's side. He grabbed Mrs. Mallet's arm and pulled her to her feet. "Move," he said urgently.

Jason jumped up, grabbed Jynieth, and ran, following their landlady. Strange, she didn't run like an old woman that never left the apartment manager's office, more like a high school track team star. He and Jynieth were having trouble keeping up. Occasionally, Jason glanced back over his shoulder. Virgil had dropped back with French, the cloud of smoke covering their escape.

Mrs. Mallet was keeping to one side of the street, hugging the wall. When she reached the next corner, she stopped abruptly. Jason and Jynieth almost ran into her.

"The hotel is around this corner on the right," she said to Jynieth. "Go, Daughter of Lilith. Get a room and stay there. Open the door to no one but me or French. We will join you in a moment."

Mrs. Mallet glanced around the corner, then shoved Jynieth and Jason forward. They ran. Behind them, they heard the old woman chanting something. Moments later, a rumble shook the cobblestones beneath their feet.

As they reached the hotel entrance, a doorman who'd been watching the battle at the corner with only mild interest, turned to them. "Checking in?" he asked.

"Yes," Jynieth yelled out of breath.

Jason turned back. He was holding a steel rod, about thirty inches long. He had no memory of picking it up. At the corner, Mrs. Mallet had lightning arcing from her hands aimed at a target back around the corner. Thunder was rumbling down the street when a blast of blue light smashed into the grouchy old woman, throwing her across the square. She recovered quickly, knelt, and began screaming in rage. Flames from her mouth and eyes leapt toward the source of the blue light.

Jason turned to Jynieth. "Inside, now!"

The two ran through the hotel doors. Once inside, a sedate calm engulfed them as if there was no massive battle occurring outside. Jason looked around, trying to remind himself that this was Hell. It was easy to forget in the gold and marble luxury of the hotel lobby. Overstuffed sofas were clustered around tables littered with travel and golf magazines, the sound of light jazz being played on a piano, and the clean smell of herbal incense intended to lighten the spirit. Jason and Jynieth ignored it all and rushed to the red and black granite front desk.

"Room," Jason said a bit too loudly.

The receptionist waited patiently.

Jason rolled his eyes. "Sorry, here," he said, pulling out his wallet and giving the dark haired woman his debit card. Thankfully, he had just been paid. He wondered how big a hole this was going to dig in his bank account.

"And how many are in your party?" the dark haired woman asked. She had very pale skin, almost white. The simple black dress she wore threw her skin into stark contrast. The hotel name tag at her lapel said *Karen*. Her lips were very red.

"Seven," he answered.

"No, six, hon," Jynieth corrected. "Ainsworth is still back at the house."

"Shit, that poor guy."

The receptionist handed Jason's card back. "Would you like to purchase insurance for the room? It's only thirty dollars more a night?" She glanced politely toward the hotel entrance. "Might be wise."

Jason wondered if this was just a scam to upcharge then decided that battles between angels and demons might get messy. "Yes, please," he said calmly.

"Room 326," Karen said happily. "It's a corner suite and has a Jacuzzi. Enjoy your stay with us."

They hurried to a gleaming pair of gold elevators. Jynieth pushed the button. They waited.

"I should never have gone after you at the Starbucks," Jynieth said softly. "I'm going to get you killed."

Jason pulled her close. "I don't care how many people try to kill us, I wouldn't change a thing. I love you babe."

He stared into her beautiful eyes and kissed her. The ding of the elevator ended the moment.

As Jynieth and Jason stepped inside the elevator cab, Virgil and Mr. French stumbled through the hotel entrance.

"Over here," Jason said with a wave.

French and the incubus hurried over. Virgil's arm was bleeding badly. A trail of red splatters followed him like a puppy.

"Where's Agrat?" Mr. French asked.

"Agrat?" Jason asked. "The Agrat? She's here?"

Jynieth squeezed her fiancé's hand. "Mrs. Mallet, honey. She's Agrat."

"She is?"

There was a poof of gray smoke that smelled of burnt smelly tennis shoes.

"Yes, I am," Mrs. Mallet said. "The Agrat Bat Mahlat, obnoxious bitch, rude nasty demon cunt, and your grouchy old landlady."

Jason turned to Jynieth. "You knew this?"

"Not until she brought us to Hell. A succubus doesn't have that power. Only one of the four Queens could do that."

Virgil chuckled. "The *Four Queens*—sounds like a bar I visited once in San Francisco. Fun place."

Mrs. Mallet pointed a finger at Virgil. "Shut it, Zen offspring. No one wants to hear about your gay romp through a hundred human buttholes."

"Such a mouth you have," Virgil replied. "I hope you don't kiss Samael with that mouth."

The corners of Agrat's mouth lifted in a smirk. "You're lucky I like you, incubus."

The elevator doors complained with a buzz.

"We have a room upstairs," Jason said, holding the impatient doors open. "Two floors up…"

Mr. French interrupted him. "Don't say the room number. A psychic impression can be read long after an incident occurs. Best to remain silent until we arrive."

Everyone piled into the elevator. Mr. French pushed the buttons for each floor in order starting with the one. Once the door closed and the elevator began moving, he also pushed the G for ground level. The Hotel followed the European norm. There was the ground floor with the lobby. Then, what

Americans would call the second floor was floor one, the third floor was floor two, et cetera.

The elevator arrived at the first stop. As the doors slid open, Mr. French placed a small bronze cube on the floor of the elevator. He then ushered them all out and then quickly back in. He did the same thing at the second stop. At the third stop, their floor, he ushered them out, leaving the bronze cube sitting in the middle of the elevator.

"This will leave an image of us leaving the lift at every floor," he explained.

"Won't fool the hounds for long, French," Agrat commented.

"True, all we can hope for is to gain some time."

Their room was at the end of the corridor. Jynieth used the key and let everyone inside. Mr. French was the last. He closed the door and made some hand gestures accompanied by muttering in Latin.

Jynieth hugged Jason. When he only hugged back with one arm, she noticed the iron rod he was carrying. "What's that?"

"This?" Jason held up the rod. "Don't know. Think it might be part of a railing. May not do much good, but I'm glad to have some kinda weapon." He turned the bar over in his hands. Writing was etched into the smooth surface. Bits of gold clung to the edges of the strange script. Whatever it was, it was old. The rod had the patina of age and long use like a cherished tool.

Virgil was at the window, peeking out the closed blinds. "There are at least twelve of them out there."

"The other Lilin should be here soon," Mrs. Mallet told the group.

Jason had trouble convincing himself that this frumpy old lady was one of the Queens of hell.

She turned to him, reading his thoughts. "Here, I'll fix that." She shook her body, shedding the image of a fashion challenged woman from the 1970's. Jason had seen something like this before when Jynieth changed into her succubi form. He found it wonderfully kinky doing the naughty with a red skinned demon with leathery wings, spike tipped tits, and sharp black claws. Besides, in that form, Jynieth was insatiable. He was getting a chubby just thinking about it.

Like Jynieth, Mrs. Mallet, now undeniably Agrat Bat Mahlat, had the red skin and wings of a succubi. Unlike Jynieth, she was intimidating as all hell. Jason smiled at his own poor choice of words. Agrat stood at least six-four, with wide shoulders and the muscular arms and thighs of a female MMA fighter. She also had the massive boobs, narrow waist, and proportionately wide hips of a succubus. Jason was wishing she would turn around so he could see what her ass was like.

Agrat scowled at Jason. "I *can* read your thoughts. Did you miss that? Besides, you're engaged to be married."

"I just like to look." He turned to Jynieth. "We talked about that. You don't mind, right babe?"

Jynieth glanced at Agrat with a smile and then said to her fiancé. "Should I take on Agrat's form the next time we have sex?"

Jason turned, looked at Agrat, looked back at Jynieth, and then shuddered. "Nah, I'd have flashbacks to Mrs. Mallet. That'd be creepy."

That elicited chuckles from everyone, even French.

Virgil was still at the window. "We've got reinforcements. Zen, Lilith, and Naahmah just arrived with a lot of armed Infernals."

A muffled explosion rattled the building. Agrat joined Virgil at the window.

Jynieth wrapped her arms around Jason. "That was close."

"We'll be okay," he told her.

Only Mr. French noticed that the incised letters on Jason's iron rod were glowing a 1200 degree cherry red. The psychic joined the group at the window.

Agrat turned to French. "That explosion was on the floor below us. A Devine team must have read Jason's comment at the elevator and attacked the wrong room."

French nodded. "We need to move. They shall discover their error soon enough."

A knock at the door drew everyone's attention.

"Hotel staff," a polite female voice said.

Jason leaned forward and peeked through the peephole. "It's Karen, the receptionist. Should I open it?" The rod in his hand was now a healthy lemon yellow 1800 degrees.

Virgil pointed at the rod. French just nodded. He turned to Jynieth. "Get behind Agrat. Jason, once she is protected, open the door."

Jason paused. Once Jynieth was in position, he unlocked the door. He took a step back, the rod ready to strike anyone that entered.

"I apologize but we will need to move you to another room," Karen, the receptionist said.

Her slight body was silhouetted against the fluorescent brightness of the corridor. Another explosion rocked the building, bringing a fall of dust from the ceiling.

"Hmm, I'll need to talk to Maintenance about this," she said waving a hand at the dust hanging in the air. "If you will follow me, we have a safe room in the basement."

"Go," Agrat said.

Jynieth ran to Jason. He put his left arm around her waist before leaning out into the hall with a glance both ways.

"We will use the employee elevator," Karen said, walking down the corridor to an unnumbered door. There was no knob—instead, she waved her hand and there was the click of a lock. Inside was a small room with stacked linens, boxes of hotel shampoo and wrapped bar soap, several laundry carts, and an elevator. It was open. Two large bellhops were waiting. They were carrying wicked looking swords.

"In here," Karen told Jason. One of the bellhops tossed Karen a weapon. Like their swords, it was the black and red of the hotel logo. This though, was no mere sword. It was a saw-toothed vicious looking thing. The finely honed razor edge caught the light.

Agrat shifted form, becoming Mrs. Mallet again. It was necessary—things were going to be crowded. After she entered the elevator, Karen and the two bellhops joined them. The doors closed and the elevator shuddered into movement.

Karen turned to Agrat. "The Devine control the ground level. Your forces are in the process of retaking the lobby but it isn't safe to pass the One on to them at this time. Hotel staff are engaged in combat on the lower level. We shall have to pass that way. There will be fighting," she said with the calm assertion of someone familiar with battle.

Jason was not so calm. He had Jynieth and their daughter to worry about. Adrenalin was flooding his system, making him antsy. He flexed the muscles in his forearm, squeezing the rod of iron in his hand.

Jynieth noticed. "Hon, your eyes are glowing."

Like a stone in a pond, his focus was broken. "Glowing?"

Mr. French, as always, had the answer. "You are carrying Agrat's rod of power. That, paired with your own magic is manifesting excess energy as light."

Jason turned to Agrat.

"You are such a weak, little thing. I thought you needed some protection," she said.

"Would it be more effective in your hands?" Jason asked. "I don't want to do anything that might risk Jynieth or the baby."

The third wife of Samael and one of the four Queens of the underworld rubbed her arthritic Mrs. Mallet hands together. "Trust me, mere mortal, I have far worse in my arsenal."

"All right," Jason said, testing the heft of the weapon. "Are there any operating instructions that I should know about?"

The elevator dinged as they reached the lower level. Agrat's answer was pre-empted as the elevator door exploded inwards. The two bellhops and Karen took the brunt of the force. The three climbed to their feet, kicking the ruined stainless steel doors aside and leapt into the smoke filled commercial kitchen. As their feet touched the slip-resistant quarry tiled floor, their bodies were no longer that of professionally dressed hotel employees. Karen was now some black horror from a nightmare. She had landed on all fours. Her head was a leech's mouth, loaded with rows upon rows of triangular teeth. Poisonous spines rippled on her back. "Kill them all," she screamed. The two bellhops, now huge armored beasts of bone and chitin, ran into the smoke.

Karen turned to the elevator. "If you will follow me," she said in her pleasant receptionist's voice. It was out of place with her whip-like medusa hair, rows of lethal spiked tipped breasts, and the sword, now covered in blood.

Jason had not seen her kill the angel that had been waiting for them. There'd been only a blur of movement as Karen had jumped from the elevator. At her feet, the angel lay nearly cut in half, golden armor and all.

"Let's go," Jason said, stepping from the elevator to join the hotel receptionist. In his hand, the rod was a white-hot instrument of death. In that moment, surrounded by the smoke, blood and stench of battle, it had spoken to him and he had responded. One blink of an eye and it had taught him how to think, how to move, how to defend, and how best to kill. He took a deep breath. "Stay in the middle of us, Jynieth."

She shed her human form. So did Agrat, Meryl, and Virgil.

"In the center with her, French," Agrat commanded. "You're our last defense."

The psychic nodded and moved up next to Jynieth.

"Here they come," Virgil yelled.

In the smoke to their right, three Devine soldiers were battling with one of the bellhops. One of the Devine raised a staff. A blast of blue light smashed the bellhop across the room, crushing several food prep tables. The three Devine turned and charged.

Agrat's fire tore into them. Flesh charred and peeled from their skulls but they didn't stop. Like a heavenly hammer, they slammed into Karen, Virgil and Agrat.

The one with the staff faced Karen. He nearly matched her speed and skill. Virgil was at a disadvantage with only his claws against a man armed with sword and shield. Agrat carried two flails with spiked balls of igneous fire. There was fear in the face of the angel she faced.

It was over in several beats of a human heart. The Devine facing Karen moved his staff to intercept her sword. The saw-toothed edge pierced the magically protected staff, which splintered in an explosion of suddenly liberated energy. Nothing was left of the angel except his wings. Karen, burned and bleeding from the explosion struggled to stand.

The blast had caught Virgil's opponent off guard. The incubus used that moment to flick his claws across the Devine soldier's face, blinding him. Within moments, he too was dead.

Agrat's opponent was a bloodied pulp on the sanitized floor. She continued pounding the body like a chef tenderizes a poor cut of beef.

Jason's spider sense screamed with the whine of four million smoke alarms. "Protect," he yelled, summoning the rod's power.

Blue and white energy tore from the smoke to their left aimed at Jynieth. Jason dove, throwing himself into the beam.

There was a moment of searing pain and the sound of pounding water like being at the bottom of a great waterfall. Then there was only silence. Jason lowered his shield. It and the armor that the rod had wrapped around him had absorbed the blast.

The smoke parted like curtains on a stage through which a Devine soldier ran towards them. His armor was not like the rest. A silver lion decorated his breastplate and he wore a lion's fur as a cape. Sparks crawled along his sword like St. Elmo's fire on a ship mast. The angel struck.

Jason's newly learned instincts kicked in. Muscle memory engaged, easily parrying the angel's first blow. Where the Devine soldier's sword struck Jason's shield, smoke burned, smelling of overheated steel.

A look of surprise crossed the angel's eyes.

"Not expecting a mere mortal to stand against you?" Jason asked.

The Devine didn't respond but swung at Jason once again. He easily parried the blow. It was a diversion. The angel turned and threw his real attack Meryl. With only millimeters to spare, she darted out of reach. Jason stepped in, the rod slamming into the Devine warrior's shield. Forced to re-engage, the angel directed all his attention at Jason His blade glowed with phosphorescence that became a mere curve of light as it moved. Again and again the angel hammered down blows and again and again Jason and the rod parried, deflected, or avoided each. Fury filled the Devine soldier's eyes. Jason waited for the anger to grow. It would make his opponent reckless.

The sword of blue-violet fire arced down. This was the moment. The angel had put too much force into the blow and was out of balance, his left foot too far forward. Jason swiveled at his waist, twisting his upper body to the right. Now his shield was parallel to the arc of the blade.

The angel's sword hit, scrapping down the length of the shield and smashing into the grit faced tile of the kitchen floor. Jason's right arm punched forward, driving the rod full force into the Devine being's unprotected angelic face.

There was no great explosion, no blast of lightning, no light or burst of sound as Jason had expected. The angel just died, his life extinguished instantly by the rod. The husk of a body in heavenly armor collapsed to the ground.

Jason scanned the silent kitchen for more opponents.

"Take that you filthy blaggards!" French yelled.

Jason turned to the psychic. "Mr. French, you really need to upgrade your insults."

Agrat laughed, cleaning bits of bone and flesh from her flails. "Yes, you are a bit of a stuffed shirt."

"Hmm, I suppose my diction is something of an anachronism."

"C'mon, this isn't over yet," Karen said. "The safe room's through here."

They followed the injured receptionist through the ruins of the scullery and storage rooms. Built into the far wall was a heavy steel bank vault door. It was open and inside was the safe room.

Karen's eyes darted to the ceiling. "Inside quickly!"

No one questioned, they just moved. Karen was last in, pulling the huge door shut.

"Bomb!" she started to say as the floor slammed them upwards. Time slowed. The lights blew out, glass shattering, spewing bits of shininess that disappeared in the darkness. They reached the apex of their flight as the battery powered red emergency lighting flickered into existence. That moment of freefall seemed to last a lifetime, then their bodies fell back down, slamming onto the concrete floor.

The red lights flickered, candle-like for a moment. Several sputtered, failed, leaving the small room looking to Jason anyway, like the bridge of a destroyer in a World War two movie. His armor had saved him from injury from the fall but what about Jynieth?

"Babe, you okay?" he asked, reaching for his wife.

"I think my ankle's broken but I'll be fine."

The small room was a pile of succubi, incubus, and a lone human.

"How about you, French?" Agrat asked. "You're part mortal. Did you survive intact?"

"I believe that several ribs were broken when I landed on Meryl's clawed fist."

Meryl chuckled. "Be glad I had my claws in."

He nodded. A trickle of blood was smeared across his forehead. "Yes, shish kebab was not on tonight's menu." He turned to the receptionist that had saved their lives. She was collapsed on the floor. "Meryl, give me a hand with Karen's injuries."

As Meryl and Mr. French did what they could to wrap Karen in makeshift bandages, Jason wrapped his arms around his wife, letting the armor fade. "I love you babe."

"I love you too, but I'm fine. You know succubi," she said. "I'll heal within the hour."

He rested his face in her hair. "Being a parent is more difficult than my mom and dad made it look," he whispered in her ear.

She bopped him playfully on the head then turned serious. "How did you do that? The Archangel, I mean. What did you do?" She glanced at the rod, still clenched in her husband's fist.

"Not sure, really. I just wanted him dead. He was threatening you and the baby." Jason held his wife a little tighter. "I guess the rod made that happen."

Outside the safe room, everything was quiet. Whether this meant the battle was over or that the room happened to have excellent soundproofing there was no way of knowing.

They sat and waited. The safe room was the size of the average suburban home's breakfast nook. Luckily, it had a pantry which Virgil raided. The cloth napkins had been an early casualty, having been torn into strips to bandage Karen's burns. A large bottle of Perrier was passed around. Jason didn't care for the fizzy stuff but his throat was parched so he choked several swallows down. He passed the bottle to Agrat.

"Here," he said handing her the rod. "Thanks. It saved my life."

She waved him off. "And it will again in the future. Keep it, at least until I come to my senses."

Jynieth eyed the rod with suspicion. "Shouldn't that have killed Jason when he picked it up?"

"Yes," Agrat said with no further explanation.

Jynieth frowned. "But you did something when you handed it to him."

"No, I didn't."

Jynieth's heavy demon-like eyebrows crushed together in anger. "You gave it to Jason not knowing if it would kill him?!"

Agrat smiled slightly. "Actually, it went to him without my knowledge. I'm as curious as you to know why."

Virgil stopped rummaging through emergency rations to turn and stare. "You hear that French?"

"Please don't get him started," Meryl complained.

"You are referring to the tale of the rod bearer, I believe," Mr. French said.

He was interrupted by a metal on metal tapping coming from outside the vault door.

"Move me over by the door," Karen told French. "The walls are blocking the staff communication feed but there's a spot in the wall by the lock that will allow the psychic vibrations to pass."

Meryl and Virgil moved the injured receptionist to the door. Her burned body was not healing the way it should be—not a good sign.

She leaned weakly against the wall then scowled. "French, do you know a human called Brother Leo?"

"He's here?" Mr. French replied.

"Yes, along with a squad from the Department of Heavenly Mitigation."

"What's that?" Jason asked.

"God squad," Virgil answered. "The Devine police. Wonder what they want?"

"If you two blathering buttwipes would shut it, we could find out," Agrat said.

Jason smiled. He liked the nasty ol' she-bitch.

She rolled her eyes to the ceiling and shook her head.

"Your friend says that Izidkiel, the archangel we fought, was a rogue. The Devine have disavowed him and his followers. They want to know if we know where he is."

Agrat shook her head slowly from side to side.

"Ok, I've told them we don't," Karen said. "Your friend's not happy about that. He says that the explosion took out the whole building. It may take a while to get us out."

***

A month later, Jason, Mr. French, and Virgil were sitting on the patio of Jason and Jynieth's small apartment drinking beer. Meryl and Jynieth were inside. Meryl had organized a baby shower.

"You never finished your story about the rod bearer," Jason said to Mr. French.

"Probably just an old wives tale," the psychic replied.

Jason pouted. "Jynieth won't tell me either."

The glass patio door slid open. Agrat looking like Mrs. Mallet stepped out. "I need one of those beers. All this girl crap is killing me."

Virgil tossed her one of the bottle from the ice chest. "Not getting along with the other Lilin?"

She twisted off the cap with her thumb. "Lilith, Naahmah, and Zen are in there worrying over baby clothes," the old woman complained. "Ignoring the fact that there's a possible war we should be worry about."

Jason took a drink of his beer. "Then you don't think our battle was what the prophecy spoke of?"

Mrs. Mallet said nothing, but tossed her beer back in one long swig.

Mr. French answered the question for her. "No. I spoke with Brother Leo. He has confirmed some of my own suspicions. Something is about to happen, something very, very bad indeed, but so far, all anyone has are rumors."

Jason slumped in his plastic patio chair. "Yeah, my spider sense is on alert too, but all I keep seeing is a wall of water, like a tsunami." He gestured with his beer at the nearby apartments. "Shit, we live in San Antonio. We're three hours from the coast—have to be one hell of a wave to get here."

"A big wave, eh? Wouldn't mind doing some surfing," Virgil said.

Mrs. Mallet rolled her eyes. "You damn Zen freaks make this so fucking hard," she complained. "Shut up and give me another beer, incubus."

Virgil smiled and pushed the whole ice chest in her direction.

What most people believe demons to be is amazingly inaccurate. Demons do not have horns, or tails, or bodies at all. They are formless hungry things from other dimensions and not hell as the Vatican would have you believe. As French finds out, trying to get them to return to those dimensions is always a bit challenging.

Fey Lines

French pulled into the office parking lot and drove around back. The first light of dawn was rose tinting the clouds.

Ainsworth frowned. "Sunsets are so much easier to appreciate."

"Agreed," French replied.

With a turn of the key, the car shivered to a halt. French glanced over his shoulder to the collection of paranormal equipment in the back seat. As usual, the convertible's top was down.

Ainsworth saw the look. "There's no chance of rain today."

"Good. There's nothing here that can't wait until later. Let's go inside."

Ainsworth nodded. "I'll bring it in before it gets too hot out."

"Thank you."

French grabbed a leather satchel from the back and headed for the house. The kitchen's screen door had been shredded by claw marks.

The psychic sighed. "Damn, not again."

Ainsworth stepped forward to examine the damage in detail. "Perhaps the game camera we placed captured the beast."

"If it is merely an animal," French added. "The claw marks are in groups of threes."

"This is the work of talons, not claws" Ainsworth corrected. "Owl talons."

"Bollocks, not again!"

French's fingers fumbled shakily with the keys as he opened the kitchen door. Tumblers of both brass and magic clicked into place.

Ainsworth followed him in, flipping on the lights. "Looks like you could use some tea."

"Indeed. The Sri Lankan Black, if you would."

French walked down the hall and into the office. At the shelves behind his desk, he unpacked the satchel. A half-burnt bundle of sage and yarrow wood, a stoppered flask of oil, and a container of Mediterranean Sea salt joined the other oddities on the bookshelf. A riveted iron box edged towards French. A brass key was in the lock. It slowly turned and the heavy lid sprung open.

"Hungry for an occupant, I see."

The box bounced like an alert puppy. French pulled a brass ring from his pocket. "Here you go."

French smiled and tossed the ring into the air. The box leapt up, caught the ring mid-air, and snapped closed. It settled on the shelf, locking itself with a quick twist of the key.

The psychic turned, more than ready to simply collapse into his wingback chair and rest. He stopped himself. Meryl was standing in the office door.

"It's about time. You had me worried." She came over and wrapped her arms around his waist.

He hugged her back. "Nothing to worry about."

"Really? Then how come your jacket's singed and you reek of sulfur?"

"A fair amount of convincing was required. That's all."

The succubus lifted her head off French's shoulder and stared him in the eye. "You're a terrible liar, French. Besides, Ainsworth filled me in."

"Ah, well, as you know, possessions can be dicey even in the best of situations."

Meryl's attractive face twisted into a frown. "It's in those dicey situations when I want to know you're safe. Remember to call next time. Your cell phone's not a viper. You don't have to be afraid of it."

French pulled Meryl close and kissed her. "I do not fear my telephone."

She pulled away from the kiss. "Oh, so you just don't want to talk to me?"

French paused, pondering a way out of this no-win solution. "You know very well that I enjoy talking to you. The truth is, as you know, that I get very focused when I'm working."

Truth it might be, but it wasn't the answer Meryl desired. "Too focused, or do you just not want to tell me when you're in danger?"

"It wasn't that dangerous. I just..."

That partial lie stoked the embers glowing in Meryl's eyes. "French, a soul eating demon brought a city block down on you!"

"That's a bit of exaggeration—only a corner of the building collapsed."

The succubus's eyes erupted like a fire sprayed with gasoline. "And with you under it!"

"I was fine. The only casualty was my jacket."

"You were fine—this time! What about the next time, French?"

He nodded, conceding the point. "You're right, I should have called. I apologize; I won't let it happen again."

Meryl's inferno waned. "You'd better."

French kissed her again. "Besides, let's hope there isn't a next time."

"There'd be no next time if you'd stop working for the Ghostapo."

French sighed. "I removed the Drecati to save the young child involved, not as an employee of the O.M.T."

"It's still their responsibility, French."

"Well, yes, but they have the finesse of a blindfolded bowler. One shouldn't muck about clueless when a child's life is at stake."

Meryl shoved out of French's embrace. "Still not your problem. The mother contacted the O.M.T., not you. It was their case."

"Brother Leo didn't feel the girl would survive their methods."

Meryl glared, incendiary daggers fueled by rage. "And got you to do their work, and now, as a result, I have to do their paperwork, thank you very much!"

She stormed to the door, slamming it as she left. It didn't latch, but rebounded, hinge squeaking angrily.

French settled into his wingback chair. He was tired. The adrenalin was wearing off. He rubbed at his shoulder where the soul stealer, angry that French had stolen its prize, had slammed him against a wall. Going to be a hell of a bruise.

Ainsworth, with the tea trolley, nudged the door fully open. "Your tea, sir."

"Ah, excellent timing. Thank you, Ainsworth."

To one of the porcelain cups, Ainsworth added the barest smidge of cream, and then filled it with tea. The heady floral scents of the Sri Lankan Black filled the room. "Miss Meryl seems rather unsettled."

"She is worried for my safety," French explained.

The manservant raised a brow. "That was an EA-2 house rattle. I would venture to say she's more angry than worried."

"EA-2?"

Ainsworth offered French the tea cup and saucer. "Enhanced Ainsworth scale—measures Meryl's outbursts. An AE-5 can destroy a city."

"I can hear you," Meryl yelled from the front office.

French took the cup. "Let's hope we never see that," he whispered.

"Anything else, sir?"

"No, that's all. Thank you, Ainsworth."

The manservant glanced towards the front office with a cat's mischievous grin. "Forgive me, I know it isn't my place, sir, but you really shouldn't let Miss Meryl get away with such behavior."

French raised a brow. "I shouldn't?"

"No, sir. Talking back to an employer—very bad form. If she were my secretary, I would take her across my knee and remind her of her place. A good thrashing would do wonders."

"Meryl's more than just an employee, Ainsworth. It's normal for her to worry."

"There happens to be time in my schedule, sir, if you'd care to have me apply the needed discipline."

"Just you come in here and try it, butler boy," echoed from the front office.

French suppressed a chuckle and blew the steam from his tea. "Thank you, Ainsworth, but perhaps not. I don't think the city would survive."

"As you wish, sir."

Satisfied smile on his face, Ainsworth left, leaving French alone with his thoughts. Things were still a bit higgledy-piggledy after the set-to with the soul stealer. He closed his eyes and breathed deep of the Sri Lankan Black's invigorating aroma. "At least there's only that matter of Mr. Stoner's to deal with today. How best to handle that?" he wondered aloud.

French exhaled slowly and glanced out the window. The sun was well over the horizon, promising another blistering Texas day. He relaxed further into the wingback chair and brought the cup to his lips—sadly, still too hot. Not surprising, properly brewed black tea needed water just short of a boil. French considered adding more cream. Ainsworth had shorted the cup purposely, to boost the caffeine content.

"Patience," French told himself. He returned the cup to the saucer and resumed stirring.

To his right, a rustic table sat underneath the open window. "Laurette, I shall need your help on a project," he said to it.

Like most of the objects in French's office, the sturdy little table seemed somewhat out of place. It had been fashioned by a farmer living near the village of Labastide-Esparbairenqu in 1790. The thick slab of wood had been hewn from the heart of an ancient oak tree. Four stout legs supported the top and other than the wood pegs tying it together, there was nothing in the way of ornament. Like everything else in French's office, the table had a reason to be there.

Wood grain shifted. What was a knot, became an eye. It blinked once.

"What bee's in your bonnet, old man?" the table replied.

"I have a client that's building a ..."

"A human?

"Yes. This client is building…"

"Building? Even worse, and you want my help?"

"Listen, please. I know you have no love for the ways of men, but your expertise would be greatly appreciated."

The eye blinked once more, and a wood grain brow furrowed. "Men and their building is why I'm here."

French sighed, taking a moment. He'd expected a certain amount of reluctance. He sipped cautiously at the still-steaming tea. "I am well aware of your situation. I helped resolve it, after all."

The wood grain tightened. "A mere seven generations of misfortune..."

"Upon the family, yes, yes, but from which they've grown wiser. Wasn't that the idea? And they did—the descendants are a botanist, an environmental activist, an ornithologist, and a park ranger."

"While I'm still bound into a table."

"Well, yes." French placed the porcelain cup back on the saucer in his left hand. "I didn't want to lose you. Are you now wishing you had died with your tree?"

Wood grained loosened. "No. I just miss the feel of soil between my toes and the breeze flowing through my fingers."

"As we've discussed, I can infuse you into a new seedling."

"No, my forest no longer exists and this foreign soil tastes too heavily of chalk."

French nodded. "Agreed, it's certainly not the hills of Langudoc."

There was little else to say. French sat silent, sipping at his tea, staring out the window. Rather than the artificial humanness of asphalt car park, he saw a sweep of French forest spreading from horizon to horizon. Like the vast prairie that once covered this area of central Texas, Laurette's pristine forest was also lost, plowed over with the vineyards and farmland of mortals.

It was Laurette who interrupted the silence. "So, old man, tell me more about this project?"

"It's a small building for a barrister's office. A building that refuses to be built."

"Oh?"

"Easier to explain once we're there."

"It'll be nice to get out of the house."

French raised a brow. "As I remember things, you found going out into the human world depressing last time."

The oaken eye closed and lines of woodgrain flowed, spilling down the sturdy oak legs. It collected as a fog near the floor, before flowing toward the psychic. The mist swirled upwards, coalescing into the form and curves of a woman. Dark hair, like curls of burl oak, spilled across her naked shoulders. She looked at French.

"Won't it be an issue, the human's recognizing me as fey?"

French didn't answer, teacup forgotten in his hand.

"Well, won't that be a problem?" Laurette asked again,

He caught himself. "Sorry, it appears your enchantment is as strong as ever."

She smiled. "You told me you were immune."

"I said I chose to be unaffected," French responded, hiding his gaze behind a long sip of tea.

She giggled. "Didn't look unaffected just now."

French glanced at her over the top of his glasses and sighed. "It's been a busy night and I'm tired. Now, to answer your question, your appearance, as magically enchanting as it is, will have the humans trailing along behind you like love sick puppies. Yes, they will certainly notice, but there shall be no complaints."

"What about Meryl? Won't my presence upset her?"

French placed the teacup on the saucer. "This concerns work. Meryl will understand."

Laurette settled onto the edge of French's desk. "Succubi are jealous. They can't help it. Whether or not you want to acknowledge it, Meryl isn't happy that you've kept your old flame around."

French sighed once again. "She is quite aware that you and I are no longer involved."

"Perhaps, but to a succubus, I'm still a competitor for your affections."

French emptied the cup, and then prodded the tea leaves in the bottom, hoping for a revelation. There was none. "I suppose it would be wise to pre-empt any bad feelings. I shall find a way to thank her in advance."

"You'd better," Meryl yelled from the front office.

French took the interruption to retrieve the teapot from the trolley. He refilled his cup, carefully weighing how to proceed with the next point of discussion.

"As to your question of the humans. We shall keep a low profile and, fortunately, my client is well aware of your fey nature. What shall be an issue, however, is you walking around in the nude.

"Clothing? Again? No, no, no. I fucking wore clothes for you once—you remember the crap that happened. Never again. Eww, it was like having the shit soiled hands of a hundred feral humans suffocating me."

French sipped at the tea. This too, he'd expected. He introduced his distraction. "How did such a shy creature of the forest learn such language?"

"From naughty creatures like you," she responded.

"Hardly. I did not teach you to drop the F-bomb."

"No," Laurette mused. "That was a couple from the village that snuck away to my forest. Amazing the things humans say and do when they think they're alone."

"You always were something of a voyeur."

"Still am, watching the things that go on in your office. It's a good thing that wingback chair can't talk. You and Meryl give it a workout."

French stopped mid-sip. "I think someone might need some time in the attic."

"Myrddin, you're such a prude. Meryl enjoys having an audience."

He was tempted to scowl then recognized the truth in the statement. "I suppose that's true—a more-the-merrier approach is in a succubus's nature, but an audience is not something I find appealing."

Laurette leaned back, crossed her arms, and looked sideways at French. "You've been around the feral humans too long. You didn't used to mind being naked."

"I did when it was cold. Clothing has practical benefits."

She scowled. "Like what?"

"Pockets," French answered.

"Your satchel would work just as well."

"But hardly as convenient."

The dryad stabbed a finger at French. "I'm not binding myself up like a prisoner just to have pockets. You can put me in the attic if you want, but I'm not wearing any fucking clothes."

French sighed. It would be far easier task to dress a cat, and there'd be less profanity involved. "It won't be like last time. Modern clothing is no longer so constricting. There are no corsets or layers of skirts…"

"Screw you, French. I won't do it. I hate clothes, and those stupid things they wear on their feet…"

"Shoes," French interrupted.

"Yes. Why don't they like the feel of the earth beneath their feet?"

Meryl stepped into the room. "It's because they fear the sensual. They would rather insulate themselves in sanitized bubbles of safeness than surrender to the pleasures of the world around them."

Meryl's auburn hair was back in a no-nonsense bun, never a good sign. French placed his teacup on the coaster. "You're certainly in a mood today. Why the sudden contempt for humanity?"

"Your paperwork for the Vatican's *Office of Minor Transgressions*. What a bunch of self-righteous, pompous, windbags—labelling *infernals* as unnatural and obsessed with sex. I'm tempted to beat that black-robed friend of yours to death with his own unused penis."

French stifled a laugh. "Brother Leo is more of a business associate and hardly indicative of humanity as a whole. If it'll help, the decanter's in my desk."

"Thanks. I've already emptied the bottle up front."

Meryl walked around the desk, leaned over at the waist, her bottom facing toward French, and opened the drawer.

He stared at the round perfection of her backside. Not because he was a chauvinist, he certainly was not. For Vaettir, respecting the feelings of others was of utmost importance. It was for that reason that he *was* staring. Meryl was feeling vulnerable. Understandable for a succubus—her lover had a gorgeous nymph alone with him in his office, a gorgeous and nude nymph that had spent nearly a century sharing French's bed. To make matters worse, Meryl was angry at an assignment he himself had given her. What a disaster.

Meryl retrieved the decanter, slowly closed the drawer, and stood.

French patted his lap. "Join us, won't you. We seem to be at an impasse."

Meryl swayed her way over and settled onto his lap. "I might as well. As loud as you two are, I'm getting nothing done."

"Don't blame me. I am not the one screaming," French stated.

"You want screaming? I can give you screaming, because you're not making me wear clothes. Certainly not shoes like those," Laurette yelled, pointing at Meryl's three-inch stilettos.

"These heels enhance my calves and ass," Meryl said defensively. "You, though, should just stay barefoot. It's summer and that won't seem unusual."

"No shoes?" Laurette asked.

"No shoes," French responded.

"And something loose like a peasant's dress," Meryl added. "It's thin cotton and hangs away from the body."

"Not all laced up?"

"No laces at all," Meryl explained. "There's one up in my room. I'll let you try it on."

"You have a peasant dress?" French asked.

Meryl nodded. "From the summer the air-conditioner broke. Like Laurette, you wouldn't let me run around naked."

"Oh yes. Blisteringly hot weather they have here, but as I remember things, I was quite happy with you *sans vêtements*. It was the repairman..."

"That wasn't my fault. My seduction wasn't even on."

French squeezed Meryl's thigh. "There's no magic needed around a woman like you."

"Dirty old man," the succubus said as she slid off French's lap. "C'mon, Laurette, let's see what you think about the dress."

The wood nymph followed Meryl to the office door. Meryl paused and turned back to French. "By the way, you owe me bigtime."

French pulled the '69 *Fury* convertible onto the construction site. He shut off the engine and stepped from the car. A man in an off-the-shelf blue business suit and yellow hard hat hurried over.

"French, glad you could come." He took French's hand and shook it with a strong grip. "As you can see, I've got a real problem." He pointed at the strangely twisted building behind him. "We build it and the next day it's like this, structural steel twisted, concrete buckled, and not a damn thing plumb anymore."

"Glad to be of help," French answered. "The beard and moustache are new, Jerry."

"Sophie's idea. Likes the rugged look."

"Speaking of women and their preferences," French gestured to Laurette in the passenger seat, "Mr. Stoner, this is Laurette."

"Ah, hello, I, ah…"

The engineer's eyes glazed over lost in the embrace of a wood nymph's magical charms.

Laurette turned to French. "I warned you."

"He'll be fine."

"Doesn't look fine."

"Hmm." French waved a hand in front of the engineer's face. "Shake it off, Jerry. You were saying."

"Uh, oh, sorry. Wow, I know you warned me, French, but it's stronger than I expected—a lot stronger than your secretary's." He took a deep breath. "Anyway, nice to meet you Laurette. I'm Jerry Stoner. So, are you, um, a succubus like Meryl?"

"We do have a similar effect on humans, but no, I'm a dryad."

French gestured at the twisted building, hoping to get Jerry's mind back on the task at hand. "Mr. Stoner, on my first visit, I identified your troubles as the result of Earth-based magic. Exactly what kind and what was causing it, however, was beyond my abilities."

"And so, he brought in a specialist," Laurette said, stepping from the car. Beneath her feet, the broken clods of rock and construction torn caliche, softened and smoothed to cushion her step.

Jerry didn't notice this minor miracle, slipping under Laurette's spell again.

French stepped between the engineer and Laurette. "You said you were going to bring your wife by, Mr. Stoner. How did that go?"

"Yes, um, yes, I did that. Sophie said something about the flux being wrong and that it might have something to do with ley lines."

Laurette squatted down, placing her hands on the ground. "Your wife must be quite sensitive. She's right, the flux is vibrating, but it's a symptom, not the cause. Is she Vanir like Myrddin?"

French quickly interrupted. "No, quite human. She did, however, spend more than a century as a ghost. That has left her with some connections to our world."

"Oh, wait, this is that couple?" Laurette stood and placed her hand on Jerry's arm. "I've heard all about you—thrilling story."

"More chilling than thrilling."

"True, but it ended well for you and your wife."

Laurette's smile had caused Jerry's eyes to glaze over again but with the mention of his wife, he snapped back to the present.

"Yes, it did, and, scary as it was, I'd do it all over again for Sophie."

French stepped forward and removed Laurette's hand from Jerry's arm. "Enough recollections. How about I invite them round for dinner, Laurette, and you can hear the story firsthand. Now back to work. We're wasting this man's time."

"Stick in the mud." Laurette squatted down once more to touch the ground. "Something strong is distorting the ley. Can I walk around the site?"

"Sure, no construction's happening until this is fixed."

Laurette zigged and zagged her way across and through the bulldozer furrows, stopping to feel the ground or wave her hands in the air. French and Jerry followed along behind.

"What's she doing?" Jerry whispered to French.

"Not a clue. Earth magic is beyond my ken."

"Looks like she's whispering to the ground, now."

French pulled a pair of brass spectacles from his coat pocket. "Likely speaking to whatever creature's responsible."

"Creature?"

French nodded. "Could be as small as a sprite or as large as a dragon."

"A dragon? They exist."

The psychic held the glasses up to the sky and scowled. "Spots. Damnation, I forgot to clean these after that incident with the Lechuza. Blasted owl saliva is like glue." He pulled out a handkerchief and wiped vigorously at the lenses. "But back to your question, yes, dragons exist, and no, we aren't likely dealing with one in this case. Most *Draconis Terranus* prefer inaccessible mountain peaks where they burrow deep underground."

"Good, no dragons."

French placed the spectacles on his nose, and squinted at the earth. After a few silent minutes of following Laurette, he turned to Jerry.

"I'm not used to you quiet. You're usually pestering me to death with questions."

"Didn't want to interrupt."

"And the smile?"

"Just amused at how much my world has changed. Never thought being an engineer would involve consulting a psychic and a dryad. As far as questions go, those sprites you mentioned, could they have done this?"

"Temperamental creatures, but this isn't their style." French looked Jerry straight in the eyes. "I'm going to assist your recollection, so maintain eye contact. Tell me again, in as much detail as you can, about the problems you've been having?"

"Things went south before I came on the job. First the slab heaved. They jack-hammered that out, excavated down another two-feet, and brought in more steel. The morning they were going to pour the concrete, they found the rebar twisted out of the formwork. The owner was pissed and blamed the engineer who was fired—and not too upset about it, either, from what I hear. Anyway, that's how I got involved. I went over the engineer's drawings. They were fine—it was obvious things were more along your line of expertise, and that's when I called. Dealing with the supernatural wasn't covered at school."

"Certainly not." French selected a piece of limestone from a pile sitting by a backhoe. After examining it through the spectacles, he tossed it away. "There's very powerful Odic signature at play here. Tell me more."

Jerry walked over to the building slab and placed his hand on a steel tube column. The precise piece of manufacturing had been twisted into a cork-screwing curve.

"Each morning, we find it like this. At first, I thought that maybe the building's spirit was telling us where it wanted to be. I adjusted the plan and that's helped, but on the whole, it just keeps tearing itself apart."

French joined Jerry and ran his hands along the steel. "It's following the distorted lines of flux. This isn't normal."

Jerry nodded. "Not even close. I read up on ley lines. Aren't they generally on a massive scale? Seems like this project's inconsequentially small for ley lines to be the issue."

"No. This isn't just a matter of ley lines, is it, Laurette?"

The dryad was twenty feet away, kneeling on the exposed white limestone bedrock. Her hands were caressing the stone. She turned her head to the psychic, chestnut hair shimmering in the afternoon sun. "No, this is the aura of an Earth spirit, a very large one, and quite near the surface."

"Something underground?" Jerry asked.

"Yes. We'll need to find it and see what it wants."

"But we looked. There's nothing down there." Jerry walked over and squatted down beside the dryad. "We used ground penetrating radar looking for voids, hoping that was the issue. There's a small one on the east side of the site, but it's under the parking lot, and not something that might cause building movement. It's all bedrock otherwise."

"This creature lives *in* the bedrock, Mr. Stoner," Laurette answered.

"In the rock?"

"Yes, Jerry," French answered. "And that cave you discovered is our way of getting down to speak with it."

"Go into the cave?"

"Well, we certainly don't want it coming up here for a conversation," French added.

Jerry glanced at the job shack and then back to French. "The GPR just showed a void, not a way in. There's no opening on site, anyway. I suppose we could drill down."

Laurette shook her head. "Not a good idea."

"Not necessary," French said. "If there's water flow in the cave, I can trace it to an opening. I happen to have just the thing in the car."

A puzzled Jerry and Laurette followed the psychic over to the Plymouth. French opened the trunk, rustled around in several black canvas bags, until he pulled out two brass rods.

"My dowsing rods."

"Really? Those things work?" Jerry asked. "Wait, stupid question, of course they work. So now what?"

"Show me where this void is located."

"Over where the parking lot's going to be, that smoothed ground over there."

They walked to the spot of earth Jerry had pointed to. Wooden stakes and string defined the parking area boundary.

Inside, limestone gravel had been compacted into an impermeable base for asphalt yet to come.

French took a deep breath, pulled his elbows into his ribs, and held the rods in front of him. He walked about ten feet. The rods remained pointing straight ahead.

"What does that mean?" Jerry asked.

"Shh," French responded. He continued walking, one slow step after another. The dowsing rods in his grip never moved.

"Old man doesn't know what he's doing," Laurette whispered to Jerry. "Cave's over there." She pointed to a spot by a large live oak tree.

"SHHH!" French hissed again.

He reached the far side of the paved area, turned and began walking a parallel path five feet to the side of his previous route. Midway back, the rod in his left had swung inwards.

"Aha!"

French turned in that direction. Both rods were now reacting. French moved slowly, keeping to a path that kept the rods crossed. He ended up at a spot by the large live oak Laurette had pointed to.

"Told you," she whispered to Jerry.

French scowled. "Do you want to do this?"

Laurette shook her head. "I can only feel the cave opening. It narrows and heads upwards in that direction, but that's all I can tell. Tracing the water's your idea, old man. Get to it."

French sighed.

"Hey, I'm impressed," Jerry said.

"Thank you. At least someone appreciates my talents."

Laurette moved behind French and began pushing him in the direction she'd pointed. "Come on, chop, chop, old man, my feet don't like standing on this stuff."

In the direction Laurette had pointed was the back fence of a large two-storied Classical Revival house.

"We can't go that way," Jerry cautioned. "The owner's an asshole and has been complaining to the city about the project. We'll have to go around the block and pick up the trail on the other side of the house."

French relaxed, placing the dowsing rods in his jacket pockets. "Lead the way."

Jerry jogged toward the job shack. "First, I'll get some rope and a couple flashlights. We'll need 'em if we're going underground."

Jerry returned with a backpack stuffed with ropes and other gear, and the odd trio began their tromp through the neighborhood—a contractor in a yellow hard hat, French in a tailored business suit, both walking on the pavement, while Laurette, in her cotton peasant's dress, danced from lawn to lawn.

"Hardly keeping a low profile," French whispered.

"That man with the watering hose didn't seem to mind."

"Neither did the jogger," Jerry added.

"Of course not, Laurette's charms are befuddling them," French commented.

"Interesting that it worked on the woman jogger," Jerry added.

"That has something to do with the Earth as mother, but it isn't well understood."

As they rounded the block, Jerry pointed to a house three doors down. "We should be able to pick up the trail there."

French retrieved his brass dowsing rods and began walking slowly toward the white Classical styled house.

"Hope the owner's not home," Jerry whispered to Laurette. "He'll call the cops on us for sure if he sees us."

"What did you do to him to make him hate you so much?"

"Nothing. He's just upset a business is going in right behind him. Personally, I think the old fart's just upset he can't run around his backyard naked anymore."

"Why can't he do that?" Laurette asked.

"Because the people in the new building would see him."

"So, it's his yard, isn't it?"

"Well, um, yes, but no one wants to see some wrinkled old geezer in his birthday suit," Jerry explained.

"Because it reminds you of aging and death?"

"No," Jerry stumbled. "It's just that…"

French interrupted from across the street. "Discussions of repressive morality later, it's this way. Hurry up." He was peering into the brush and trees of an urban wilderness area.

"That's Olmos park," Jerry commented. "Creek's near here."

French, dowsing rods twitching, stepped into the brush, followed excitedly by Laurette.

"I love the feel of leaf litter underfoot. So much better than that concrete and it smells so good."

Jerry followed the dryad into the underbrush, wrinkling his nose. "Smells like moldy mulch and deer poop to me."

Laurette turned and scowled at the engineer. "To the forest, this smell is just as important as flowers in the spring."

French interrupted. "Really, will you two hush so I can concentrate. The water is quite shallow now. Look for a depression or sinkhole."

Laurette pointed ahead and to their left. "It's that way. I can smell the water."

Jerry took point, pushing aside the undergrowth in the direction the dryad had pointed. "You'd make a good bird dog, but I don't suppose you'd approve of hunting."

"Predation is a part of the forest. As long as you eat what you kill, and don't waste anything, it's fine."

Jerry stopped, turning to face Laurette. "Sensible. Funny, I'd figured you more of the tree-hugger type."

French interrupted a third time. "More looking, less talking!"

Several minutes passed before Jerry yelled out, "I see it. There's a sinkhole over here."

The engineer disappeared into a depression nearly invisible amongst the juniper and yaupon holly. French and Laurette joined him, scampering down the leaf litter and loose rocks of the sinkhole. At the bottom, water runoff fed into a concrete drain covered by a metal grate. A heavy-duty padlock secured the rusty steel bars.

Jerry kicked at the lock. It didn't budge. "Crap! Got a way to open this, French?"

The psychic made his way to the grate and examined the lock. "Of course."

"Going to use magic?"

"There's no need to exert oneself. I can easily pick this."

French rummaged in his satchel before pulling out a small cloth pouch tied closed.

"My lock picks. They've saved me from many a bad situation. Good opportunity to practice my skills."

Jerry leaned down and peered through the grate. "Looks fairly deep. I'll tie off a rope."

Laurette pointed to a large live oak. "This one over here won't mind."

As Jerry showed Laurette how to tie and secure the anchor line, French inserted one of the fine tools into the lock. He jiggled the tumblers until the lock clicked open.

"Success!"

French pulled open the grate. A burble of flowing water whispered from the darkness.

Jerry tossed the rope into the open hole. "Either of you know how to rappel?"

Laurette shook her head "No."

"I'll go down, see what we've got, and then come back up to help you two with the harnesses."

Jerry put on one of the steelwork safety rigs from work, clipped onto the line, and eased himself over the edge. The limestone was slick with algae. Several feet down, he slipped and fell into the wall.

"You okay," Laurette yelled down.

"Yeah, just slipped. Walls are really slick"

Jerry repositioned himself and began descending again. The pungent smell of rotting vegetation was growing stronger. Mingled with it was another smell, something else, like cement or mortar when it's wet.

"Found anything?" French yelled down.

Jerry stopped his descent. "Nothing so far. I'm about fifteen feet down. Sounds like there's a fair amount of water at the bottom."

He glanced down, switching on his helmet light. In the water below was a mound of trash washed in from the neighborhood—aluminum cans, plastic bottles, decomposed cardboard, a Burger-Bar Styrofoam cup, and other litter. Around this garbage island, the water was clear and looked only ankle deep. It flowed into a Hobbit-sized opening in the wall.

"Found your water, French. Didn't think to bring boots," Jerry yelled up. "We're going to get wet."

"My attire has survived far worse," French replied.

"Ooh, are there are fish!" Laurette asked.

"It's not that deep, but maybe. Probably get washed in when the creek floods. I'm more concerned about snakes."

"Hurry back up. I want to see too!"

Jerry glanced around one last time. "All right, I'm coming up."

Jerry unclipped an ascender from his belt, attached it to the line, and made his way back to the surface, one arduous pull after another. At the grating, he heaved himself onto the concrete. Mud and plant scum smeared his business suit.

"Going to be a hell of a cleaning bill."

Laurette poked at Jerry's safety harness as he stood. "Do we have to wear one of those?"

"Yeah, I've got one for each of you. Not real climbing harnesses, just OSHA safety rigs, but it'll do for this."

"French, you said no tight clothes!"

"It's more of a belt than clothes," French replied.

"I don't like it and it won't work with my dress."

"You won't have it on for long," Jerry added. "Just until we get down the hole. It levels out into a tunnel after that."

"I can take it off?" she asked.

"Yes," French replied.

"Good, I'm tired of this dress anyway." Laurette pulled the peasant dress up and over her head.

Jerry stood silently, a fall-protection harness half-out of his backpack, with an astonished smile on his face.

"Oops," Laurette said.

"Oops, indeed." French shook the engineer. "Mr. Stoner?"

There was no response.

French moved to eclipse Jerry's view of the naked dryad. "Jerry?"

The engineer slowly returned to reality. "Wow! Sorry, you're really beautiful."

"Nothing to apologize for." French glared at Laurette before turning back to the engineer. "Someone should have warned you first."

"My bad," Laurette added.

French turned again to the Dryad. "Where did you pick that up?"

"Charlotte, she says it a lot."

"Right, yes she does. College students and their slang."

French turned his attention back to the still befuddled engineer. "Mr. Stoner, think of your wife. Picture her in your mind."

Jerry nodded.

"Okay, when I step away, keep thinking of her and try to avoid looking at Laurette. Can you do that?"

"Yes. Shame though."

Laurette giggled.

"Focus, you two. We have a job to do, and yours, Mr. Stoner, will be most challenging of all—you have to get Laurette into that harness. Avoid touching her skin, it will bring on the charm. Ready?"

"Yes," Jerry answered.

As French steeped away, it was clear that Jerry wasn't. His eyes glazed over immediately at the sight of Laurette's pale skin and delightful curves.

"Jerry, concentrate!"

The engineer shook his head, deliberately staring at the harness in his hands. "I can do this," he mumbled.

With his eyes focused deliberately on the ground, Jerry moved behind Laurette and laid out the harness.

"All you have to do is step into the two loops, then pull up," he told her. "Buckle it at the waist and chest, then tighten the leg straps. Make it tight! You don't want any play. I'm going to turn away now."

The dryad pulled the harness on and belted it. "I don't need this, you know. I can climb stone perfectly well." She tightened the one leg strap, cringing as she did.

"Humor us," French replied. "We worry about you."

Laurette tightened the opposite strap. "Speaking of which, shouldn't you call Meryl?"

"Hardly a life-threatening situation," the psychic replied.

"You don't know that."

"Fine. I'll text her after I have the harness on."

Laurette feigned mock-surprise. "You can text?"

French steeped into his harness and belted it at his waist. "Yes. I can use modern technology, I merely prefer the classic look and feel of period design."

"Ancient and obsolete is what he means, Jerry, just like he is."

French tightened his leg strap. "I'm not obsolete."

"But you are ancient," Laurette giggled.

"Perhaps." French turned to Jerry. "And, luckily, in all that time, I have managed to rappel before. I shall assist Laurette. You head back down, and Jerry, don't look up."

That set Laurette to giggling more. Jerry found it to be an intoxicating sound. He eased over the edge, this time descending without incident. He stepped gingerly into the water.

"Shit! Be careful, the water's deeper than it looks," he yelled up the shaft. "And it's cold."

"We're on our way down," French replied. "On belay."

Jerry kept tension on the line by feel, his eyes set firmly on the spot of stone directly in front of him in the circle of his helmet light.

Movement on the rope stopped. "Laurette, what are you doing?" French said, alarmed.

"This is silly," she replied.

There was the sound of buckles and straps. Jerry didn't look up.

"Stop that this instant!"

"I know what I'm doing, old man."

A safety harness skittered down the shaft, splashing into the water. Jerry glanced up to see Laurette gracefully climbing down the wall to his right. Hand and footholds appeared in the rock surface as she moved. The dryad landed with a light splash of water.

"See, I didn't need the rope."

Jerry continued to stare, eyes wide in wonder.

"Oh no." She waved her hand in front of the engineer's face. "Looks like I did it again, French."

"I shall be there in a moment." Without the benefit of an earth creature's natural talents, the psychic was moving slowly, inching his way down the slick walls.

Laurette shimmied her shoulders. Jerry's mouth dropped open.

She giggled. "Humans makes such funny faces." She continued flaunting her figure, eliciting even wider stares. "This is fun!"

"Would you stop harassing the poor man."

French landed with a miscalculated sploosh. "Oh, bollocks!"

The thrash of limbs and spray of water was enough to misdirect Jerry's attention. "French, sorry, are you okay?"

French pulled himself upright and shook off. "Yes, merely drenched. Nice to have you back with us."

The engineer shook his head. "Yeah, she's a whole lot stronger than your secretary."

The psychic chuckled. "Oh, you haven't seen Meryl at her best. She too, has quite the figure."

"I doubt Sophie would approve of my seeing that, "Jerry replied. "Or this, come to think of it."

"Just keep your eyes down," French instructed, "And take the lead."

Jerry nodded and crouched down to squeeze through the narrow opening. Centuries of flowing water had carved the tunnel from a fracture line in the limestone. The walls were smooth and reflected his helmet light. The limestone surface above was another matter. It was moving.

"Lotta crickets huddling on the ceiling in here. Keep your head down!"

Jerry crab-walked into the tunnel, thighs complaining. A swirl of mud disturbed by his boots, flowed on ahead, obscuring his footing. The tunnel turned to the right. The sound of falling water grew louder.

"Tunnel bends," he yelled back. "Sounds like there's a waterfall ahead."

Flashes from French and Laurette's flashlights darted chaotically across the tunnel surfaces, casting Jerry's shadow as a menacing silhouette in the muddy water before him. The tunnel curved and the source of the falling water became apparent.

"We're gonna get wet. Water's sheeting in from a fracture in the rock above. Looks like the tunnel slopes down at that point. Keep hold of the rope."

"You don't need to yell," Laurette said. "We're right behind you."

"Sorry, can't look."

Jerry stepped through the sheet of frigid water, glad for his helmet. At least his head was still dry. Despite the heat of the summer, the cave's interior was quite cold. This side of the waterfall, the tunnel widened into a small room. The water was growing deeper, and was now at Jerry's waist. In the center of the room, a plastic cup from Taco Riviera swirled in an eddy. Below the surface was a child's tricycle. Rust had consumed much of it but enough chrome remained on the bell to reflect the light.

Laurette pushed through the cascade of water. She noticed what Jerry was staring at. "That's creepy."

Jerry fought the urge to turn to her, focusing instead on the tricycle. "Yeah. Must date to before the City blocked the opening. Wonder how long it's been here?"

French splashed into the chamber. "Why are we stopping?"

"Spooky tricycle," Laurette answered. "Think the child's ghost is hanging around?"

"No, I would feel it if it were. Now keep going, we need to find this earth spirit."

"There's no place else to go." Jerry shone his helmet light to where the flow of water disappeared into a hole at the center of the pool. "Look like that's the end of this adventure."

"Why?" Laurette asks.

"We'd need scuba gear to go on from here."

"No, we don't. It comes out in a large chamber just over there."

"How far *just over there*," French asked.

"One breath," she answered and dove into the water.

"Shit!" Jerry shed his backpack, struggled to kick off his Red Wing 971's, then dove in after her. Sucked down the confined tube, he struggled to stay in the center of the rushing flow of water. With no up or down, there was only the claustrophobic walls pressing in from the darkness. His lungs were beginning to burn. He needed air. How far did she say it was—one breath? Hers or his?

He was spat out into open water. Jerry gasped for air, his eyes struggled to focus. Everything was black, not dark, but black. Darkness implies light and here there was none. The earthy cement smell was strong here.

"Laurette! Where are you?"

The gritty sound of a foot shifting on rock came from his left. He dogpaddled cautiously in that direction.

"Laurette! It's Jerry. Are you all right?"

No answer. Was she okay? Had she drowned? He kicked harder and his groping hands found a sandy bottom. He stood, waist-deep listening for some sign of the dryad.

"Laurette!"

There was very little echo so the space couldn't be that large. More sounds of movement in the dark ahead of him. Someone or something was there.

"Laurette, is that you?"

A stone-on-stone rasping of a voice answered him. "Huuumaaan."

Something touched his foot.

Jerry jumped away from the touch, screaming like a panicked 1950's movie heroine. At least he didn't trip.

The thing that had touched him surfaced, expelling air, and taking a deep breath.

The engineer readied himself for a fight.

"It's me, Jerry," French said.

Jerry relaxed. "Thank goodness. I can't find Laurette and there's something in here with us."

"Something?"

"Yeah. Deep voice, very raspy."

"What did it say?" French asked.

"*Human*, just the one word."

French began rustling through his wet jacket. "Somewhere in these pockets is a light sphere." After a few moments, the cavern was bathed in light.

"Tooooo briiiight!" the raspy voice screamed.

French covered the glowing marble with his hands.

"Is this acceptable?" French asked, allowing only the smallest amount of light to spill between his fingers.

"Betterrrrrr."

In the dim illumination, Jerry could make out the shape of the cavern, Elongated, and about the size of a bus, water spilled in from a hole high on the wall near the back. It had created a deep pool, the turbulent reflective surface hiding anything hidden in its depths. They were near the center of the space. On the sandy bottom around them, animal bones gnawed white lay like seashells. At the far end of the cavern, about where the bus driver would sit, was something toad-like, hard, and white like the flow stone of the walls. It was this gargoyle-like thing that had spoken. Beyond the creature was an open tunnel.

"What is that, French?"

French took a step closer. "This, if I remember correctly, is called a Druell. Am I correct?"

The rock creature turned its head, watching the psychic carefully. "Yeeessss."

"We were with a dryad. Has she passed this way?"

"Yeeessss."

"Most excellent." French turned to Jerry. "This way then. I believe we are close."

"Youuuuu shalllll notttt passss."

"Your friend's gone Gandalf on us, French. Does Gollum show up next?"

"Merely a miscommunication." French stepped over to the Druell. "We would like to follow our companion. We have come to speak with the Old-One who dwells here."

"Youuuuu shalllll notttt passss."

"I've always hated the word *Shall*," Jerry complained. "Used in contracts all the time. Past tense is *Should*. If you want me to do something, tell me *You Will*, not *You Should*. That gives me an option, like now—should we try and pass? What happens if we do?"

"I shalllll crusssshhh youuuu."

"Ah, see, that's the loophole. You *should* crush us, but will you actually do so?"

"Yeeessss."

"Hmm, too bad. I was hoping to tell Mrs. Pritchert that the grammar she pounded in my head in fourth grade was finally helpful."

"Good grammar is its own reward," French countered. He turned back to the Druell. "Why may we not pass? Did the Old-One command this?"

"Yeeessss. No humannnsssss shalllll passss."

"Well, this is something of a gluepot." French looked around, considering other options.

Jerry nodded. "If you mean we're stuck here, then I agree with you. Even with the rope, there's no pulling ourselves back up the way we came, not against that current and I don't know about you, but I'm freezing."

French fumbled in his leather satchel and brought out a piece of amber the size of a skipping stone. He handed it to Jerry. "Put that in your pocket. It'll keep you warm as a kettle."

Jerry took the stone. The amber itself was cool, but a feeling of warmth radiated throughout his body. "Thanks, that's better."

French turned back to the Druell. "Can you tell a Vaettir from a feral human?"

"Yooou arrrre neitherrrrr," the creature responded.

"True, I am not, but can you tell that my companion is not a feral human? You can detect the aura of his Odic energy, can you not? He is Vaettir."

The Druell peered at Jerry, its eyes as white and stone-like as the rest of its body. "Ittttt doesssss rradiatte maaaaggicccc."

"Exactly. Ergo, not a human," French pronounced proudly.

"Youuuuu stillll shalll notttt passss."

"So much for logic," Jerry sighed. "What now?"

"The Druell obviously has other instructions we aren't aware of." French looked around the cavern. "There do not appear to be many alternatives."

"What if we rush it?"

French turned back to the engineer. "There are far more than just the one."

"There are?" Jerry asked.

"Yes. Look carefully at the walls. You will discern at least twelve pairs of eyes."

Jerry looked around. In the darkness, many pairs of the same stony white eyes stared out from the stone. "Crap."

"Indeed. We shall just have to wait and see what Laurette achieves."

With little else to do, Jerry toyed with the end of the rope still hanging in the torrent of water. Without the ascender, just climbing up to the point where the water exited the wall was going to be a bitch.

The engineer waded back into the pool. "I'm going to try and climb back up."

"To what end?" French asked.

"My phone's in the backpack. I can call for help."

"Try if you must, but there are other alternatives."

Jerry took a firm hold on the rope, pulled himself up the wall, and plunged into the deluge of water ejecting from the hole. Several feet in, with his legs hanging out and offering no real purchase, he managed a yard or two of advance before the strength in his arms failed and he was spat back out into the pool.

He surfaced, expelling water, and swam to the psychic who was calming relaxing in the shallows.

"What other alternatives," Jerry asked.

The psychic began rummaging through the contents of his satchel. "I believe that I have the things needed to create a portal back to the house. Better solution all around, actually. I rather doubt we could get Laurette back into her dress."

Both French and Jerry jumped when the Druell interrupted "The drryaddd rreturrrns."

From the passageway the rock creature was guarding, Laurette stepped into the cavern. "Where've you two been?"

French closed his satchel. "We, it seems, are *persona non grata*."

"Crap, aren't you freezing?" Jerry asked. "Do you want my jacket? Sorry, it's so wet."

"How come you aren't gawking?" Laurette asked, puzzled.

"Dryads are immune to cold," French explained.

"Must be nice." Jerry pulled the slab of amber from his pocket. "This works, but I've still got goosebumps."

"Similar magic, but Laurette's is a part of her nature."

Laurette stepped over and wiggled her boobs at Jerry. "How come you haven't gone all stupid human?"

Jerry shrugged. "Don't know. More worried about you, I guess."

"Hmph, that's no fun." She cupped her breasts in her hands and bounced them. "Nothing? Not even a twinge?"

Jerry glanced down and his eyes began to glaze over. "They are quite nice."

Laurette smiled. "That's better."

"Please stop that!" French exclaimed. "We need Jerry intelligent if he is to meet the Earth Spirit and resolve this issue."

"Just worried I was losing my touch."

Jerry forced his eyes closed. "No, you're still quite potent."

French stepped between the Dryad and the engineer. "What did you find?"

"We're dealing with a Jord," she replied

"A Yord?" Jerry asked.

French nodded. "Spelled with a J but close enough pronunciation. Shortest description would be a stone giant."

"Living here in the bedrock?"

"Yes," Laurette answered. "Your building is making it itch."

"And when it scratches, my building tears itself apart."

"Exactly."

Jerry looked up, examining the rock surrounding him. "So, I've got a giant with allergies. What do I do, or is it hopeless?"

"Is it possible to discuss this with the Jord?" French asked.

A deep resonance, like the fluid tones of a double bass, filled the cavern.

"Good acoustics in here," Jerry commented.

"That was the Jord speaking," French explained.

Laurette nodded. "He wants to talk."

Behind her, the Druell merged back into the stone of the wall, leaving only his pale, limestone eyes exposed.

Laurette turned and bounded down the passageway. "Come on." She disappeared into the blackness.

French and Jerry slogged after, struggling in the knee-deep water.

"How does she do that so easily?" Jerry asked. "Climbing walls, running through water, that sort of stuff."

French opened his hands a bit wider, illuminating more of the tunnel. "Dryads are a part of the Earth. As such, the Earth makes way for them. It's also how the Druell and the Jord move through rock—it simply flows around them."

French paused. Ahead, the tunnel opened up into a cathedral-like chamber of stalactites, stalagmites, flowstone, and columns. Laurette was standing before an altar-sized speleothem. It turned to regard the newcomers with large, pupiless eyes.

"Come Closer," Laurette told them. "The Jord wants to look at you."

"No distance vision," French added, stepping forward. "Useless in stone."

Jerry joined French and Laurette. "I would like to apologize," he told the Jord. "My construction has disturbed you."

Jerry was answered by the bass pipes of a church organ.

Laurette turned to Jerry. "He wants you to touch his face."

Jerry stepped up to the Olmec like formation. He reached up and placed a hand on the limestone forehead.

Tectonic plates flowed like paper boats. Forests came and went, pushed aside by great sheets of ice. A cavern grew, this cavern, Jerry realized, once a fracture in an old sea bed, now opened by water, stalagmites thrust upwards joining stalactites, and then something the Jord found interesting, changed everything.

"He's curious about us?" Jerry asked.

Laurette took the engineer's hand. "Yes, that's why the Jord's here so near the surface, to watch humans."

"He's so old."

"As old as the Earth."

"Yes, unlike other lifeforms, a Jord is not born, nor does it die," French added. "They simply are."

"Amazing."

A marching band of tubas sounded a single note.

"The Jord's excited to meet you too."

Jerry smiled, the shared connection expressing both their feelings. "He's fascinated that humans build things."

Laurette smile quickly faded. "The Jord wouldn't be if it were his forests the humans built their stupid houses and ships with."

"Hush," French said. "We're here to help Mr. Stoner, not complain about things that happened 250 years ago."

"It's still happening! They're still cutting forests down."

"Shush! Mr. Stoner, ask the Jord what you need to do to fix your building."

Jerry focused once more on the cave. "It's more of shared feeling and images I get, nothing verbal."

"I'll ask," Laurette interrupted.

She turned to face the pair of overlarge limestone eyes, her own tightly closed.

She ran her hands along her back. "Mr. Stoner, you will need to start by removing all the things stabbing down into the Jord's back."

Jerry nodded "That would be the concrete piers—all twenty-two of them?"

"Let me see." Laurette swayed slowly, moving her back from side to side, sympathetically feeling what the Jord felt. Her lips counted silently. "Yes, that sounds right. It's the metal in them that's causing the issue."

Jerry nodded. "Steel rebar—does that mean above ground structural steel is out too?"

Her hands traced out from points on her back. "Feels like it. Is that bad?"

"Maybe not." Jerry pulled at his beard, thinking. "Could use load-bearing masonry walls topped with glu-lam beams. The Jord won't have trouble with wood connected with small steel plates, will he?"

"No, some metal is okay," Laurette answered. "The houses that used to be here didn't bother him."

"They were pier and beam and, unfortunately, I need to place a slab." Jerry turned to French, thinking out loud. "Might be able to do this with fiberglass rebar in the concrete."

"Fiberglass?" Laurette asked.

"A product of silica, soda ash, and limestone."

Laurette nodded. "Seems okay. We can try it and see."

***

As Jerry pulled up to French's office, the dryad waved from the porch. He wasn't nearly as affected anymore but it was still a thrill to see her.

"You ready to see if our experiment worked?"

"Yep. I think Uraghild is too."

The experiment was the construction design for the building's slab. The fiberglass reinforcing had been put in place with no incident. Laurette said he couldn't really feel it. Today they would discover if the mass of concrete that had been poured yesterday was still in place.

"Who's Uraghild?" Jerry asked.

"The Jord," she replied, getting into the truck. Jerry had the windows rolled down despite the oppressive heat of the afternoon. It was the only way Laurette would ride in a car.

"That's a mouthful. Say it again."

"Uraghild," the dryad said easily."

"Yurg-hilt," Jerry said.

She shook her head. "Deeper in your throat and it's got to resonate."

Jerry tried again. "Youraggghild."

"Better."

By the way Laurette said that, he could tell it wasn't better by much. "How about I just call him *Urgh* for now until I get some practice?"

She nodded, her chestnut hair shining in the early sun. "I think that will be easier than teaching you to say the name properly."

"Thanks."

Jerry pulled out onto Broadway. Mid-afternoon, there wasn't much traffic but that would change in a few hours. The area had become a mecca for up and coming hipsters. Property values were going through the roof.

"So French is still planning on selling his office?"

"He sold it yesterday," Laurette replied.

"But he hadn't even listed it?"

She shook her head. "One of his former clients is a realtor. She put him in touch with an investor that wants to redevelop the property. They're going to build more stupid human houses."

"I'm glad Urgh doesn't share your opinion of human building."

"There are just so many humans and they trash everything," she replied. "Humans need a predator to keep your numbers down."

Jerry turned onto Mulberry. "Seems like humans do a fairly good job of killing each other ourselves."

"It's why everyone else is scared of them."

He glanced quickly at the dryad. "Everyone else who?"

"The Vaettir, all the earth spirits, the Infernals, not to mention the Devine, but they're so aloof that they pretend not to care."

"But they're so much more powerful than humans," Jerry objected. "What do they have to fear from us? Humans don't even have magic."

Laurette turned and stared. "Humans created weapons that destroy a city in the blink of an eye and that leave the earth poisoned for generations. There's no magic powerful enough to do that. Even if there was, no one would use it."

Jerry was quiet for a moment. "That only happened twice."

"Humans only killed their own kind with it twice," she corrected. "But those weapons have been used to blast the earth many, many times."

"Oh yeah, I forgot about the testing."

Laurette clutched at her chest. "Humans don't feel the death and pain that they create but I do and those like me do. We feel it every time."

It was quiet in the cab of the truck for several miles. Jerry didn't know what to say to apologize for what his race had done. Hell, she hadn't even brought up all the plastic in the ocean. Maybe humans did need a predator.

"I'm sorry for everything we did."

She cocked her head, looking at him confused. "You haven't done anything."

"I mean humans," he explained.

"But you're not human, your Vanir."

Vanir?" Jerry said. "French said that when we were underground in the tunnel. What does that mean?"

"The Vanir are like humans but evolved," she answered. "You can use magic and respect life; well most Vanir do, anyway."

"I can use magic?"

"That's probably why you were able to meet your wife."

Jerry smiled, thinking about Sophie. She was six months pregnant and really starting to show. She'd gotten the hang of shopping and his bank account was feeling it.

"I just thought I was sensitive to spirits."

"Nope," she said. "That's from being Vanir. If it wasn't for the siphons you'd be able to do magic too."

"Siphons?"

"When the magic races created their own world to escape humans, they left siphons behind which harness excess life energy. One side effect is that it keeps any Vanir in this world from using magic."

"Why'd they do that?" he asked.

"The siphons power the magic that keeps their world apart from this one."

Jerry pulled into the construction site. The foundation was intact.

"Hey, looks like our experiment was a success."

Laurette opened the car door and stepped out. She reached down and touched the ground. "Uraghild says it doesn't bother him a bit. He's wondering what the walls will feel like."

"I'm using limestone masonry. I got the impression when I shared with him that natural stone would be fine."

"He thinks so too," she said. "He's looking forward to the weight."

***

Two months later and the first of the autumn leaves were falling. In San Antonio, that happened around mid-November. French and Laurette were in the convertible on their way to the grand opening of the barrister's office she and Jerry had worked on.

"I wish Meryl had come," Laurette lamented. "I would have felt better if she were here."

"I'm still surprised to see the two of you getting along so well."

Laurette had her feet up on the dash. Her yellow cotton dress billowed in the rush of air. "Meryl likes having someone to vent to when you're in one of your funks."

French glanced over and scowled. "I do not have funks."

"Yes, you do, like the other day when the Vartilliamenthum bit you."

French found a parking space and pulled the Plymouth up along the curb. "That was not a funk. Why that beast has such an attitude towards me is incomprehensible. I should have left it on Enewetak where I found it."

Laurette undid her seatbelt as French shut off the car. Getting her to wear a belt had been another long fight. "The new girl says the Vartilliamenthum's grumpy because it's cold."

French stepped from the car and shut the door. "Her name is Caitlin." He looked up at the clouds.

"No rain today, you're safe with the top down," she said. "I like the new girl. She likes animals."

"Once she's trained, her empathy level will be nearly as strong as yours…wait, the Vartilliamenthum's cold? In the Texas heat? Bloody hell, how hot does it want it?"

"Don't know, but the new girl's got Ainsworth building an addition to the greenhouse. He's happy because it gets him out of the office."

French joined Laurette. She was standing next to the sidewalk, bare toes wiggling happily in the grass.

They started walking, French's *Crockett & Jones* Oxfords clicking smartly on the pavement with Laurette's bare feet padding along on the lawn.

"And why doesn't Ainsworth want to be in the office?" French asked.

"Charlotte gives him bad vibes," Laurette answered. "Haven't you noticed that he's not around much since you moved her into the guestroom?"

"The poor woman had nowhere else to go. To the humans, she's dead, or undead, well, officially dead anyway." French pondered a possible solution. "Perhaps there's something available at Meryl's flats."

"Might not need to ask. Charlotte and the new girl were talking about sharing a place but I don't think that'll work out. The new girl's gay—Charlotte okay with that?"

"Caitlin, the new girl's name is Caitlin, and she's gay?"

"Yep."

They reached the corner. Two lots down, a limestone building, rock still creamy and fresh from the quarry, beckoned them on. Tall wood-framed windows, mimicking those of the houses to either side, spilled light into the growing November gloom. Inside, people mingled, sharing stories of legal battles won and lost.

"Fairly big shindig," French commented.

Laurette vaulted over a sidewalk. "Yep. Owner's spending a small fortune on the catering. He's hoping to attract some rich clients."

French stopped and turned to face the dryad. "How do you know all this? First, the Vartilliamenthum, then Charlotte and Caitlin, and now this."

"I listen. Meryl stays on top of the gossip and Jerry told me about today."

French shook his head and headed up the walk. "And I thought Virgil was a good source of information."

The psychic pushed the oversize wooden door. It pivoted on a bronze pin set into a large block of limestone. The babble of excited humans flowed out the opening.

"Interesting door."

"Didn't want to use steel hinges," Laurette explained. "Irritates Urgh."

"Urgh?"

"Jerry's simplification of the Jord's name, Uraghild."

"His name is Uraghild? I didn't realize they named themselves?"

"Uraghild thought it an amusing idea and named himself."

French stepped through the elaborate opening. Laurette, however, paused at the threshold, her eyes on the crowd of people in formal dress.

"There's so many of them." She glanced back toward the car.

French put his arm around the dryad. "No need to panic. Things will be fine. Unlike us, the humans prefer large groups."

He escorted the dryad inside and scanned to room. A table with hors d'oeuvres was at one end. "Why don't we find something to eat? It might settle your nerves."

She nodded.

Taking Laurette by the arm, French led them to a table loaded with imported cheeses, caviar, salmon, and other delicacies. The babble of conversation faded as the guests noticed the dryad.

"I wonder where Jerry is?" she whispered nervously.

French picked up a plate, selecting the smoked salmon as something Laurette might enjoy. "Probably going on about some beam or whatnot. He does so love his work."

Laurette brightened. "Oh, here he comes."

The engineer hurried over, making a large gesture toward the dryad as he came. It was unnecessary—the crowd was already focused on Laurette.

"Everyone, a toast please for Laurette, the Chi Master that made this building possible."

Eyes unglazed and a smattering of applause echoed off the heavy limestone walls.

"So, she's a Chi Master now?" French whispered as the engineer joined them.

Jerry glanced sideways at a man in a tailored linen suit. "The owner's a believer in Feng Shui. Easier to explain Laurette's involvement that way."

Laurette gave the engineer a big hug. "Is your wife here?"

Jerry pointed to a corner of the building where windows framed a view of an old juniper tree. "Collapsed on the couch at the moment. Being eight-months pregnant means standing isn't her thing at the moment."

Laurette stood on her tiptoes, trying to catch a glance. "I don't blame her. She seemed quite uncomfortable when you came by for dinner."

"She is and could use some company, if you'd like to join her. She's hiding from the crowd. She's still acclimating to the present."

Laurette nodded "Me too. Call if you need me."

"Thanks."

Conversation dwindled as Laurette crossed the room.

Jerry pulled his eyes away. "Glass of wine, French?"

The psychic shook his head.

The engineer nodded towards Laurette. "Still making Meryl jealous?"

French nodded. "Yes, and although the two are getting along famously, my list of honey-do's grows on a daily basis.

With this project complete, things can go back to normal—
me in my office and Laurette in her table."

Jerry swirled the pinot noire in his glass before taking a
sip. "Around you, French, nothing's normal, but I wouldn't
be too sure things will settle down."

"Why do you say that?"

"Just something Sophie told me."

"What was that?"

Jerry took a long sip of the wine, making the psychic
squirm. "Laurette has been asking questions—did you know
that the two of them went shopping the other day?"

"Laurette left the house?"

"Yep, took an Uber. Meryl helped her. Did you try the
prosciutto and ricotta?"

French shook his head. "What kinds of questions?"

"She was asking Sophie what it was like, living in the real
world."

"Really?" French pondered that for a moment. "And what
did your wife say?"

"That it was exciting, but scary. They had a good time at
the mall. Sophie helped her buy the dress she's wearing."

"Laurette bought a dress?" French said flustered. "I
thought it was another of Meryl's."

Jerry shook his head and finished his wine. "Big, bright
sunflowers are hardly your secretary's style, French."

"Hmm, yes, I was rather surprised by that."

French glanced across the room. Sophie was using her
phone to show Laurette an ultrasound image of the baby. The
two were laughing.

He turned back to Jerry. "I think I will have that glass of
wine. Several actually."

Aliens from outer space are often lumped in with phantoms, demons, and earth spirits under the term Paranormal. Do they actually belong under the same umbrella or are little green men something completely different? Perhaps, but it is up to Mr. French to find out.

The Hex Files

It was an unusually quiet Thursday in November when Edward Cruz, panicky and out of breath, burst into the office.

"Mr. French, you've got to help my friend Bill."

French gestured for his long-time friend to sit. "I'm happy to help as always, but why all the tizzy?"

This wasn't Edwards first time in French's office. Back in the days when polyester was king, local DJ and discotheque impresario, 'Cruising' Eddie Cruz, had boogied into French's office with a ghost problem. The successful business man had been an acquaintance ever since.

Edward collapsed onto the settee, arthritic knees complaining with a pop. He leaned forward, perched on the edge like a nervous sparrow. "Thanks, French. I told Bill you're the best. He's really desperate."

"I'll ring for some tea. In the meantime, tell me about your friend's problem? Ghosts? Demonic possession? Earth spirits? Not another banshee, I hope?"

The elderly businessman shook his head. "No, no, nothing like that. Bill was abducted by aliens."

French stifled a cough. "You know, Edward, I deal with the otherworldly, not the off-worldly. Aliens aren't quite my bailiwick."

"I know, but the UFO investigators found nothing. Doctor Beauzlavo, the UFOlogist, recommended Bill seek mental help."

There was a knock at the door. Ainsworth entered with the tea trolley.

"Thank you, Ainsworth." French turned back to Mr. Cruz, "Not a particularly stirring referral, Edward. Cream?"

The man nodded. French poured a small amount into the cup, added the tea, and passed the steaming cup over. The businessman stared at the porcelain cup in his hands without seeing it.

French prepared a cup for himself. "So, how do you know this Bill?"

"Long time. He's been an employee on and off for years. Heck he was there when you dispelled that banshee at the club."

French thought back. "I don't seem to remember a Bill."

Edward's gaze shifted to the ceiling but his eyes were focused on the past. "You know, you're right. When that banshee showed up, it scared the pants off Bill and he quit. Those were some crazy times. Anyway, he works for me as Warehouse Manager at my Northside *El Electronico* store. He's a unique individual but I know he's not batty, these are real aliens."

"You seem quite certain."

The older man's eyes grew wide. "I am. I've seen the aliens too," he said in a whisper.

The spoon in the psychic's Earl Grey ceased it's back and forth stirring motion. "Really? Tell me more. Start at the beginning."

"The aliens had been bothering Bill for several days before he contacted Dr. Beauzlavo at the university. They brought a team out to investigate."

French hid his scowl with a sip of tea. He placed the cup back on the rough-hewn table next to his wingback chair. "I am somewhat familiar with the Doctor. He and his paranormal research teams have crossed paths with me before."

Mr. Cruz nodded. "Yeah, I don't like him either. Bit of a self-important prick."

"Let's not judge. Though hopelessly misguided, he means well."

Edward chuckled. "So, what Beauzlavo was looking for was evidence of what they call an encounter of the second kind, you know, scorched ground, or footprints, that kind of stuff."

French nodded. "But they found nothing."

"Yep, not even evidence of a forced entry into Bill's house. That's when the Doctor said Bill was crazy. Well, that just pissed Bill off and at work the next day he asked to borrow some cameras from the store to catch the aliens himself."

"Somewhat improper of an employee."

"Yeah, but the guy was looking bad, eyes all dark and sunk in from losing sleep. I gave him some Argus-3 infrared security cameras, top of the line in night vision technology."

French leaned forward. "And how did that go?"

"Zilch, just blank pictures of the yard and his house."

"Do you have access to the videos?"

Mr. Cruz patted his jacket pocket. "Yes, I brought 'em, but all they show is Bill getting up from bed and walking out of his room."

"Then why are you so sure that these aliens are real?'

Edward slumped back into the settee. "Cause I was there, and I saw 'em, walking around in silver spacesuits and everything."

"Really? Tell me more."

The elderly man drained his teacup. "You got anything stronger, French? I could use it."

"Of course." French walked over and retrieved the decanter of whiskey from his desk. He poured a healthy shot into Edward's cup. "So, you were saying…"

"Bill'd told me the aliens showed up late at night, so we set up a camera in his yard and several in the house. Bill went to sleep and I stayed in the kitchen, monitoring everything. Just before morning, lights started flashing in the yard but not a goddamn thing showed on the digital setup. It was the damndest thing. I went over to the kitchen door to investigate and damn if there wasn't a glowing ball of light sitting in the yard."

"Which also didn't show up?"

"Right. When the aliens headed for the house, I hid in the kitchen pantry. There they were, French, honest to god aliens. They passed right through the door like it wasn't there, went to the back of the house, and took Bill away. After about an hour, they brought him back. I don't think they ever saw me. I'm telling you, French, I was scared enough to shit bricks."

"Was Bill injured in this abduction? No anal probe or any such thing."

Edward shook his head. "Nah, nothing physical, and he doesn't fully remember what happened. He said it was like being drugged or really drunk—just fuzzy images of the aliens staring at him and asking him questions."

"And none of this was captured on your security cameras."

"Nada. It's like we were in another reality from the one the cameras were filming."

That sparked an idea. French sat back in the wingback chair. "Interesting. And you're sure the aliens are from outer space? Several types of Infernals and numerous Earth spirits don't show on recording devices."

Edward nodded vigorously. "Like the banshee that haunted my disco. That's what made me think of you. I was hoping you might have some way to record them."

The psychic drummed a finger on the chair's embroidered armrest. "There are several methods, but they are based on Odic energy signals. It's questionable whether they will work on aliens."

"But they may. So, you'll look into this?"

Edwards desperation mixed with enthusiasm was both encouraging and discouraging at the same time. "I'm glad you think I can solve this but, remember, aliens are outside my sphere of knowledge."

"If anyone can solve this, you can."

French stood. "We shall start with the video. There's a large screen TV in the next room. Let's retire to view it there."

The elderly Cruz followed French across the hall and into what had been the formal dining room when the building once served as a home. Now, the large table was strewn with an assortment of research and evidence from ongoing investigations.

French moved a Pyrex serving dish filled with human bones to one side. "Ainsworth, do we have any biscuits?"

The door to the kitchen slid open. "Yessir. American or British?"

"Mr. Cruz is having whiskey. Something appropriate."

"Bourbon, scotch, or Irish whiskey?" Ainsworth asked. "We have shortbread, Thin Mints, or Oreos. The Oreos go well with a single malt scotch."

French curled a lip. "Really? Sounds a bit too sweet for my tastes. Hmm, bring a plate with all three, we'll let Mr. Cruz experiment."

"Yessir."

French turned to the elderly businessman. "You said you had a flash drive?"

Edward fumbled in his coat, pulling a red flash drive embossed with the *El Electronico* logo from his inner pocket. He handed the device to French who inserted it into a computer sitting on the mahogany buffet opposite the bay window. The large screen flashed to life as the computer booted.

Ainsworth reappeared, placing a tray of cookies on the table. Edward selected one of the Oreos. "The file's called *Bill 01*."

French scrolled down, found the file, and double clicked. On the screen, the images from six cameras appeared in a grid.

"This is when we were setting up." Edward pointed at an older man in a t-shirt and jeans. "That's Bill. Fast-forward to 5:04. That's when the lights started flashing."

On the screen, Bill speed-walked to the bedroom and jumped into bed. Occasionally he would toss or turn but in the rest of the house, nothing moved. French slowed the video as the timer reached 5:03.

Edward took a bite of Oreo, chewed several times, before washing it down with the whiskey. "Okay, watch the camera in the kitchen. You'll see me run to the back door. I'm seeing lights but not a damn thing's on the video."

French watched closely. Things went exactly as Mr. Cruz said, including Bill getting up from bed and leaving.

French paused the tape. "That's interesting."

"What?"

French rewound to a point where Bill was still in bed. "Watch closely." He started the playback. "Here's Bill getting out of bed. Notice how he looks as if he's in a trance or sleep walking. Bill crosses into the living room, walks over to the door to the kitchen and poof, he disappears."

French stopped the replay. "There is something happening. Whether it's aliens or not, I can't say, but this is proof."

"What do you mean?" Edward asked. "I didn't see anything."

"Exactly. Camera four shows Bill leaving the living room and going into the kitchen but camera two, focused on the kitchen, never shows him enter."

"But he did, I saw him. He went through the door escorted by two of the aliens."

"And this happens every night?" French asked.

Edward nodded. "Between five and six, like clockwork."

"Then that's where we shall be tonight."

***

Bill lived on a farm out in La Vernia, sixteen miles to the east of San Antonio. As they drove up to the farmhouse in French's convertible, an elderly man sitting in a weather-beaten recliner, stood up. He waved, his grin spread ear to ear.

"That's more like the Bill I know," Mr. Cruz said. "Always a smile on his face, that is until all this mess started."

French parked and shut off the engine. Like the recliner, the farmhouse had seen better days. Time and neglect had taken its toll. Peels of paint littered the porch and the panes of glass in the windows shook with each of Bill's steps, threatening to fall out.

Bill let the porch screen door slam behind him. "You came!"

Mr. Cruz met him halfway to the car and shook his hand vigorously. "Told you we would."

"They were here again last night, Eddie, asking their questions. Cain't get no sleep at all anymore."

"Mr. French can help." Edward turned to the psychic. "Mr. French, meet Bill Foley."

"It's very nice to meet you Mr. Foley. I hope I can help."

Bill shook French's hand with the same enthusiasm he had extended to Mr. Cruz. "Damn glad to meet you, Mr. French. Tain't never met a psychic afore."

"We shall see if my talents can be of any use."

Bill motioned to the house. "Well come on in. Cameras are still set up like you left 'em, Eddie."

French, instead, walked to the rear of the car. "I shall be with you in a minute. I have some things in the car boot I wish to bring inside."

"Need help, French?" Edward asked.

French shook his head. "No, just my equipment."

"Well get'cher stuff and come on in. Don't need to be formal and knock or nothin," Bill said.

As Bill and Edward entered the house, French pulled a beaten suitcase from the trunk of the car. *Stoner Paranormal Investigations* was stenciled on the front in white paint along with the silhouette of a ghost.

"Between the two of us, Jerry, we might solve this case," French muttered.

After grabbing a box of his own from the back seat, he lugged both to the house. Inside, Bill and Edward were in the kitchen discussing the cameras.

"… and you disappeared. Not on the kitchen camera like you should've been." Edward was saying. "Would never have noticed that without French."

Bill turned to the psychic. "Put your things down anywhere. Care for a beer, they're cold?" He turned to Mr. Cruz. "Eddie, you wanna get the Fritos and chili outta the cabinet?"

Edward nodded. "Can opener in the drawer?"

"Nah, just washed it. By the sink."

With the successful local business man and millionaire busy heating chili in the microwave, French took the opportunity to question Bill.

"I was told the aliens interrogated you. What were they trying to discover?"

"Um, don't know, really. Um, kinda messed up in my head when they's got me in their ship."

"Does this feeling persist long after you're returned?"

"Nope. Goes away pretty darn quick, in fact," Bill answered.

The microwave dinged.

"Chili's ready." Edward tossed three snack-sized bags of Fritos onto the table, and then brought over the steaming bowl and some spoons. "Think the aliens are using some kind of brain control device on Bill?"

French shrugged his shoulders. "Anything's possible."

Bill and Mr. Cruz pulled open the tops of their Frito bags and began ladling in chili.

"It's Frito pie," Edward explained. "Kind of a southern traditional food."

"Ahh." French pulled open his own bag of corn chips and followed suit, adding several spoonfuls of the chili straight into the bag. "Bill, do you remember any of their questions?

What is it they're trying to discover? That may tell us something. Are they asking what planet this is, or the country, or even who you are?"

"They knows me," Bill answered confidently. "Maybe they's lookin for something, but I ain't got nothin no aliens would need."

French put a spoonful of the odd mixture in his mouth. The salty chili corn chip mix was quite tasty. "So, these aliens seem to be looking for something."

Bill nodded. "But I ain't got nothin," he said around a mouth full of Fritos. "No gold or nothin they might want. I done told them that, but they come back ever night anyways."

"Interesting."

Bill gestured at the refrigerator. "Hey Eddie, wanna hand me another beer? I'm about empty."

The businessman nodded, turned and opened the refrigerator. "How about you, French? How're you doing?"

The psychic swirled his half-empty bottle. "Still good."

The banter went on for half an hour. French discovered that Edward and Bill had gone to high school together, dated several of the same women along with some personal information he'd have been quite happy to not know, but nothing more about the aliens.

About 2:30, they sent Bill to bed. Edward pulled out a laptop and connected with the cameras. He nodded at the items French had brought from the car. "So, what mysteries you got in your boxes?"

"I shall show you." The psychic opened the worn suitcase and extracted two devices. "These I borrowed from a friend that is a ghost hunter."

"Ghosts? You think this is ghosts?"

"No, but the equipment might tell us something that my own methods fail to register."

French placed an orange piece of equipment on the table, followed by something that looked like George Jetson's cell phone. "The big one is a phased K3 meter. It monitors changes in electromagnetic fields."

"And the fancy walkie talkie?'

"It's called a spirit box and allows ghosts to speak using radio waves," French explained.

Edward cast a skeptical eye at the spirit box. "A bit macabre for you, isn't it French?"

"Yes. I brought the device for the way it skips through radio frequencies. I thought that might assist us in communicating with the aliens, whose existence I am now beginning to doubt."

"You back to thinking Bill's crazy?" Edward whispered.

"No, something is definitely occurring but I think Bill knows why," French replied. "Did you notice how evasive and nervous he became when I asked about the aliens?"

"Well, yeah, they scare the willies out of him. Me too."

French shook his head. "His reaction was dread, not fear and, as the night went on, he told me less and less, like someone trying to keep their story straight."

Mr. Cruz paused a moment. "You know, I did notice that. When Bill first told me about the aliens, he wouldn't stop blabbing about it, and the bit about the aliens wanting gold was new."

French lifted the other container from the car. It was an antique traveling case with brass on the corners. The leather was a faded green and embossed with a crown, shield and, griffon. Judging from the look of the thing, one might guess it had sailed with Shackleton on the *Endurance*. The polished brass corner reinforcements clicked on the table's Formica surface as French sat it down.

"What in there?" Edward asked. "Some sort of Geiger counter?"

"Not quite, but close."

The psychic twisted four brass latches one by one. "I believe that the gold Bill mentioned, or something like it, may be precisely what all this is about."

With a turn of the last latch, the box popped open. Within, nestled protectively in a red velvet lining, was a glass sphere set in a silver housing. French took the apparatus out and set it gingerly on the table. Dials and indicators within the sphere were identified in a stylized Germanic script.

Edward peered over French's shoulder. "What's that thing—some sort of barometer?"

"This *thing* is an Odeometer," French answered. "It measures Odic potential within a given area; what you would call magic."

"You know French, if I hadn't seen that banshee with my own eyes I'd think you were feeding me bullshit."

The psychic nodded. "Your disbelief is a product of your history. It's easier to believe my kind never existed, rather than admit to exterminating us."

"We did that?"

"You tried. Since then, the Vaettir and other creatures of magic have kept a low profile, which the Vatican is content with."

"The Vatican knows about you?" Edward asked.

French sighed. "Unfortunately, yes, and I believe the file on me is a rather large one."

"So, if this isn't aliens, what is it?"

"That, I believe, we shall discover this evening."

***

The two men sat monitoring their equipment, talking occasionally, until around 4:30 when one of the Odeometer needles began to bounce, slowly climbing along its graduated dial.

As French made minor adjustments to a group of small set screws on the Odeometer, the K3 meter began chirping. "Interesting. Things are afoot."

"What is it?" Edward asked.

"Not quite sure as yet."

French reached into the Odeometer's box and pulled out a small book bound in blue leather. He flipped the dog-eared manual open and thumbed through the pages. After finding a set of tables, he turned to stare intently at the dials. A few more consultations in the book, and he sat back and pulled a compass from his pocket.

Staring down at the compass, he pointed to the back of the house. "Somewhere, in that direction, a gate is being opened."

"A gate, like a cattle gate?" Edward asked.

"No, nothing so innocent." French steepled his fingers. "This has the signature of fairy magic."

"Fairy? Like Tinkerbell?"

"Yes, although Tinkerbell is very powerful and quite dangerous to deal with."

French referred to the blue manual once more, flipping several times to reference information in the back.

"This has the pattern of the Aos Sí."

French turned to Edward. "Bill's surname, Foley, do you know if his family is from Ireland?"

Edward nodded. "I do. They came over 'cause of the potato famine."

French abruptly stood. "I'll be outside for a moment."

"Outside?"

The psychic didn't respond, merely hurried out the door. Edward caught up to French walking down the gravel drive. The psychic reached a point where the road crossed a small stream and stopped.

He scanned the tree line. "It needs water, so it'll be around here somewhere."

"What? Your gate?"

French stepped into the underbrush. "No, a hawthorn tree."

"A tree? What do we need a tree for?"

"It will serve as a key," the psychic said cryptically. "Ah, here's one!" French reached up and snapped off a small twig.

"Now back inside," he ordered. "They'll be here soon."

"Who, the aliens?"

"These are not aliens, they are some form of Aos Sí—Irish fairies. That's why they don't show up on camera. The Aos Sí world is parallel to ours, coming closest at dusk and dawn. I think they are here to retrieve something stolen from them long ago."

"The gold," Edward said. "But I've never known Bill to steal."

"Not Bill, one of his ancestors. To the Aos Sí, however, the burden of that crime is carried down through the generations. The only thing we can do is to return whatever was taken."

Edward pointed to a light beginning to glow behind the house. "Crap, they're coming."

The two men broke into a run.

"They're opening the gate," French said.

"I can see why Bill thought it was aliens," Edward added. "Certainly looks like a saucer."

In the area behind the house, a bulging cylinder of xenon fluorescence was growing larger.

"The gate is nearly open," French yelled.

"I was thinking it'd be more like a door," the elderly businessman said, out of breath. "Not round and wide."

French reached the house and hurried Mr. Cruz inside. The cylinder of pale blue light was now the length of a Volkswagen Microbus. Figures in silver stood within the blue glow.

"The Aos Sí are connecting our world with theirs. Once the gate is fully open, they'll come for Bill. We need to prepare."

French shut the kitchen door and stepped to the table. Yellow lights within the Odeometer were glowing brightly.

"Aren't you going to lock that?" Mr. Cruz asked, pointing to the door.

"Not necessary. The Aos Sí can pass through anything in our world as if it doesn't exist."

"So, what do we do?"

"Start by waking Bill. It's time for the truth, and then some diplomacy."

Edward ran to the bedroom, screaming for Bill to wake up. The two returned to the kitchen. Lights were strobing in the yard outside.

French pointed at the table. "Sit!"

"But they's here," Bill answered, eyes full of fear.

"Yes, they want something, don't they? Now sit."

Bill slowly settled into the chair, staring with dread at the door and the light flooding through its yellowed vinyl blinds.

French pulled out a chair and sat, staring Bill in the eyes. "Mr. Foley, we are about to be visited by a race of very powerful beings. They are not aliens, but I suspect you've figured that out by now."

"Why's they here?"

"I think you know why." French leaned forward. "Mr. Foley, what did your ancestor take from them?"

Sweat was beading on Bill's forehead. "Nothin"

"You'd not be so nervous if it was nothing."

"Twern't nothing we weren't owed," Bill said defensively.

"Explain."

"The Shee done took one of the girls—Ilish was her name. My great-great-something granpappy went after the Shee to get Ilish back, but he couldn't find her, so he done stole a bucket of gold in exchange."

"Shee? The banshee from the club?" Edward asked.

"He means Sidhe. Sounds similar. It's another name for the Aos Sí," French explained. "Interesting connection, though. The Aos Sí may have sent that banshee to find Bill."

Edward nodded, it now beginning to make sense. "And Bill knew, and that's why he quit so sudden."

"I had to hide," Bill blubbered. "The gold's all been spent. I nain't never seen none of it. What'em I gonna do, Mr. French? Will they kill me?"

French shook his head. "Unlikely, and certainly not over gold. I shall speak with them and see what it is they do want."

French headed for the door, then turned to Edward. "Get him another beer from the refrigerator. Keep him drinking. It will calm him down."

Out in the yard, the gate was now fully formed. In its blue radiance, five individuals stood wearing armor, of a style similar to the German Gothic of the 1400's—these were the silver spacesuits Edward described.

French was wishing he was wearing his own armor as he opened the door and stepped from the house. He crossed the lawn and stopped about twenty feet from the gate. "I am Myrddin Wyllt of the Vaettir. I bid you welcome."

One of the armored visitors lifted the visor of his sallet. "I've heard tales of ye, Myrddin. Ye knew my father, Finvarra."

"He was a good and fair king," French replied.

"Indeed." The armored man stepped forward. "And are ye intervening on behalf of this mortal?"

French joined the Aos Sí near the edge of the gate's glow. "I would hear your side of the issue before making that decision."

Another of the Aos Sí stepped forward. "Majesty, I would tell that story, if ye would permit me, my king."

The first Aos Sí beckoned the man forward. "It is to return your property, Forannán, that we are here."

Forannán took the hand of the armored Aos Sí standing with him. The two stepped forward and raised their visors. The second figure was a woman.

"I am Forannán and this is me wife, Ilish. I am of the Aos Sí, she is of your world."

French bowed his head, acknowledging the two. "Are you the Ilish that was supposedly kidnapped?"

"I was not kidnapped. That is a lie spread by my father," the woman snapped.

"Indeed," French answered slowly. "Should I presume that he did not approve of your marriage?"

"No, he did not, and the fool followed us to the Sidh to kill Forannán, stupid old man."

French glanced back at the house. "Mr. Foley failed to mention that."

"And did he also fail to mention that my father stole the wedding gift given to me by my husband?"

French turned back to the couple. "There was mention of some gold. Mr. Foley insists it was spent long ago."

Ilish turned to Forannán, a puzzled look on her face.

"There was no gold," Forannán said. "Twas a small cauldron, quite powerful, created long ago by my ancestors before we came to your world."

Behind Forannán, a warrior bearing a staff stepped up to the king. "Your Majesty, the dawn comes quickly, Sire," she said.

The Aos Sí King nodded. "Ruarcc, retrieve the human. We have spent far too long on this. We shall resolve this at the Sidh."

The largest of the five Aos Sí warriors marched towards the house. Things were not going as French had wished. Hopefully, Edward would have the sense to hide again.

French turned back to Forannán. "I recognize the historical, ancestral, and magical value of this cauldron, but it has been over two centuries. I do not know if the mortal even knows of the item."

The king stepped forward. "He does. He has admitted it."

French scowled. "Then things are not as they seemed and do not look good for Mr. Foley. Your claim, it appears, is quite justified."

The King shifted his gaze from the house to the psychic. "Ye are as my father said, fair and honest, despite being neamh-mhairbh."

"I choose to live through the grace of others, not as a taker of life."

"So my father told me." The King's gaze shifted back to the house. He scowled. "Who is the other human Ruarcc returns with?"

French's shoulders dropped. The Aos Sí champion had both Bill and Edward in his grip. "It is a companion of mine," French said. "He is unimportant in this matter."

Ruarcc, brought Bill and Edward forward. Both seemed disconnected with reality. "This other mortal was with the thief, both hiding like rats."

"Bring them," the King commanded.

French stepped into the gate followed by Ruarcc and his prisoners. With a nod from the King, the warrior-mage raised her staff. Reality shifted and the blue glow faded. Around them were the finely cut stone walls of a courtyard. They were in Mag Cíuin, stronghold of the Sidhe.

Above the courtyard, the first hints of dawn were driving away the stars. The constellations were long unfamiliar to the psychic. "Are we your prisoners?" French asked.

"No. Merely guests for now," the king replied. "I shall convene court later to determine the fate of the thief. After that, you and your companion will be free to go."

"And Mr. Foley?"

The Aos Si king glanced contemptuously at Bill. "That will be determined in court."

He turned to the guard holding Bill's arm. "Ruarcc, take them to the east tower. Almaith's room will do."

"Yes, my liege."

The large warrior turned to French and Edward. "This way, milords."

"What'd you get me into, French?" Edward said under his breath.

"Me? This is your affair, Edward."

The businessman's head swiveled back and forth, taking in the marvels of the Sidh. "Is it magic that makes those floating balls of light."

French nodded. "Yes, a simpler solution than generating electricity."

"The magic make it kinda purple?"

"Not entirely, what you call magic is Odic energy. That energy is focused at a point, ionizing the air, which releases that excess energy as light. In this case, it is the nitrogen and oxygen in air making that color—altogether not unlike a fluorescent bulb."

The businessman turned to French. "Sounds more scientificky, than magical."

"The two share science. Magic simply is an energy form your scientists have yet to discover."

"Oh."

They continued down a wide passage, through a monumental hall, and up a grand flight of stairs. Ruarcc nodded down a hallway to the right.

As they made their way along the palace-like hallway, Edward was frowning at the paintings hanging on the walls. "How come the faces don't move," he whispered to French.

"Why should the faces move?"

"They do in Harry Potter," Edward said.

French sighed. "We are in the Mag Cíuin of the Aos Sí, not Hollywood."

Ruarcc stopped in front of a large pair of ornately carved doors. "You'll be staying here." The warrior swung open the doors revealing an opulent room resplendent enough for the highest nobility. Cobalt blue curtains of velvet framed windows reaching up to the ceiling twenty feet up. There, a fresco of gods and goddesses lounged in clouds, appearing to look down and observe the room's occupants.

Edward turned to the guard. "Holy crap, were staying here? I thought you were taking us to a prison cell."

"It may as well be a prison cell," Ruarcc answered. "Do not leave unless ye are summoned."

"You trust us?"

Ruarcc ushered them inside. "No, but there is no place in Mag Cíuin that you can hide, so do me a favor and get some sleep. I've not been in me own bed for weeks now, searching for the likes of this one." He nodded at Bill. "I am tired and wish to spend time with me wife, so get some rest. His Majesty will call for you later. Tis best ye are rested for the trial."

Ruarcc closed the doors and Bill started sobbing. "What'em I gonna do? They's gonna kill me fer sure."

French took a hold of Bill's shoulders and cast a small charm to ease the man's panic. "We shall deal with that tomorrow," the psychic said calmly. "Now lie down and get some sleep."

Bill walked over to one of the oversized beds, pulled the embroidered satin bed cover aside, and climbed in like it was something he did every day.

French turned to Edward. "I have mildly sedated Bill. He will need his rest."

"Like we don't? We've been up all night, French."

French walked to one of the windows, opened it, and stepped onto the balcony. Below, the tree-lined streets were hedged on either side by four-story buildings. There was little movement below.

The psychic motioned his friend Edward to join him. "Strange, don't you think, not much activity for a morning. You'd expect to see some hustle and bustle in a city this large."

Edward peered over the railing. "Maybe it's a holiday?"

"Perhaps," French replied, not convinced.

There was a knock at the door. French walked over and opened it. An attractive woman in her thirties entered pushing a trolley "Good sirs, I have brought ye something to break your fast."

On the trolley's upper shelf were platters of meats, boiled eggs, sausages, and bread. Below, there were bowls of baked beans, mushrooms, grilled tomatoes, and potato cakes along with butter, jellies, jams and marmalade.

With the mention of food, Edward quickly joined French. "That smells good."

"Thank ye, good sirs."

French nodded. "No, we thank you. This is a fine repast. I am called Myrddin and this is Edward."

She curtsied. "I am Clíodhna. I am very pleased to meet ye. Tell me, are ye the same Myrddin that slay the beast Firgach?"

Edward elbowed the psychic. "You killed a beast?"

French sighed. "Yes, although in truth, I banished it rather than killed it. I prefer not to take life where possible. It belonged in that other realm, I merely returned it."

Clíodhna smiled. "I heard the tale when I was but a wee child. I never thought I would meet ye."

Edward turned to the psychic. "How old are you, French?"

"Old enough." French turned back to the woman. "Clíodhna, it seems that there are far fewer of the Aos Sí than on my last visit. Is this so?"

"Aye, in times past, there were many Aos Sí, but no longer." The woman placed a delicate hand on her stomach. "Unfortunately, our fields have grown barren no matter how much they are plowed."

French nodded his head slowly. "These are ill tidings. And naught can be done?"

"Nay. Only the goddess can save us now."

Clíodhna cast her eyes down and hurried to the door. "Twas a grand pleasure meeting ye, Master Myrdden."

French followed her to the door. Outside, there was no guard. He pulled the door closed. "Interesting."

"Interesting? They're in the midst of a famine and that's interesting." Edward strode away from the trolley piled high with food. "I can't eat if they're in a famine."

"I'm not sure a famine's what Clíodhna meant," French commented. "I think it was a metaphor. Besides, a famine should hardly affect them—they could easily harvest food from our world or simply create it with magic. Eat, Edward. Letting it go to waste will help no one, certainly not Bill."

***

In the afternoon, Ruarcc returned. "You are summoned before His Majesty."

Bill hid behind Mr. Cruz. "This is it, they's gonna kill me, Eddie."

"Not if French can do anything." Edward turned to the psychic. "Right, French?"

"I am hopeful that will be the case."

"Best not to keep the King waiting, Master Myrdden."

"No, of course not. Lead the way."

They followed the Aos Sí champion down to the great hall they had passed earlier that morning. One end of the great table was now filled with men and women in a mix of medieval finery and the Gap. It was not what French had expected. This was more like a board room than an imperial court. King Máeldor wasn't seated in a throne or even at the head of the table, but instead, alongside his nobles.

The group at the tables hushed as Ruarcc ushered the prisoners in.

"Thief, you come before my court seeking mercy," Máeldor stated.

Bill stepped forward. "I didn't steal nothin. I weren't even borned then."

French had instructed Bill not to snivel or grovel. So far so good.

"In our law, the guilt of your forebearers carries unto you."

"French done told me that. Stupid way of runnin' things."

French sighed inwardly. Luckily, the King ignored Bill's comment and turned to Forannán and Ilish. "Make your claim, Lord and Lady Tairngire."

Forannán stood. "William Kevin Foley, do you wish to make amends for the wrong done to me and my wife by your family and to return the Coire Brígh?"

"Amends? I don't know what you mean." Bill turned to the psychic. "What's he askin' me, French?"

French stepped forward. "For the clarification of this court, the Coire Brígh, what is it?"

Ilish answered. "It is an iron cauldron forged in antiquity. My father took it when he escaped."

French turned to Bill. "The bucket, you said your ancestor filled a bucket with gold, do you know where it is?"

"Yessir, sorta."

Bill was getting panicky. French took him by both shoulders. "Bill, you can set things right and get out of here. You just have to give that bucket back."

Bill started to shake. "But I don't have it. I ain't never even seen it. My Pappy done buried it 'fore I was born."

"Where, Bill?"

"The back ten acres somewhere. Crops done real good in that field no matter we got rain or not. My Pappy always said the bucket was why, but he never showed me where it was."

The King stood. "That is unfortunate. Without the return of the Coire Brígh, William Kevin Foley, by law, your life is forfeit."

With that announcement, the nobles at the table stood. Máeldor left the great hall followed by the others. Only Ilish and Forannán remained.

"I ain't never even seen it, ain't never even seen it..." Bill collapsed to his knees, sobbing, cursing his ancestors.

Ilish regarded her descendant with sympathy. She walked over to French. "I should offer explanation, there's far more to this than just the return of a stolen item. The Coire Brígh isn't just any cauldron; it was crafted by the Goddess to bless all those who partook from its bounty."

French nodded. "And the Aos Sí believe it can help with their fertility issues."

She cocked her head in surprise. "Yes. Some even claim that removing the Coire Brígh from our land is why we are having our troubles. It isn't true, of course, the problem is much older than that. It is why the Aos Sí sought human partners for many centuries before Forannán and I were ever married."

"It has affected you two as well?"

"Yes, and I would so love children."

"How soon will the sentence be carried out?"

"Dawn tomorrow."

"Swift justice here," Edward commented.

Ilish gave a slight shrug of her shoulders. 'The laws are old. Yet, we've no need to update them—there's almost no theft here. With the reduced population, we have far more than any individual needs."

French nodded, brow furrowed in thought. "But if the cauldron was returned?"

"Bill would be spared, of course."

French nodded. "Then that's what has to be done?"

"How?"

"I shall go back, find the cauldron, and return before morning."

The woman looked around. "I doubt whether you will be allowed to leave," she whispered.

"I was not intending to ask for permission."

***

At dusk, French made his preparations.

"Won't they notice you're gone?"

The psychic placed a small coin on the floor. "This shall distract them."

French slipped from the room, first pulling a small cloth bag from his pocket. Clutching the bag of chameleon bones, he quietly made his way to the courtyard where they had arrived by gate. He waited until a pair of women left before stepping to the center of the court. From the inside of his coat, he pulled out the hawthorn branch he'd taken that morning and placed it on the worn paving stones. He took a deep breath and focused on the branch. Behind him, somewhere in the castle, an alarm sounded.

So, they'd noticed he was gone. French refocused on the branch. A green sphere of light appeared. The sound of running footsteps grew nearer. French did not let it distract him, instead focusing on enlarging the sphere. It was now the size of an exercise ball.

Voices echoed, yelling for attention, summoning guards, but they were thrust from the psychic's conscious to be ignored. Within the ball of light, there was grass, not the stone pavement of the courtyard. The sound of steel sliding against steel grew near—the guards in their armor. French squatted and threw himself through the green ball of light. He snatched up the hawthorn branch and the sphere extinguished.

French was alone in Bill's backyard. He ran to the house. It wouldn't take long for the Aos Sí to follow. In the kitchen, he grabbed the Odeometer and its blue manual. He paused. Trying to locate the cauldron with the Odeometer was going to be tricky enough. He needed to narrow down where in the field he should start.

French glanced at Edward's computer. Google Earth might have the answer. French started the software and zoomed into Bill's property. The fields were bare—either winter or post-harvest. Were there other images? French searched for past photos, finding a clock icon, and clicked. An image of the property in summer appeared, fields lush with growth.

French zoomed in. One field stood out, north of the house, far greener than the others. That must be the back ten acres. French zoomed in further. An area to the east was decidedly greener than the remainder of the field. French made a mental note of the location, grabbed the Odeometer, and headed for the door.

It was kicked open by Ruarcc. "You're not doing this thing alone, neamh-mhairbh."

French paused. That was not the pitch of voice he'd expected. "You are here to assist me?"

"No, I am here to retrieve you, but if we happen to stumble upon the cauldron along the way, so much the better. You ready, wizard?"

French smiled. "Yes, I believe I know in what area the cauldron is buried. The Odeometer will help us pinpoint the location."

"You plan to pluck it from the earth with your hands?"

French hurried through the kitchen door. "There should be shovels in the barn."

***

Once in the field, French held the silver framed sphere of the Odeometer in both hands and walked slowly, eyes fixed on the intricately painted dials.

Ruarcc followed the psychic a pace or two back. "The Coire Brígh will not be found easily. The goddess created it as a tool, not some artifact of power."

"Do you think it will help your people?"

"I don't know. So many of us are now half human. Honestly, I'm not sure if the Aos Sí even exists truly as a race anymore."

One of the needles twitched. French turned to the right. "That way."

The two men crossed the tillage covered furrows. French swung the Odeometer side to side, following the needle bounce like the click of a Geiger counter. Finally, there was a point where the needle peaked.

The psychic placed the Odeometer on the ground. "I think this is it."

Ruarcc handed French a shovel. "Any idea how deep the Coire Brígh's buried?"

"Several feet, at least. Deeper than a plow would go."

Ruarcc nodded and the two began digging. They were four feet down when the Aos Sí champion struck metal.

"I think you've found it, Master Ruarcc."

The big man squatted at the bottom of the hole, feeling through the dirt. "There's something here all right. Iron, but warm to the touch." He glanced over at French. "You do good work, neamh-mhairbh."

"I try not to make that aspect of myself public anymore. Just call me Myrddin."

A little more excavation and they had their prize, a shallow black cast iron cauldron. Runic lettering covered the surface.

Ruarcc heaved the Coire Brígh up and out of the hole. "We've three hours 'til dawn, Myrddin. Is there anything to quench our thirst in the house of that thief?"

"Yes, I believe there is, but it may be too weak for your taste."

"Better than water, old man."

***

Just before dawn, the gate opened. The King, Forannán, and Ilish stood within the pale blue glow. Ruarcc had French by the arm, the Coire Brígh in his other hand.

"I have retrieved the prisoner, your Majesty."

Ilish ran forward. "And the Coire Brígh!"

"Aye, the neamh-mhairbh is not without talent."

The King turned to someone on the other side of the gate. "Step forward Edward Cruz and bring the thief with you."

"I'm not a thief."

Forannán extended a hand to Bill, "With the return of the Coire Brígh, that tis true. Your family no longer carries the shame of thief."

Bill shook the Aos Sí warrior's hand. "I'm damn thankful fer that."

Ilish pulled Bill to her and hugged him. "Someday, you should come and see more of the Mag Cíuin."

"I'll do that, and remember, y'all are always welcome to visit my world."

She smiled, stepping into the radiant ball of light. "Oh, we do. We have nothing like Starbucks *Caramel Macchiato* in Mag Cíuin."

As the luminescent magical link between worlds snuffed out, Edward turned to French. "There's never a dull moment around you, is there?"

"No, I'm afraid not."

In an emergency room, the trauma team is usually ready for just about anything. A malevolent spirit escaping from the body of a dead priest, however, is something new even for seasoned veterans. French is called in to capture the spirit and send it on its way.

Black Mist

Meryl escorted French's new client into the office. As usual, the man was far more interested in the curves revealed by her form-fitting red dress rather than the collection of apparatus and paraphernalia on the walls and shelves of French's office. No surprise there.

"Meryl, would you bring us some tea, please," French asked.

Meryl nodded and left. The man's eyes followed her until the moment she was out of view. It was time to get the client's mind onto business. French stood and shook the man's hand.

"I'm Mr. French. My secretary tells me you have a bit of a problem that I might help with."

The man nodded. He had a firm and controlling handshake. He was someone used to things in a certain way and a certain order.

"I'm Dr. Martin Aguirre," he said. "I'm a surgeon at Methodist Hospital."

French gestured to the velvet upholstered Victorian couch. "Sit and make yourself comfortable, Doctor."

Despite the authority of the handshake, the man was nervous, obviously out of his element. French settled into his wingback chair by the window. "What can I do for you, Dr. Aguirre?"

"It isn't for me. It's for my neighbor."

The Doctor was in his fifties with short Grey hair, tall and thin in the manner of his Spanish heritage, around 6'-1" and fit, probably a cyclist. His hands were immaculately clean. He was certainly not typical of French's regular clientele.

"And what is it you wish me to do for your neighbor?"

Dr. Aguirre leaned forward. "I'll be honest, I don't believe in your psychic hooey but I've seen something and don't know where else to turn."

"What is this thing you saw?"

"I work in the E.R. and eight days ago, we had a patient ambulanced in suffering from chest pain. I thought cardiac infarction at first but it was far worse than that. It was a TAA, thoracic aortic aneurysm, a rupture in the artery from the heart. The patient bled into his chest cavity. There was nothing we could do, he'd died in transit."

"And this thing you saw? Was it in the patient who died on the way to the hospital?"

"Yes. Upon receiving the patient, Dr. Atkinson checked for vitals and declared the time of death. As the intern was removing the endotracheal tube, a black mist erupted from the body. It was overpowering, like the smell of gangrenous necrotic tissue mixed with the sulfurous odor of a chemical plant. The intern and Dr. Atkinson passed out and fell to the floor. I was further away and watched as the mist collected in a corner of the ceiling. After a moment, it evaporated through the wall."

Mr. French knew the smell. This was not good news. "It didn't behave normally, did it?"

Dr. Aguirre shook his head. "No, if it had been just decompositional gas, it would have gone to the vents. Surgical rooms are designed to evacuate contaminated air. This was a demon."

French had come to that conclusion as well. "Interesting, why do you assume this?"

The Doctor paused for a moment. "I know it's a demon because later it found me. In all the confusion of dealing with Dr. Atkinson and the intern, I'd put the patient file down and left it. Later, when I went to retrieve the file, the demon found me."

"It found you?" French asked. "You mean it possessed you?"

Dr. Aguirre shook his head. "Yes and no. I felt it enter my body. I could sense it but there was no overwhelming sense of evil and I didn't start puking up pea soup. It was just there, in my mind, watching me. The next several days, I made excuses not to be intimate with my wife, staying late at work, picking up extra shifts in the E.R, anything not to be at home. I didn't want this thing seeing my wife naked, who knew what might happen, right?"

French pulled a set of spectacles from his inner jacket pocket. The lenses were a pale apricot pink. Most of his clients referred to them as his John Lennon Hippie glasses. He put them on and looked at Dr. Aguirre. There was no spore tinting his aura.

"You aren't possessed now," French stated.

"No, two days ago it left me. I was in the bathroom when I got violently ill. I vomited and the mist spewed out along with my stomach contents. It stared at me for a moment and then disappeared through the bathroom window. I think it's gone next door and possessed my neighbor."

French was puzzled. This was not like any demonic possession he'd ever heard of. "Why your neighbor?"

"I don't know, just a felling I had. I immediately went over to warn her. She's an old retired woman, the type that keeps cats. When she answered the door, it was there in her eyes. I was too late."

"But you never felt any malevolence. Why were you worried?"

"Because I could feel that it wanted something!"

Meryl rapped once on the door. She had the tea trolley.

"Tea, Dr. Aguirre?"

"Uh, no, well sure, why not."

Dr. Aguirre had the uncomfortableness most Americans had around tea. It was the fear of not knowing what fork to use at dinner. It's just tea—you get a cup and you drink it. French knew that if he had offered Coca-Cola, Dr. Aguirre would have had no difficulty deciding.

Meryl pushed the trolley over to the Doctor. Leaning forward, she poured the tea into a cup and handed it and a saucer to the Doctor. As she no doubt enjoyed, the Doctor's eyes went straight to her ample cleavage. One might think a doctor would be immune to human anatomy. Perhaps so, but this was Meryl and she was a succubus.

"The sugar, cream, and lemon are on the cart," she said as she stood.

Traditionally, as host, it was his duty to serve, but seeing as Meryl was having to deal with a great many of the psychic's ongoing issues, it seemed fair to let her have her fun. The Doctor certainly didn't mind. He had added two cubes of sugar and a slice of lemon to his cup without ever looking down.

French stepped over to the tea trolley and nodded for Meryl to go.

"You said that this demon wanted something. Any idea what that might be?" French asked.

"I don't know. I went to my Priest. That was awkward. I guess they get this type of thing a lot—people misdiagnosing mental illness with demonic possession. It was only when I told him my patient was a priest named Father Carter that he changed his tune. I was referred to St. Brigit's and Father Joseph."

French poured a small bit of cream into the teacup. Adding cream was an old English habit that dated to the eighteenth century. Cream or milk added to the cup first kept the fragile porcelain of the period safe from thermal shock. It also prevented staining by the dark, black tea. Modern porcelain requires no such careful treatment but the English, once they have grown accustomed to things, tend to keep at it.

Things made sense now. "And that's how you found me," French said. "I've had the pleasure of working with Father Joseph before."

"Father Joseph thinks it's a demon that Father Carter exorcised from a girl back in the fifties."

Mr. French leaned forward in his chair. "And it's been in the Priest all this time?"

The Doctor nodded. "Father Joseph told me that at the exorcism, Father Carter took the demon into himself to free the girl. Afterwards, he carried it with him, his burden to bear, to prevent it from attacking others."

This was new. For the most part, the demons that possess and control humans are of two types, either a Verthag or Shatha'agral. They are extremely belligerent and cause no small amount of suffering. Luckily, they were rare, even in French's business. Whatever this was, it was something else entirely.

"Please don't blame your priest. The Church now recognizes that most possessions are misdiagnosed schizophrenia or some other mental disorder and so they train priests to look for this first. In the case of your neighbor, I shall have to make a visit. Can I get the address?"

Doctor Aguirre pulled a business card from his pocket. "I'm at 7154 Oakridge. Mrs. Ashwood lives at 7112."

French stared at the card, pondering what he might need to do. Demonic possession was never a simple affair. "I'll call you when I know something," he told the Doctor.

***

Dr. Aguirre and the Ashwoods had done well. Their address was in Oak Hills near the Medical Center. Fixer-Uppers in the area started at $350,000. The 1960's era house was the typical long and low ranch from the period. It was all grey brick with a shallow sloped roof and three-car carport. There must be a garage beyond—no cars were visible. Not so typical was the large chunk of real estate it sat on. The sprawl of St. Augustine grass that was the front yard could have held two more homes.

French pulled into the circle drive and parked his vintage candy apple red Plymouth convertible. He walked the concrete path to the front door and pushed the bell.

It was warm and muggy. From the looks of the sky, a thunderstorm was rolling in. Not the best of weather in which to expel a demon.

A deadbolt rattled and a small woman in her late seventies answered the door. "Excuse my looks, I'm cleaning." She was wearing an apron and had her hair covered by a scarf.

"My name is French…" he began.

The small woman interrupted. "Oh, fantastique. Je m'appelle Adrienne."

Not again. You would think that the British accent would be a dead give-away, but no, this was the second time this month. "Désolé, mon nom est *French*, comme le majordome á la télévision."

The spark of excitement in her face faded with the realization that her visitor was not some exotic foreign visitor but likely just another salesman. "Oh, please excuse an old woman. I'm always looking for a chance to use my French. I don't get the opportunity to travel anymore."

She cocked her head to one side, looking her visitor up and down. "You know, you even look like Sabastian Cabot. I loved watching the *Family Affair* when the kids were young. We would sit in front of the television and eat Swanson TV dinners, sort of like a picnic."

This was certainly not the encounter French had prepared for. The woman seemed quite normal. A small ginger and white cat wiggled past her leg to escape.

"Bitsy, come back here. Oh, would you grab my cat, please?"

French scooped up the fugitive feline. Bitsy was not upset, turning her head for French to rub the side of her face.

The woman motioned French to enter. "Come on in before the others escape, won't you."

French followed the elderly woman inside. The 1960's era house had never been remodeled. Even the mid-century modern furniture was correct. A flat slab sofa on splayed wooden legs was against the left wall. Cylindrical arm rest pillows sat at either end. If it had been harvest gold, it could have come off the set of *The Brady Bunch*. Instead, the sofa and pillows were a burgundy which matched the painting hanging on the wall above. That was an abstract of high-energy brush strokes in wine red, black and pale grey. The grey matched the brick of the wall which was the same brick as the exterior of the building.

"So tell me, what are you here to sell me Mr. French?" The woman asked.

French lowered Bitsy to the floor. "Nothing at all. I am here on the behest of several people that are worried about you. Have you noticed anything unusual lately?"

She ushered French toward the couch. "Sit. I'm afraid I don't have anything at the moment to offer you. My grandson is coming by this weekend to take me shopping."

Was she being evasive? "So, no voices or feelings that someone is watching you?" he asked.

"You can just say it, Mr. French. You're here about Laba'al. Are you from the Church? Did the Doctor send you?"

"Laba'al?" French didn't remember any demonic reference with that name. "No, I am not from the Church. I am a psychic. Who is Laba'al?"

"A demon," she said with a smile.

She seemed to be in quite a good humor for one possessed. French retrieved his aura reading glasses from his jacket and put them on. There was no doubt—there was a demonic tint within her aura.

"You don't believe me, do you?" she asked.

French was about to answer when the old woman lifted into the air, slowly revolved and then carefully, oh so carefully settled down to the ground. "Father Carter liked to do that too." There was something different about the voice. It was deeper.

"Am I speaking to Adrienne or Laba'al?" French asked.

"We are both here," Adrienne's voice replied. "I could get you some ice water if you like?"

"No, I am fine," he replied. "This Laba'al is rather different from the demons I have removed in the past."

"No blood from the eyes, foul language, green vomit, and that sort of thing," she added.

"Well, yes, that is what Hollywood would have us believe, isn't it."

French removed the glasses. There was no overriding blackness to her aura, no red of fresh blood dominating a human soul, no yellow of flames burning with the freedom from perdition, there was just a faint shadow curled like a cat on its owner's lap.

Mr. French returned the glasses to his inner jacket pocket. "No, I was referring to the fact that Laba'al seems content to just lie there."

"Goodness, you are very perceptive, Mr. French," she replied. "And you are right, he just wants a home and I am happy to have someone to talk to."

How very odd. "The Priest, Laba'al's former, um, shall we say, home, did they talk?"

"Only when Father Carter was alone. He worried that his fellow priests might consider him insane or senile," the deeper voice of Laba'al replied. "We had some interesting discussions on theology. He was very intelligent and kind. I shall miss him greatly."

This was not the type demon typical to possessions. "You have the feel of an Infernal—an incubus or succubus rather than a Verthag or Shatha'agral."

The elderly woman nodded. "Yes, like the incubi, I consume the life energy of my host."

"Yet you were with Father Carter for years?"

"I need very little to survive and he was kind enough to provide. By the end, I was drawing from the lives around us to sustain his body. Ultimately, it was not enough and the flesh failed."

"Thoracic aortic aneurysm," French said.

The woman nodded. "It was quick and painless, like falling asleep. However, I was completely unprepared."

"Unprepared?" Mr. French asked.

"Those like myself, we generally choose children for our hosts. Children are not afraid of us. We become playmates."

"Imaginary friends," French added.

"Yes. As they get older, they find their own friends. After that, we just watch out for them, nudging them in directions when they would make a bad choice."

"But there were no children at the hospital."

"No, just that intolerant Doctor and his religious prejudices. I did nothing to harm him yet all he felt towards me was loathing."

French nodded. "Humans can be that way, they fear that which they fail to understand."

"Exactly. I fled and was lucky enough to find Adrienne." The voice shifted. "I really am glad to have Laba'al living with me," Mrs. Ashwood said.

French stood. "Well, I had better be going then. I see that you're in the middle of tidying up and I don't want to keep you."

A smile brightened Mrs. Ashwood's face. "You aren't going to do an exorcism?"

"You both seem happy enough," French replied. "At some point though, I would like to learn more, perhaps over sandwiches at the Bakery Lorraine?"

"That would be excellent. I get out so little these days. Most of my friends are in homes or have passed. I'd love the chance to…"

She stopped herself.

"Oh fiddlesticks, Laba'al says you're not single. What a shame."

French smiled, something that he not done much recently. "He is correct. Meryl and I have been together for over forty years."

Mrs. Ashwood's eyes grew large. It had nothing to do with the length of time. "What? A succubus?! Why Mr. French, how wonderfully naughty of you!"

French smiled. "It's actually rather common. I'm guessing that he can sense her presence on my aura?"

"Something to do with tangerines, he says." She stood. "Perhaps the two of you can explain it all at the restaurant. You know, when you arrived, Laba'al told me that you were much older than you looked. When I didn't see a ring, I was hoping…"

Mr. French sighed. "I'm afraid Laba'al is correct. I am very, very much older than I look. As to a ring, I suppose that at some point, Meryl and I should make it official. There always seems to be too much going on."

The older woman retrieved Bitsy. "Yes, you should. Women like that sort of thing. Shame on you making her wait so long."

She opened the door and French stepped out onto the stoop. "It was nice meeting you Mrs. Ashwood," French said with a nod of his head.

A sly smile spread across the older woman's face. "Someday, I'm going to have you tell me what it's like to be with a succubus. Au revoir, monsieur French."

Normally, when someone goes missing, you search for them until they show up. If that fails, you might call the police or even a professional detective. But what if you are one of the heavenly Devine in charge of purgatory and you've lost several recently deceased I.T. developers? Call Mr. French on the Q.T. is what.

Inhuman Resources

Being in the aether was like floating in the universe. Pinpricks of light sparkled in the darkness like stars. These stars, however, were the energy of life itself. Some were massive, swollen large with vitality. Others were dim, red, and near death. Some floated alone, or with one or two partners in a paired orbit. Others were gathered together in massive colonies, creating galaxies, hot and burning with life.

French approached one such galaxy. Its center pulsed with blue-white argon brightness; the metaphysical equivalent of a heartbeat. Around the galaxy edges, tendrils of multi-color brilliance radiated outwards. They swayed in slow-motion choreography like an anemone's tentacles caught in the ebb and flow of some aether ocean.

French moved within range of one of the tendrils. Sensing him, the fuscia with sparks of lemon tentacle extended, curious to discover what this new thing was.

The neon radiance that was French extended his arm forward. There was only the most tentative touch at first. Then, upon recognizing French, it curled itself about the psychic's wrist.

This galaxy was the collective lifeforce of the plants and animals in French's menagerie and the reason why the psychic was here in the aether. A conduit was needed to harness the galaxy's wildly excessive energy.

French opened his palm and dots of light spilled into the darkness. They joined with the tendril sending ripples of arc light vibrating through the swirling galaxy.

At the far edge of consciousness, Mr. French heard the ring of the doorbell. Odd, during the day, most people just entered the office.

He paused, letting his connection with the galaxy establish itself. This was but the first step in creating a conduit to transfer the menagerie's excess Odic energy to the storage objects in his office. Once done, the amber stones would serve as magical batteries for both himself and the forces that protected his office. Quite honestly, he'd put this off for far too long. Things had just been all sixes and sevens since he'd moved house and there simply hadn't been time to create the energy conduit.

Easing toward full consciousness, he heard Meryl answer the door.

There was a mumble of conversation. Meryl was speaking with someone—hopefully, it would not be a client that actually needed his attention. French had put off this conjuring long enough. Until it was in place, he would have to continue walking across the street each night to retrieve the amber storage stones. Caitlin's multitude of rats had settled into the warehouse quite well. The girl even had them doing a number of small tasks. The girl had been a most excellent addition to his staff. The rats' excess energy alone filled three of the stones.

In his office, French's physical body drew a circle with a candle flame beginning the conjuration. He concentrated his thoughts, visualizing the lump of stone which served as the focal point for the conduit in the real world. It was an ancient piece of Baltic amber. Inside, an ant was forever trapped. The ant and the amber, both having once been living things, were ideal for the storage of Odic energy. French felt the conduit as it snapped into place. Good, now just to tie it down at this end.

"Mr. French, you have a visitor," Meryl said, interrupting his thought.

"One moment please," he answered, struggling not to lose the tenuous grip his mind had on the energy flow.

His succubus secretary sighed. French looked up, divorcing himself partially from the aether. In the doorway, standing next to Meryl, was a Devine. Considering that the two races were immortal enemies; that his secretary merely sighed showed a major amount of restraint.

French moved the conjuration to the back of his mind. "I don't often get visitors from your realm," he said to the winged angelic being.

She smiled pleasantly. "No, generally we try to solve our own issues."

Meryl exited the room and his Devine visitor visibly relaxed. Devine and Infernal proxy wars had led to many of the mortal world's greatest conflicts but there was no longer open warfare between the two species. Instead, they had made the wise and deliberate choice of simply avoiding one another whenever possible. That had been an advantageous solution for everyone involved.

"You come highly recommended, Mr. French."

The Devine's voice was a near whisper which was rather odd. Most Devine are bigger than life, overflowing with good looks and vitality, but not this one She was no taller than five-four, mousy brown hair, plain face, and wearing round glasses—a very odd thing for an angel. French knew that this completely unassuming image was a deliberate choice. Just as succubi chose their shape; so do the Devine. The question French was asking himself was whether this was an aspect of her personality or was it intentionally manipulative?

The psychic bowed his head. "Thank you. Brother Leo told me to expect someone. How shall I address you?"

"There's no need for formality, simply call me Palial. I manage the accounting section of the Transfer office."

The Transfer office is what most Catholics would call Purgatory. The Devine created it in response to human expectation and at the Vatican's request.

French motioned for her to sit. "Tea?"

"Yes, please. Brother Leo told me of some the cases the two of you solved together. Very exciting. I don't get much adventure in my line of work, thankfully."

French poured a smidgen of milk into each of the two cups on the tea trolley. "What is it that you do in the Transfer Office?"

"I work directly under Patriarch Lamechiel. We are responsible for processing the incoming supplicants. Very important occupation."

French tipped the tea into the cups. The warm vapor of Earl Grey filled the office. "Sugar?"

Palial leaned forward. "Yes, please." She pointed at the mound of sugar cubes in the bowl on the tea trolley. "That lump there, and this one here, if you would."

French placed the carefully selected sugar cubes into Palial's cup.

"Stir twice clockwise, please."

French typically stirred by moving the spoon in a silent sideways arch but did as directed, then handed his guest the cup and saucer. "Outside of Britain, I have not met anyone quit so fastidious about their tea."

Palial glanced down apologetically at her teacup. "I'm afraid that I am a bit nit-picky in everything I do. I suppose that's a good trait in an accountant."

"Just so," French replied. "And how is it that I am to help you, Co-Adjutor?"

Palial's brows rose. "You're familiar with Devine hierarchy?"

French nodded. "I did some research prior to your arrival."

She paused. "Then you realize how embarrassing it would be for someone in my position to lose several supplicants in my accounting."

"These supplicants were lost?"

Palial leaned back in the settee. "The four chose to wander out of the safety of the evaluation containment facility. Completely not my fault. They were told to wait."

"They escaped purgatory?"

Palial nodded. "Non-believers. It weakens the containment."

"Where could these escapees go from there?"

"One of two places and they are not in the Devine realm. That I have searched quite thoroughly. As they may have gone in the other direction, I was hoping you might be able to look into the matter."

"Ah, of course as I am far less noticeable." French offered the plate of sweets. "I assume Hellish Intelligence is not to know."

"Most certainly not," Palial replied. "Word would get back to my superiors. Gabriel himself intervened the last time this occurred in the 1720's—before my time, of course. Heads rolled after that incident."

She shivered involuntarily and took a biscuit from the plate to cover her reaction.

"Were there any witnesses to their escape?" French asked. "I assume there were other individuals present in purgatory at the time."

"Three other supplicants shared the detention block. My interviews with them and a subsequent search are what led me to believe that the four have escaped to the nether world."

French noted that Palial took precise and very calculated nibbles from the Nabisco sugar wafer. Absolutely no crumbs escaped to fall to the napkin on her lap. If she managed purgatory in the same fashion, such an escape as she described seemed unlikely.

"Tell me about the four individuals," French said. "Is it possible they had help?"

Palial handed French a manila folder. "Inside are mugshots and background files taken from our database." She took a calculated sip of her tea. "The four supplicants left the earthly plane as a result of a car crash. They had attended an Internet security conference together and were returning home when a drunk driver crossed into their lane."

French glanced through the photos in the folder."

"You will note that they are two men and two women, all in their mid-forties, with no religious affiliation, and highly intelligent. Of the four, Mr. Davis is even more so, definitely at a genius level in his profession. In point, Mr. Davis was one of the keynote speakers at the conference."

"Any sign of foul play?"

"Not one of my parameters," she said flatly.

"I'll get on the case immediately. Anything else I should know?"

"Just be discrete. I've worked really hard to get where I am, schmoozed the right people, cultured the right connections, I really don't want to lose all that."

Mr. French escorted Palial to the door. After the pleasantries were done, she left, driving off in a white Mercedes AMG GT coupe. He walked back to his office deep in thought. Not the easiest nut to crack—just getting to hell was going to be an issue.

***

There was a knock at the door. Jason glanced up from the dining room table and the partially finished model for architecture class. He and his succubus fiancée Jynieth didn't get many visitors. Probably just a salesman or Jehovah's Witness—not much else got past the protection barriers placed by the succubi queen Agrat.

Jason was still coming to grips with the reality that succubi and angels weren't just the stuff of bible school. They did exist, he was engaged to one, and he had the battle scars to prove the two didn't get along.

Jason summoned the rod into the real world. Could be anyone or anything on the other side of that door and Jason had learned to be cautious. The rod was an artifact of some other dimension. No one really knew what it was. What little that was known, no one was sharing with Jason, which was annoying. The rod had found him when a bunch of rogue angels had showed up intent to kill his and Jynieth's unborn child. Good thing it had, they'd needed it and there were a few less rogue angels now.

Jason peeked out the spyhole—it was Mr. French. Odd, why would he show up without a phone call? Jason opened the door, the rod held ready.

"Hey French, what's up?"

"Something, but I can't discuss it out here."

The rod cooled in Jason's grip—must really be the psychic and not something pretending to be him. "Jynieth and the baby are resting. We gotta be quiet."

French entered. Jason carefully shut the door.

French's eyes dropped to the rod. "Good, we shall be needing that if you decide to help me," the psychic whispered.

"We gonna go bash some more Devine butt?"

French shook his head. "Nothing so dramatic. I'm trying to locate four individuals who may be hiding in hell. You and the rod can get me there."

Jason looked at the rod, still glowing brick red in his hand. "Um, it can do that?"

"Yes," French answered. "It is one of the five planar objects. Not only can it transfer between realms, but with you focusing it, the rod can take us directly to wherever my missing software engineers might be."

Jason didn't like the idea of leaving Jynieth's side, even for a little while. "Agrat's in the apartment manager's office, why don't you ask her?"

"This is something of a hush-hush business. Neither Agrat nor Hellish Intelligence is supposed to know."

"These missing guys dangerous?"

"No, just misplaced. My client, a Devine who shall remain unnamed, would find it inconvenient it this became public."

Upon hearing Devine, Jason's grip on the rod tightened. "Why should I help one of those assholes?"

"Don't be so quick to judge," French interjected. "The Devine may be a bit pompous at times, but most are not like the terrorists we fought. They and the Infernals are the same race after all. The division is purely ideological."

Jason listened, trying to keep an open mind as French explained the situation.

Once the psychic was done, Jason mulled things over. "I suppose I could tell Agrat I need to run to the store," he said at last. "She likes being around the baby. She's a lot less grumpy acting like a grandma. If she sees you though, she'll know something's up."

"Agreed," French said. "Getting past Lilith's pet polar bear was hard enough. I don't believe that my magic would confuse Agrat."

"The polar bear's name is Donijex. Good security guard but he makes me nervous. Doesn't talk much."

"You expect chit chat from one of Hellish Intelligence's trained killers?" French asked.

Jason shook his head. "No, but he's not H.I. Six, at least not anymore. Karen said he's good but a bit of a lone wolf and didn't quite fit within her agency."

"You've been speaking with the Director?"

"Agrat brought her by to test the defenses. Not sure what they found but Agrat made some changes."

"Most interesting. You'll have to tell me more at some point but for the moment, we need to get started. Meet me at my office. We'll leave from there."

***

Jason wasn't that interested in helping the psychic and had no idea why these missing dead guys were so important but it was the first chance he'd had to learn more about the rod. Everyone seemed to know more about it than he did. Jynieth said it was important that he not know. He had pressed for more but the subject made her cry. She wouldn't even explain why. It was all really pissing him off. That it could transport him to hell was new. Perhaps, if he was lucky, maybe French would drop some more hints on this little mission of his.

Once at the office, French handed Jason a photo of a guy in his forties.

"This one of the missing dudes?"

French nodded. "Yes, now concentrate on the photo of Mr. Davis. Think about going to his location. My research indicates that once found, the rod will connect the two points and shift anyone in contact with you along that line."

Good to know. "So simple a three-year-old could do it," Jason added.

French scowled. "Perhaps, but a three-year-old playing with an object of this power would not be advisable."

Another clue. What else could this thing do? Even the rod was being close-lipped although it didn't really communicate as such. Jason just suddenly knew things, like with the fighting. French's implication was that it could do a great deal more.

Jason redirected his attention. "All right, I'm focusing on the photo. Now what?"

"Once you feel his location, go there!"

"I can see him…"

They were no longer in French's office. Instead, they stood next to an office cubicle. Inside Mr. Davis was typing away on a computer.

Mr. French stepped forward. "Mr. Davis…"

The computer geek kept typing away. A LeBron James bobble head was on the shelf above his monitor along with several photos of Hawaii.

"Mr. Davis?" French tried again.

"He can't hear you. His headphones are up too high." Jason reached forward and tapped the guy on the shoulder.

Mr. Davis jumped, turning quickly. "Who are you?"

"I'm Jason. This here's Mr. French," Jason answered. "So you escaped purgatory? Pretty sweet. You likin' it down here?"

"Definitely. Workload's way less hectic and they've provided top end machines with forty-two terabit per second data transfer. Better yet, the Admin isn't some poser in a suit but actually knows the subject."

Mr. Davis paused, eyeing Mr. French and Jason quizzically. "How did you get here?"

"Why? Where do you think we are, Mr. Davis?" French asked.

"Hellish Intelligence, cyber security division four. You two aren't wearing badges."

Mr. Davis reached for his phone.

"We were sent to confirm that you find these afterlife accommodations accessible," French said smoothly. "You did bypass the normal function of things."

Mr. Davis settled back in his chair. "Oh that. Yeah, we found a backdoor in the security and ended up here. H.I. Six found us and offered us a job. Good benefits, lots of vacation, realistic deadlines, what's not to like."

Mr. French nodded. "Excellent, I will pass that along."

He then turned to Jason. "I believe that you and I have taken more than enough of Mr. Davis's time."

"Sure. Nice meeting you Mr. Davis..."Jason began.

A flash of light and smoke filled the maze of cubicles followed by the appearance of multiple well-armed H.I. Six operatives.

"Drop your weaponzz and do not move," hissed the squad leader. He was a mix of spider and gorilla with saguaro cactus tentacles.

French politely bowed his head to the spidercactusrilla. "Ah, Agent Vergulakkkt, if I remember correctly. Can you tell the Director that..."

"Zztop! Do not attempt to ztspeak or make any movement. My team will zzshoot."

The spidercactusrilla turned to Jason. "Drop your weapon!"

"I'm trying. It won't leave my hand."

One of the guards behind Jason placed the muzzle of his gun against the young man's head."

"That is Agrat's rod," French explained. "It will not leave his person. Now will you please tell the Director..."

"You can tell the Director herself," a familiar voice said.

Jason relaxed. He knew this person. It was Karen. "Thank goodness you're here."

She did not look happy. "Jason, why are you and French deep, deep within my security?"

Jason remembered their mission was secret. "Experimenting with the rod. French mentioned that I could travel to hell with it. Sorry. Thing should've come with instructions."

Karen sighed. She turned to the psychic. "French, can you please talk to Agrat and get her to do something? That thing should not be in the hands of a novice."

"Agreed, but the rod, not Agrat made that decision," French replied. "We are at its mercy, I'm afraid."

Karen's spines were up. "That damn thing can raze continents!"

French shook his head, signaling the H.I. Six Director to end the discussion. "Jason is not to be told the abilities of the rod nor the prophecies of the rod bearer."

"I'm standing right here you know," Jason interjected.

French and Karen ignored him. Instead, the Director of Hellish Security swiveled her eyes to the rod. "Not telling him is foolish. A soldier must know their weapon."

"As you saw at the hotel, the rod provides Jason the knowledge he needs as he needs it, not before. It has not chosen to reveal its capabilities to Jason, and we believe it best to abide by that."

Karen's leech face scowled. "Damn dangerous. We don't even know where the thing came from."

"True but of the five objects, the rod has always acted in our benefit," French countered.

Karen turned and stared at Jason. It wasn't a comfortable place to be, under her glare. Finally, she spoke. "Out of my building. You have a wife and baby to protect."

She didn't have to tell Jason twice.

***

French floated in the aether. The conduit was complete. The menagerie was happily going about their lives and their excess energy was being transferred into the stones in his office. To the left, Meryl's distinct chartreuse, carmine, and violet aura approached along with a smaller but very energetic energy comprised of lemons, magentas, and teals.

French withdrew back to reality as Meryl knocked on the door.

"Visitor for you."

French took a deep breath. "Show her in please."

The meek and subdued image that was Co-Adjutor Palial entered the room.

"You have found them?"

French nodded. "They are quite happy in their current location. It might be best not to request their return. It could make things difficult."

"Difficult, how?"

"They are working for Hellish Intelligence," French explained.

Palial's shoulders dropped. "Is H.I. Six aware that…"

French shook his head. "No, but they do find their abilities useful and so would fight extradition. As such, I took the liberty of finding a loophole for you to exploit."

"A loophole?"

"Yes, with regards to their status as non-believers," French explained. "Article 350 section B subparagraph ten of the First Vatican Accords specifically states that those outside of the faith structure are not to be processed through purgatory."

Palial raised an eyebrow. "That was superseded with the Council Edict of 1901. My office processes all supplicants now."

"Actually, the Edict made it discretionary. If you recall, hardliners on the Council insisted on the option. This, I believe, would be an excellent time to exercise that clause. If these four were never officially in purgatory, then how could you have lost them? Isn't that so, Co-Adjutor?"

She smiled. "It means burying the decision in a tidal wave of paperwork but nothing that someone of my caliber and expertise would find difficult."

The angelic middle manager stepped forward and wrapped her arms around French. "Thank you so much. My job means everything to me. Please call me if you ever need anything."

French had been hoping she might say that. There were few things he had in mind.

Once again, the Vatican's Office of Minor Transgressions has botched a job. Can Mr. French correct their error and find a woman who has escaped a demonic possession by retreating into her own mind?

Possession is Nine-Tenths of the Law

"Hey French, Brother Leo just called. The O.M.T. fouled up another exorcism."

French was a psychic; the only one that guaranteed his work. "Did he give any particulars, Meryl? Will I be dealing with a Verthag or Shatha'agral?"

"Neither," she replied. "Those idiots managed to drive the demon out but nearly killed the patient in the process."

Meryl was Mr. French's secretary. She was also a succubus and so had no love for the Vatican's Office of Minor Transgressions.

"I shan't need this then." The psychic returned the Anhedron to its lead-lined box. "Is the patient conscious or unconscious?"

"Conscious but unresponsive, but she isn't your concern, French. Let the O.M.T. clean this mess up themselves."

French paused. "This woman is my concern, Meryl. Doing everything I can to heal the rift between humans and those of our kind is what I have chosen as my profession."

The succubus scowled. "That's your guilt speaking."

"It is and I know that no amount of good deeds will ever atone for what I have done. That does not mean that I shall not try. Now, did Brother Leo give you any information on her medical condition?"

"Yes, quite a lot actually." She glanced down at her notes from the call. "The Patient withdraws from noxious stimuli but shows no purposeful movement. Her pupils are equal and reactive to light. Heart, lungs, abdomen, and extremities are unremarkable. Serum and urine toxicology are normal. The chest x-ray, ECG, CBC, serum chemistries, urinalysis, and liver function test results are also unremarkable. For a change, the O.M.T. was smart enough to do a C.T. scan of her head thinking the demon might have slammed her around but there were no abnormalities."

French tsked. "Sounds like another case of post traumatic withdrawal."

"You really should talk to Brother Leo about updating their methods; they're straight out of the inquisition."

The psychic frowned over the top of his glasses. "You make it sound like the O.M.T. is using burning pokers and thumb screws."

"Might as well be," Meryl replied. "In these cases, you usually use a pet to coax the patient out. Is that your plan?"

"Yes, simplest solutions first. Please contact the family and see if the woman has an emotional bond to an animal."

"Already done." Meryl handed the psychic a piece of paper.

"Oh, bollocks, it's a bird."

"Thought you'd like that."

"Quite. After that incident with the lechuza, I've had my fill of things avian." The psychic paused. "Hmm, perhaps this might be an opportunity to use Caitlin's abilities."

"The rat girl?"

French scowled. "Yes, although her abilities extend to far more than rats."

"And I suppose you'll want me to contact Dr. Maximillian?"

"If you would, please."

"You do realize that Infernals and the Devine don't get along."

The psychic tsked. "Dr. Maximillian is hardly a typical Devine. Like the Infernals, she has chosen to work for the sustenance she needs."

"It isn't just that, French, and you know it. They have this air of superiority like they're God's gift to the world."

He stared over the top of his glasses. "The humans gave them that role."

"One that they abuse! Feeding off prayer and delivering nothing is wrong!"

"Whereas Infernals provide carnal pleasure."

"Better than being a leech."

The psychic frowned.

"French, you know I wasn't referring to you. You're different. You respect the creatures you draw from."

"As do the Devine, for the most part."

Meryl rolled her eyes. "To them humans are just livestock. The Devine only do the bare minimum to keep them happy."

"That was not their choice. The Vatican requested they keep a low profile," he replied. "Besides, the humans believe the Devine were brought here by a higher power."

Meryl shook her head. "We both know that's just Vatican propaganda."

"I reserve judgement until facts are provided either way."

"Sounds like your mother talking."

French shrugged. "She was a product of her time whereas Dr. Maximillian has adapted to the modern age. Please give the Doctor a call and tell her to expect us."

"Fine, when?

"Tomorrow. I shall have to call Miss Caitlin and see if she is free in the afternoon."

***

Caitlin had no idea what she'd volunteered for, something to do with a possessed woman and her pet parrot. It was quite typical of French—not much explanation, just encouragement that this would be an opportunity to practice her talents. What talents? So far all she could do was *feel* what the rats in French's menagerie wanted. There was no real communication although they seemed to understand when she spoke to them. That and the other animals in the psychic's menagerie seemed to like her. Not much of a talent but who knew, maybe the psychic was right. Well, not all of the animals liked her; the Vartilliamenthum raised its spines every time she passed. Then again, it was more plant than animal and seemed to hate everyone.

French pulled up to the walk. Caitlin had never ridden in the psychic's convertible. Unfortunately, the top was up. She opened the door and slid in.

"Hi, Mr. French."

"Good afternoon, Caitlin. Thank you for joining me."

Caitlin pulled on her belt. "No prob. Hope I can help."

The psychic put the candy apple red 1969 Plymouth Sport Fury convertible into gear and pulled onto the road. "Don't worry, you'll do fine."

"I don't know; I've never been around a parrot."

All her family had at home was a dog and two cats and there were no birds in the psychic's menagerie. Would her talent work on a parrot?

French turned onto Fredericksburg. "It shall be as easy as dealing with Bob."

Caitlin sighed. "Bob does most of the work. He seems to know what I'm thinking, not the other way around."

Bob was the alpha male rat in the menagerie. He spent most of the day sitting on Caitlin's shoulder. He was probably wondering where she was right now. "I did some research. Don't most parrots pair-bond to their owners?" she asked.

French slowed to a stop as the light changed. "Yes, but this is a Caique. They're different, also much smaller than other parrots."

"Meryl mentioned that this was a Caique. Do they bite?"

"All birds bite," he answered testily.

Meryl had told Caitlin in confidence that French had issues with birds. That was probably the real reason she was here.

"Should I have brought gloves?"

The idea of being bitten frightened her. The rats sometimes nibbled her fingers but that was all in play, they weren't trying to hurt her…well, that wasn't completely honest, the rats had tried to eat her once but they were starving at the time and following the commands of a lunatic.

"I doubt that gloves shall be necessary," the psychic answered. The look on his face was not reassuring.

"I guess I just find birds a bit of an unknown and that makes them scary," Caitlin admitted.

She turned and looked at the psychic. "Of course, you must be used to scary things. Most everything you do seems scary, to me anyway. Can you at least promise there won't be a ghost this time?"

He nodded. "No ghost and the demon has been exorcised."

That wasn't completely reassuring.

"So, demons are real?" she asked.

"In a manner of speaking but they aren't from hell. What humans call demons are formless malevolent entities that existed on the plane the Infernals and Devine came from. Unlike them, demons cannot take on a form so must inhabit a human."

French slowed and signaled to turn. Caitlin looked up; it was just another concrete and glass storefront mini-mall. The sign on the building read *Angel of Mercy Health Clinic*.

"Funny place to have fought a demon?"

"I had the patient transferred here," French explained. "Dr. Maximillian is quite well versed in the maladies and disorders of the paranormal."

"Really? People study that in medical school?"

He shook his head and turned into the parking lot. "No, Dr. Maximillian is a Devine who chose to live here on Earth. As such, she has a great insight into problems like this case."

It hadn't been that difficult for Caitlin to wrap her mind around the idea that Meryl was a succubus. The woman certainly looked the part with gorgeous auburn hair and a super sexy physique. That angels were also real, although from another dimensional reality and not Heaven, was a bit much for her to fathom.

"Meryl doesn't like her." Caitlin said flatly.

"Meryl is biased," French countered.

There was a break in the traffic and the psychic pulled into the parking lot and found a space. As he and Caitlin walked up to the entrance, he added "I do have gloves in the car boot if that proves necessary."

She glanced back at the car wondering if she should just get them now. "Thanks."

***

Caitlin didn't really know what she'd expected, maybe something from a mad scientist's lab or gothic steampunk maybe, but the clinic was quite normal. Everything was sanitarily white, there were golf magazines on the waiting room tables, and the nurse at the counter didn't have angel wings.

"The doctor will be ready for you in a moment," the woman told French.

Like every other doctor's office Caitlin had been in, there was an underlying smell of alcohol. "So what exactly are we doing to this possessed lady?" she asked.

"Formerly possessed," French corrected. "You and I, along with the bird," he said that last part with some distaste, "Will be entering the patient's mind. She is in a self-imposed coma. We are going to encourage her to return to the outside world."

A light flashed on the nurse's phone. She looked up and motioned for French. "The doctor is ready."

They followed the nurse down a hall of patient rooms. At the end was a pair of doors with a warning sign lit up above- *Electromagnetic Field Generator in Use*. As they passed through, Caitlin felt the back of her head begin to throb.

French noticed. "Yes, uncomfortable, but necessary. We shan't be able to feel it once we are in the cradles."

Caitlin was afraid to ask what they needed baby cradles for. The nurse led them through a second pair of doors and into a modern clinical lab. One wall was lined with hospital beds surrounded by monitors on stands that flashed and beeped. On the center bed, a woman was lying unconscious. She must be the possessed woman. Instead of a pillow, her head lay in a padded cylindrical shell.

Caitlin also noticed that the beds on either side also had similar devices. On the furthest, a clear acrylic box sat between the two halves of the cylindrical shell. Inside the plastic box was a parrot.

It squawked, sounding like a home smoke alarm.

In Caitlin's brain, alarms were beginning to go off as well.

A statuesque brunette in a lab coat motioned them toward the beds. "You're right on time, French." The woman was really beautiful, with large eyes, full lips, and a nice figure. Dr. Maximillian was really hot. Caitlin's fear faded.

French stepped forward and shook the woman's hand." Dr. Maximillian, this is Caitlin. She will be helping with the bird."

Dr. Maximillian offered her hand. As Caitlin shook it, a mild charge of electricity flowed through her.

The doctor turned to French. "Your patient is ready. I'll monitor things and pull you out if your vitals seriously jump."

The bird squawked again. Unlike the parrots Caitlin had seen in real life, this one was small, about the size of a robin. It. had green wings and a yellow body with a black head. From what she'd read, caiques were supposed to be friendly but also a little ADHD. Funny, who would have thought animals could have the same issues as people? Of course, who would have thought that pets could get possessed along with their owners? Caitlin struggled to imagine Blossom, her cat, puking up anything other than a hairball. Not so scary.

"If you will both lie down, I will set up the monitors."

Caitlin settled onto the bed. She pointed to the padded cylinder. "Dr. Maximillian, what does this do?"

The woman smiled. "Call me Dr. Maks." She reached up and placed her hand on the device. "We call this a cradle. It works sort of like an MRI but is tailored to interact with the electrical field of the brain, not just image it. With the cradle, a group of people can share and experience each other's thoughts."

The alarms in Caitlin's head began blaring again. So much of her life was secrets—things she kept from her parents, her feelings for Jenn, and things she hadn't told French. Would this machine make that all public?

Dr. Maks must have seen the fear on her face. "Don't worry; only the thoughts you allow to be shared can be accessed," she said reassuringly.

French was already settled into the bed on the opposite side of the possessed woman and had his head securely in the cradle. "Caitlin, we may experience some bizarre and disturbing things. This poor woman has experienced a great deal of trauma. It is important to keep in mind that everything you see and hear is not real. It is all just figments her mind is creating to block out what happened to her."

"I think I'd want to block out a demon possessing me too."

"Quite."

Caitlin lay back and placed her head in the cradle. The pillow was warm. "What do I do?"

Dr. Maks clipped an oxygen monitor on her finger. "Nothing. Just lie back and relax."

That didn't sound so bad. "So, no cybernetic needles sticking into my brain?"

"No needles at all," the Doctor said as she placed a blood pressure cuff on Caitlin's arm. "Nothing like that. This is more Vulcan mind meld than Dr. Who."

"Brain needles might be okay, if I got a Tardis."

"Afraid not," French said. "Lie back and close your eyes. Once the machine is turned on, you will feel a bit of a shift, sort of like you're falling. Once that happens, you can open your eyes again. At that point, we shall be in the ready room."

"Ready room?"

"A virtual space before we enter Ms. Endicott's mind," he explained.

"That's the woman's name?"

"Yes, now shut your eyes."

Caitlin closed her eyes and tried to relax. "What's the parrot's name?"

"Siegfried," Dr. Maks answered. "Okay, everything's ready. I'll countdown from three. Ready? Three. Two. One."

Caitlin felt the sensation of movement although nothing had moved. She opened her eyes. They were in a room constructed entirely of white plastic. She sat up. They were lying in real beds, not hospital gurneys. French was there and so was the bird although there was no plastic cage. French jumped as the parrot flew over to Caitlin's shoulder. Wow, French must really not like birds. Caitlin, on the other hand, hadn't been startled at all, she had simply known Siegfried was about to fly.

"I can feel the bird," she told the psychic.

"Will he do what you tell him?"

She shook her head. "Don't know. I can just feel that he's glad to be out of his cage."

French gestured at a door in the plastic wall. "Once we open this, we will be in the world of Ms. Endicott's thoughts. Things may be strange. She is likely to hide from us at first. That is why we brought the bird."

Caitlin turned to look at Siegfried sitting on her shoulder. He had round, black eyes with red around the edges. He leaned over and played with her hair in a friendly, affectionate way. "I think he knows what we're doing."

"Really? Should we follow him, then?"

At first Caitlin thought the psychic was making fun of her. Then she realized he was serious. "I don't know. Once we open the door, I'll see what he feels."

French nodded and opened the door.

The white plastic room disappeared and they were assaulted by the smell of stale popcorn and sideshow organ music. Around them were walls striped black and red with a beige tent canvas for a ceiling. There were circus posters and pictures of carnival clowns plastered on the walls. Occasional outbursts of crazed laughter completed the nightmarish illusion.

Caitlin shivered. "Ooh, I hate clowns."

French nodded agreement. "That is a fear shared by many. The artificial emotions on the face inspire distrust."

On their right, a barrel of fun was slowly spinning. To the opposite side, three garishly painted doors were numbered one through three.

"Does the bird have any suggestions," French asked. "I for one do not wish to discover what is behind those doors. In my experience, such a choice is never beneficial."

Caitlin looked to the parrot on her shoulder. He leaned, pulling to the right and the barrel of fun.

"I think Siegfried agrees with you."

French walked over and gently put his foot on the horizontally spinning stainless steel cylinder. "Seems safe but we must remember, this is not reality. We could just as easily fall through what we perceive as solid."

The bird flew off Caitlin's shoulder to land at the far end of the rotating tunnel.

"I think Siegfried's impatient," she said.

French harrumphed and strode forward. Catlin followed, having a bit more issue with the moving surface. Once on the far side, Siegfried stared up at her from the floor.

"You want back up here?"

Obviously.

"Oh, sorry."

Caitlin reached down and the parrot deftly climbed onto her finger. His feet were warm and pleasant.

At this end of the rotating tunnel, there was only blackness around them. "Which way?" she asked the parrot.

Siegfried's little black head snapped from side to side and then stopped, pointing directly ahead into the darkness.

"Forward it is." As the psychic took a step, lights snapped on. A dazzling collection of glass, mirrors, and chrome lay before them.

"A hall of mirrors?"

"Ms. Endicott's mind is erecting barriers," French commented.

"Think it's safe?"

The psychic climbed the steps up to the sideshow attraction. "Very. Remember, everything we are experiencing is a product of her imagination."

Charlotte wasn't convinced. This was all too similar to a horror movie. All that was missing were a bunch of evil clowns. "But we're trying to help. Why is Ms. Endicott trying to keep us away?"

French ran a suspicious hand along the glass panels. "My guess would be that Ms. Endicott no longer trusts her own faculties. We could be just another manifestation of the demon."

Siegfried nipped her ear.

"Ow! What was that for?"

Hurry.

"The bird bit you?" French asked.

"Just a bit. He's impatient and wants us to hurry up."

"I shall only be a moment. If Ms. Endicott is constructing defenses, there may be…"

The parrot launched off Caitlin's shoulder and flew into the maze.

Caitlin charged after him. "Shit! Siegfried, come back here!"

Two turns in, she ran into a glass wall and was nearly crushed by French who was right behind her.

"But the bird just went through here?" she said.

"I would hazard a guess that Ms. Endicott has recognized the parrot and has allowed the bird to pass."

There was no glass to her left. Caitlin turned and began going forward with her hands held before her. No more running into walls. "Good for him, but it means we've lost our guide."

They felt their way along the glass and mirror corridors. Unlike a true maze, so far there had been no dead ends or intersections with choices to make.

At a turn to the right, Caitlin caught a glimpse of someone else in the maze; someone dressed in a baggy orange and yellow bodysuit with floppy shoes and white makeup.

"Mr. French, there's a clown is in here with us!"

"Where?"

"That way but I only saw him for an instant."

French scanned their surroundings then turned, looking back the way they had come. "I don't see anything. Perhaps it was merely a reflection of one of those paintings we saw earlier."

Caitlin shook her head. "Don't think so. It looked real. At least it was far away."

"Shall we continue forward, then?"

"Okay."

Several twists and turns later, Caitlin asked the question that had been bothering her since they had first entered this place. "If I was to imagine a safe place to escape a demon, the last thing I would put in it would be clowns."

"It may be that Ms. Endicott is using the carnival imagery in an attempt to keep the demon at bay."

"Oh, that makes sense; even demons must find clowns scary." Caitlin turned left and there was a thud behind her as French hit a wall.

The psychic ran his hands up and down the glass panel now standing between them. "Rubbish! It seems, Caitlin, that we are destined to continue on separate paths."

"But the clown?"

He gave her a mild look over the top of his glasses. "Whatever you encounter, it cannot harm you. It is no more real than you allow it to be."

Caitlin made a mental note to say no the next time Mr. French needed help. "All right."

"Steady on, then." French felt the walls around him. "I am to go to the right apparently. We shall meet at the exit."

Caitlin nodded. French was ignoring the fact that there might not be an exit. What if this was a trap?

As the psychic disappeared around a corner, multiple reflections of his well-dressed English gentleman's silhouette appeared scattered in all directions.

Caitlin sighed and moved forward. A turn to the right, several steps forward, one left, one right. French's reflection was getting further away. How big was this place? She turned a corner. Standing in front of her, with only a glass panel to keep it away, was the clown.

She screamed and threw herself backwards, slamming into a glass wall that just moments before had been open space. With no other option, panic took over and Caitlin dove past the leering clown. She ran blindly, smashing into walls and corners, overcome with the fear that the grinning specter was right behind. Finally, ever deeper into the labyrinth, the reflected image of the clown was gone.

She collapsed. Her heart was beating like an unbalanced washing machine. She took a deep breath, trying to manage her panic. As her pulse rate slowed, Caitlin glanced around. She was in a corridor of fun house mirrors. She placed her hands flat on the glass and pulled herself to her feet. Her reflection was a short, fat hobbit. Across the corridor, she was stretched into a bean pole with incredibly wide feet. There was something about the distorted images that was threatening. She glanced away, looking instead at the end of the corridor. If she kept her head down and focused on the ground, she could get past the mirrors and their surrealist interpretation of reality. Caitlin began walking; the image of her tennis shoes all she focused on. She reached the end of the corridor. It was a glass wall. She checked right and left; more glass. Was this it? Was there no end to the maze?

Panic tried to take hold again. It's all fake, she told herself, repeating French's words. She'd have to backtrack. If there was an exit, she would find it and somewhere back there was Mr. French. At least the psychic was in here somewhere too. That was a comforting thought.

And then her sub-conscious interrupted- *So is the Clown!*

Fucking stupid sub-conscious. Caitlin steeled herself for the walk past the mirrors. Why were they so scary? She forced herself to look. She appeared like a top with a tiny head and feet with an oversized belly between. Not a good image for anyone with anorexia. Opposite, her face was stretched into a cylinder perched on her body so that she looked like a wooden toy soldier. The next mirror was empty. Why was there no reflection? She reached forward to touch the curved glass.

There was none. Instead, the small space was a flipped image to the corridor she was in. Caitlin entered. There was a sign far to the left- *Exit This Way!*

She hurried forward, turned a corner, and right into the clown.

She screamed.

To her right, French was trapped behind a glass panel. He slammed his knee into the glass and the shattered, glittering fragments spilled everywhere. He took a stand protectively between her and the clown.

"The clown's blocking the exit! What do we do?"

"I think not." French stepped forward and applied his foot to the clown. It fell to the floor lifeless.

Caitlin starred at it. "The clown's a cardboard cutout?"

"Logical. Ms. Endicott doesn't wish to harm us, just frighten us away."

Caitlin looked around. Once again, there seemed little else other than the blackness.

"Where to now?" she asked.

A large sign in the shape of an arrow dropped from the darkness overhead. On it, the words THIS WAY pointed downwards. Flashing marquee lights emphasized the less-than-subtle hint.

"Ask and ye shall receive," French said.

"I'm not sure I want to go through anymore of Ms. Endicott's playland," she told the psychic.

French stepped forward to examine the sign. "These are tests. Her brain is trying to determine if we are who we appear to be."

"Well I am a very scared high school girl." She joined the psychic under the sign. "What's it pointing too?"

"I'm not sure," French answered. "There's nothing on the floor."

The ground beneath them fell away and Caitlin found herself in a tube sliding downwards in darkness. The trip ended with a thump into a large pile of cushions.

French stood and brushed himself off. "Ms. Endicott has a sense of the dramatic." He turned, eying their next challenge.

"A balance beam over fire?" Caitlin asked. "There's no way something like this could be in a real carnival!"

"No," he agreed. "And because of that, I shall go first."

He gingerly stepped onto the beam. It was around a foot wide and the psychic had little trouble for the first several feet.

"It will not be this easy. Something will most certainly…"

He didn't get the chance to finish his sentence. A blast of air tried to throw him off balance.

The psychic quickly righted himself. "Ha, you shall not get me that easily."

There were several more air blasts and then French was at the far side of the chasm.

"Can you remember where the wind occurred?" he yelled. Caitlin waved. "Yes!"

Remembering where the air blasts were, however, was not the same as wanting to try and cross.

"Come on then."

Caitlin starred at the beam and the glowing coals below. She sighed. "Say no, always say no when French asks you for help," she muttered under her breath.

She stepped onto the beam and walked to the point where the first blast of air had nearly dislodged French. She reached forward and waved, hoping to trigger the sensor.

Nothing happened.

Stupid balance beam. Caitlin crouched down and took a step forward. Again nothing happened. She waited. Still nothing.

Relieved, she allowed herself to relax. "I think the air is either off or the pattern is random," she said as she stood.

A blast of air hit her from the opposite side.

"Oh fuck you. I hate this. It isn't fun at all."

She crouched back down and began angrily marching forward along the beam. 'This is so stupid. Only reason I'm here is for a dumb bird that flew away the first chance it got."

She reached the end of the balance beam with no further air blasts. Waiting for her were the psychic and Siegfried.

"Your *raison d'etre* has returned," French said.

Caitlin bent down and retrieved the parrot. "How come you bailed on us? We were having such fun."

Slow.

"Yeah, well we can't fly."

Caitlin glanced up at Mr. French. "Where to now?"

The psychic pointed to a school bus yellow archway. "A rotor or gravity whirl is the colloquial, I believe."

Caitlin followed the psychic inside. It was a cylindrical room with a yellow swirl painted on the black floor.

"What's a gravity whirl do?" she asked.

As she said this, a panel slid down with a *whang!* blocking the exit. The loud sound startled Siegfried and he flew up and into the darkness.

"Oh no, not again."

"Perhaps he knows something we do not."

The room began to rotate.

"It seems he does." The psychic motioned to the wall. "If you would stand flat against the surface, as we spin faster and faster, the floor will descend but we shall stay affixed quite firmly to the wall," French instructed.

The ride was rotating quite quickly now and Caitlin had little choice but to find a spot on the inside surface of the cylindrical room. "Centrifugal force. Basic physics," she commented.

"Yes, although in this place I would assume we should expect something more than an entertaining ride."

By this point, the speed was making Caitlin somewhat nauseous. "Ms. Endicott will deserve it if she makes me puke. No way in hell will I clean it up."

"Ah, see below us, the floor is descending."

Beneath them the black floor with its hypno-spiral had dropped a good three feet.

"What happens if the ride doesn't stop?" Caitlin asked.

"That is a question we shall deal with if such a thing occurs," the psychic replied.

Below, the floor was now over ten feet down and dropping ever faster. The walls, however, ended just below their feet. The ride began to slow.

Caitlin frantically searched for any sign of a hand hold. Of course there was nothing. She felt herself begin to slip. "What do we do?"

"Fall, unfortunately," French answered. "I see little else we can do."

"Not helpful. That part I'd already figured out."

Caitlin's feet had slipped below the wall and her shoes were threatening to fly off her feet. She placed her palms against the steel wall hoping to slow her descent.

For a few moments, that worked but as the rotation slowed further, she began sliding.

French fell first, and then Caitlin.

She hit the floor wrong, falling forward and onto her out flung hands. There was a pop and her wrist erupted in excruciating agony, causing her to cry out.

French was there almost immediately. "What is wrong?"

"My wrist, I may have broken it."

"Let me see."

She let the psychic take her arm. He held her gently, taking care not to move her much. He trailed his fingers bare millimeters above her skin.

"Radial wrist sprain. Ligaments are torn but not severely."

"Feels severe," Caitlin countered.

"The good news is that once we emerge from Ms. Endicott's mind, you will no longer be injured. In the meantime, I have something that will make the pain abate."

The psychic reached into his inner jacket and retrieved an enameled Victorian pill box. From it, he pulled a small blue tablet which he handed to Caitlin. "Take this. If your wrist continues to hurt, I can give you another."

Once on her tongue, the tablet dissolved almost immediately. She nodded toward a door that their descent had made visible. At the door, Siegfried was once again waiting. "We going through there?"

"In time. First, we shall take a few moments to discover if the medicine is working."

As they waited, French pulled forth a handkerchief from his vest pocket. Handkerchiefs? Who carries handkerchiefs anymore? In the moment while she had pondered this, the psychic had fashioned the embroidered piece of silk into a sling. He put it round her head and Caitlin carefully positioned her arm inside.

"That's helping. It still hurts but not like it did."

"Good. Wait here and I shall do a recce to discover where that passage goes."

Caitlin wasn't sure what a *recky* was but patiently waited as French walked over to peer through the opening. In the psychic's absence, Siegfried waddled over and stared up at her.

"Messed my wrist up," she told the bird.

He flew up and onto her shoulder. There was the distinct feeling that she was being judged and found wanting for not being able to fly.

"Not my fault, I was born with arms, not wings."

French hurried over from the door. "There is a corridor beyond. At the end is an exit sign. Perhaps we are close."

"Or it's just the exit to the ride like at the hall of mirrors," she replied.

"Positive thoughts, my dear. Shall we proceed?"

Caitlin nodded and stepped forward to join the psychic. Beyond the opening was a rather normal corridor reminding Caitlin of a hotel. There were wall sconces and carpet and no signs of anything carnival. As French had said, at the end was a door with a very mundane exit sign. Siegfried began bouncing.

"He's happy. We really must be at the end."

"I too am glad that we have reached our destination," he replied. "Shall we?"

"Yes, let's," Caitlin answered playfully.

As they stepped onto the carpet, the corridor end stretched away like a cheesy movie effect. The exit was now hundreds of feet in the distance. To make matters worse, the floor beneath their feet began to move like a treadmill, forcing them to run just to stay in one place.

Siegfried flew down the hall and landed by the exit door.

"I so fucking hate this place!"

"Normally, I would chastise you for your language, but in this case, I am afraid I must concur with your assessment."

Despite the pain in her arm and desperately having to run, his comment made Caitlin smile.

They were gaining some ground but only slowly. "Will we be able to reach the end?" she asked panting.

"Perhaps but that is the least of our troubles. Look behind us."

Caitlin glanced back. At the door where they had entered, there stood a clown and a huge bird with a woman's head."

Caitlin ran faster. "What the hell is that?"

"A type of witch known as a lechuza," the psychic replied. "I had quite a difficult time with one recently. Ms. Endicott is drawing from our own fears to populate her labyrinth."

"Shit, shit, shit."

French glanced again over his shoulder. "Hmm, I wonder…"

"You wonder what?"

"Stop running."

"What?!" Caitlin asked.

"Stop running. We shall face our fears."

Caitlin wasn't too sure that would work but one thing she did know that she was quickly growing tired. "Okay, whenever you're ready," she told French.

"Now."

The two stopped, turning to face the clown and the lechuza. The clown raised his machete, and bounded toward her. To the clown's right, the lechuza jumped into the air and flew with her talons outstretched aiming for French.

"This is all an illusion," he said calmly.

Caitlin hoped so because the clown had his machete back to strike.

The hotel corridor disappeared, replaced with the quiet of a Victorian drawing room. At a bay window, a woman was sitting with Siegfried perched on her hand. The woman looked at Caitlin, then back to the bird.

"So this is the girl you were telling me about?"

The parrot made a chattery buzz sound.

French nudged her forward.

"I'm Caitlin Stevens and this is Mr. French. We brought Siegfried. We came to help you."

"My life has been quite confusing of late," she said. "Are things back to normal?"

"Yes," Caitlin answered. "The demon that possessed you is gone. Mr. French drove it out."

"Actually, it was Brother Leo from the Vatican that preformed the actual exorcism," he corrected. "I am here as a courtesy to let you know you no longer need to hide."

"So nice to know that's over."

With that statement, they were no longer in Ms. Endicott's drawing room but once again lying on the hospital beds.

Caitlin extricated herself from the cradle and glanced over. Ms. Endicott's eyes were open.

Caitlin gestured to all the medical apparatus. "This is how we entered your thoughts."

On the bed behind Caitlin, Siegfried squawked from his acrylic box.

"Sorry, I'll get you out of the box." Caitlin walked over and opened the acrylic cage. The parrot happily jumped onto her finger and she walked him over to Ms. Endicott. He flew the last several feet to land on her shoulder.

"Someone has been missing you a lot."

On Ms. Edicott's shoulder, Siegfried squatted, wiggled his butt and pooped.

"Oh no!" Caitlin exclaimed.

She found a tissue and handed it to Ms. Endicott. The frail woman dabbed at the mess then turned to Caitlin. "When you own a bird, this is something you get used to. For birds, you see, the whole world is a toilet."

"Good to know," Caitlin replied. "Not sure I'll be letting him ride on my shoulder anymore."

This was the very first Mr. French story I ever wrote. It dates back quite a while and no longer quite ties in with the reality I have created for the psychic and his allies. It is something which I thought that should be included in this book just so readers could see Mr. French in his first incarnation.

The Car

I found the psychic on the internet. Mr. French was his name. I don't generally believe in this crap, but his ad was not like all the others. No mumbo jumbo bullshit, no goofy name, and the ad said that Mr. French guaranteed his results.

His office was in an old house off of Broadway. The car *only* tried to kill me twice on the way there. The house was painted purple and had a huge hand-painted "Psychic" sign on the balcony. I pulled in and parked the car. I could feel the damn thing glaring at me as I shut the door and walked up to the building.

There was a sign on the front porch as well. Apparently Mr. French also performed tarot readings, aura evaluations, and exorcisms. An exorcism! That's exactly what my car needed.

I opened the door and stepped inside. Heavy velvet curtains, once red but now aged to a dust covered, lethargic pink, lined the walls. As the door closed, the darkness of the room enveloped me like a shroud. On the wall to my right, an old oil lamp sat on an antique half-moon cherry table. Its guttering flame provided a meager sulfuric-yellow light. I waited while my eyes took their damn time adjusting to the gloom.

On the table, there was also an open guestbook. I walked over. Mr. French was a pretty good psychic- my name, Kevin Blake, was already written on the top line.

Behind me, I heard the curtains draw back.

I turned. An old man in a well-tailored black suit stood there.

"So, Mr. Blake, you have finally come to Mr. French for help." His dark hair was streaked with grey at the temples as was his mustache and beard.

"I think my car is possessed," I said.

"How odd, Mr. Blake. You don't believe in psychics, but you *do* have faith enough in me for your automobile?"

Smug bastard. "You're right, Mr. French, I don't believe in psychics, but I don't generally believe in possessed cars either. However, I can't deny the fact that my car is quite definitely trying to kill me."

"Interesting," was all he said.

Silence hung between us so I filled it with more of my story. "The damn thing will be driving fine and then suddenly, it tries to swerve into traffic or to veer off the road into a tree. It isn't anything mechanical. I've torn the steering system down to nuts and bolts. Something is taking control of the car that wants me dead."

Mr. French stared at me; his eyes like a doctor making a triage diagnosis. "There is indeed something that wants you dead," he said at last.

That was a relief. However hokey this psychic crap was, as long as it worked, I'd be happy.

"Please follow me," Mr. French said after a few moments, "And stay close. It would not be wise to get lost in my house."

I followed him through the curtains. We were in the original foyer to the house. A stair led upwards and several doors gave no hints as to what lay beyond. Mr. French chose one to the right and it opened onto a dimly lit room filled with arcane mechanisms cast recklessly against an Egyptian sarcophagus. We quickly walked through the room and into a corridor piled high with ancient books and embalmed creatures in bottles. We passed a glass paned door through which I could see a table laid out with the assorted accoutrements for holding a séance. The planchette on the Ouija board was moving as we hurried past. At the end of the corridor, we stepped through a door into a space so dark I could only follow Mr. French by the sound of his voice as he hurried me along. The smell was horrible and I could hear things moving in that foul darkness. From that stygian space, we stepped into another corridor, at the end of which was a door. It was painted red and had a brass number eight nailed to the frame above.

The old man reached into his coat pocket and retrieved a ring of old-fashioned brass keys. He unlocked the door and turned the faceted glass knob. "Inside we will find your answers."

The room was a sitting room and appeared little changed from the time the house had been built in the late 1800's. He motioned for me to sit. I settled into the green satin upholstery of a button back settee. The room smelled of age and incense. Mr. French took a seat opposite me in a Victorian mahogany armchair.

"Tell me about your car," he said as casually as if he was asking about a pet or family member, and not some demented piece of machinery that was intent of seeing me dead.

"I bought the car from a vehicle auction," I began. "It had been in an accident."

"The previous driver having perished in said accident," Mr. French added.

"Yes." I was beginning to wonder if I even needed to tell the story at all. "I guess that should have raised some warning flags but I wanted the car. I had one like it back in in the 70's in high school."

He nodded. "A 1969 Plymouth Sport Fury convertible, candy apple red. Am I correct?" he asked.

"Yes."

Smoke from the incense was thick in the room and was making me light headed. Normally, I would have been irritated that French was finishing my sentences for me. Instead, I just continued on.

"It sat in my garage for several years until I finally had the time to work on it. The accident hadn't done that much damage. When I bought the car, I was told that the driver had not been wearing a seatbelt and had been thrown from the car."

"And now you think the previous driver is haunting the vehicle." Mr. French pulled a pair of wire frame glasses from inside his jacket. "May I see the keys?"

I handed him my keyring. "Can this ghost be removed?"

"Oh, I can easily remove unwanted spirits," Mr. French said casually. "I am just not convinced that it is the previous owner that is trying to kill you."

"If it isn't a ghost, then what is it?"

Mr. French handed the keys back. "There is definitely something trying to kill you and it is for a very specific reason." He carefully closed the arms on his glasses and returned them to the recesses of his coat.

"You say that like I am not going to like the answer," I said. "Is it a demonic possession? Am I driving *Christine*?"

"No," he said firmly.

He didn't offer anything more. "Well, what is trying to kill me?"

Mr. French leaned forward in his chair. Smoke from the incense curled about him. "Let me try to explain," he said. "There is a boundary between this world and the world of the afterlife. Sometimes, for reasons not understood, a soul does not cross over."

"Then it *is* a ghost," I said excitedly.

"Yes, but allow me to finish." Mr. French wrung his hands for a moment. "These souls, by remaining in this world, create an unbalance. It is a precarious existence these souls find themselves in and the *Universe* will do all that it can to move them on to the other side."

"I've watched enough *Ghost Adventures* to know that spirits need to move on, but what does that have to do with my car?"

"It isn't your car that is trying to kill you," Mr. French said.

He must have expected me to understand but I still had no clue as to what he was trying to tell me. "What are you saying?"

"It is the *Universe* that is trying to kill you," he said. "The Universe is trying to even the balance. You see, you are the driver that died in the accident."

And I had just started to believe this guy. "What a load of crap!" I yelled. "Guaranteed results my ass, you're just trying to pull a scam."

Mr. French was quite calm in the face of my tirade. "Do you remember selling the car you had in high school?" he asked quietly.

"Of course I do…" I began, but then I found that there was no memory there. In fact, there was no memory of the car at all after high school. I thought about it. Why would I have ever sold the car?

"I have seen several cases like this before," the old man said. "Few have been as impressive as yours. Most spirits that remain on this side are little more than wisps of misplaced energy. You, on the other hand, have managed to create a physical form. Quite remarkable, but I suppose that was necessary for you to drive the vehicle."

"Stop it! I'm not dead." I pinched myself. "See, real flesh!"

"As I said, very impressive," the psychic said calmly. "But I am afraid that it is far past your time."

He pulled something from his pocket.

"What is that?" I asked. "What are you going to do?"

Mr. French opened his hand. He was holding a small hand bell. "This will open the portal for you."

He shook the bell and the room was filled with light and the rush of air.

"You see, I do my guarantee my results," I heard the old man say through the maelstrom.

I was being dragged into the glare. My hands were passing through the settee like it was made of sand.

"I hope you enjoy the other side, Mr. Blake."

About the author.

Michael Lane is the adopted son of an engineer and an artist. He is indebted to them for nurturing his mind to balance both logic and creativity.

The first piece of writing Mr. Lane sold was to a radio station when he was in high school. He earned ten dollars for the story but managed to miss the broadcast when it was read on the air.

It was also in high school that Mr. Lane first learned to wield a sword in the Society for the Creative Anachronisms. Fighting in armor is something he enjoys but seldom finds time to do anymore.

In college, Mr. Lane nearly failed out of school, discovered punk music, learned to do the Time Warp in heels, had a stint as a newspaper cartoonist, and found a passion for architecture. It was in this field that he received his master's degree.

After college, Mr. Lane moved to San Antonio where he spent ten years working in an architect's office. In 1999, he began teaching at several San Antonio colleges and universities.

Currently, Mr. Lane is married to an artist that he loves dearly and is employed as a project manager at Alamo Colleges where he herds cats.